I0547891

TO BELIEVE IN YOU

Texas Roots Book 2

Charity Christy

Copyright © 2018 by **Charity Christy**

All rights reserved. No part of this publication may be reproduced, distributed or transmitted in any form or by any means, including photocopying, recording, or other electronic of mechanical methods, without prior written permission of the publisher, except for brief quotations embodied in critical reviews and noncommercial uses permitted by copyright law.

This is a work of fiction. Names, characters, places, and incidents are a product of the author's imagination. Locales and public names are sometimes used for atmospheric purposes. Any resemblance to actual people, living or dead, or to businesses, companies, events, institutions, or locales is completely coincidental.

Book Layout © 2017 BookDesignTemplates.com

Book Cover Design © 2018 Victorine Lieske

Book Cover Photo © 2016 Lauren Elizabeth Powel

Author Photo © 2016 Lauren Elizabeth Powel

To Believe in You / Charity Christy.
ISBN: 978-0692091012
ISBN-10: 0692091017

Books By This Author

Texas Roots

I Get to Love You – Melissa & Blake

To Believe in You – Aly & Colt

Jade & Luke (COMING SOON)

Cami & James (COMING SOON)

From the Author

Dear Reader,

I want to first say thank you for reading *To Believe in You*. I cannot tell you how much it means to me that you have taken time to read this story! My writing process and strength as a writer has grown dramatically with this second book.

To Believe in You is an contemporary clean romance. I have absolutely fallen in love with Colt and Aly. I've spent countless hours with them, individually and together, and feel like they are a part of my family. Their story is one of forgiveness, honesty, trust, heartbreak, and love. I wrote this book to help inspire men and women everywhere to see that through God's grace we are all capable of change. The desires of our heart matter to God and His plan is always at work. No matter who may be against us, God is for us. With renewed faith, God can help us to live inspired and love in the deepest way possible.

If you enjoyed this book, please leave a review at Amazon and Goodreads. Reviews are a major asset to authors and help allow them to continue to write more stories.

I'd love to get to know you! Visit my blog at www.charitychristy.com. You can also find me on Facebook, Twitter, Instagram, and Pinterest.

XO

Charity

CONTENTS

Prologue

Three Weeks Ago

It was going to be a long day, and it wasn't even noon yet. The phones rang continuously in time with the pounding of Aly Meyers' growing headache as customers called to make their insurance payments before the 4th of July holiday.

A door opened, and a breeze blew past her desk, bringing with it her favorite spicy cologne. She didn't even bother trying to hide the smile on her face. It was crazy that she was so attuned to him. When he was anywhere near, she sensed it. A few seconds later, his fingers glided through her hair and caressed the back of her neck.

Greg.

Aly turned her head up as he walked past her. His wink and sexy smile made her heart flutter even more. Then he disappeared behind his office door—the one that read "Greg Winters, CEO." It probably wasn't the best idea to be secretly dating her boss. She figured it wasn't entirely a secret, but they kept everything professional while at work. She returned her attention to her overflowing email inbox.

When she first started working at Winters Insurance, LLC, she was a sophomore in college, and the job had been an answer to her prayers. Did she like insurance? Not especially. But it came at the right time and she needed the stability. The flexible hours allowed her to maintain her class schedule. She not only needed the money, but also the experience to go along with her business degree. Greg had given her valuable insight in running a business and some one-on-one coaching. Falling into a secret relationship with him hadn't been part of her plan, but it happened.

Twenty-seven email replies later, Aly entered Greg's office. He looked up and shot her that devilishly handsome smile.

She returned it and said, "I have the reports for you to sign off on."

"Great." Greg took the papers from Aly in his right hand. With this left, he pulled her closer to him, her legs pressed against his side. "I missed you this morning."

He leaned into her for a hot and steamy kiss. Aly melted like butter in his hands. How did she get so lucky?

"I missed you too. Can we do something this weekend?"

He released her and leaned back in his chair. "I'm not sure that's going to be a possibility. I've got some things to take care of."

Her stomach dipped. They didn't discuss his personal life at length, simply because he didn't want to talk about it. "Well, maybe just dinner tonight?"

He continued to scribble across the reports. "I actually need to go to Austin tonight. I'm not sure when I'll be back. It may be a week or two."

Aly nodded. This was the way their relationship had to be for now. He technically lived in Austin, where the headquarters for Winters Insurance was based. She hoped one day he might consider moving to Dallas permanently… or ask her to move down there. But that was crazy talk right now. They didn't see each other all the time but did stay in touch almost every day. It wasn't ideal to be long distance, but if it meant she could still have Greg, she would do whatever it took.

The rest of the day was rather uneventful, something Aly was thankful for. Greg had been tied up in his office with several conference calls, and she only entered when she needed his signature.

At fifteen after five, almost everyone was packing up to leave. Aly was doing her best to get everything done in hopes of spending a little time with Greg before he had to leave for Austin. She cleaned off her desk and began filing reports in the cabinet behind her.

"Excuse me."

She looked up to see a stunningly beautiful woman. Her perfectly curled brown hair fell past her shoulders. She had on a form-fitting black dress and heels.

"Hello. I'm sorry, but we're about to close. Is there something I can help you with?"

"Oh, I'm not here for insurance. Is Greg in his office?" The woman gestured to the closed door.

Jealousy rose in Aly's chest, hot and fierce. Why would this woman come to see Greg after hours, especially dressed like that? "Umm, he is. I can let him know you're here."

The woman waved her hand in the air, dismissing Aly. "I don't need an introduction. I'm here to surprise him." With that, the woman glided across the floor to open the door.

Aly was usually the only one allowed to enter without knocking. She followed quickly behind, and they entered Greg's office.

He was leaning over his desk, thumbing through some files. Without looking up he said, "Aly, sorry I've been busy today. I didn't mean to be—" His voice cut off. "Angie?"

The look on Greg's face was a mix of surprise and horror. Aly wasn't sure why but she couldn't bring herself to leave the room. Greg's eyes darted between the two of them. Who was Angie?

"Greg, darling! I came to surprise you. I wanted to have a weekend getaway for our anniversary. I left the kids with your parents, so it's just us!" Angie threw her arms around his neck and kissed him.

Everything inside Aly came to a screeching halt. He was in a relationship with someone else. Someone who would surprise him with an *anniversary* present. And kids? He had children with this woman?! Tears burned the back of her eyes. As she turned to flee, Angie called to her. "Dear? Could you please close the door as you leave? I need some alone time with my husband." The giddy laugh was like fingernails on a chalkboard to Aly's temple.

Her husband?! He was married. MARRIED!

Aly didn't even look at Greg though she felt his gaze burning a hole through her back. The reality of his lies would surely be found in his eyes. Increasing the twist of the knife stuck in her back. She couldn't breathe and a storm churned in her stomach. She bolted to her desk noticing how empty everything seemed, just like her heart now. She unlocked her cabinet to retrieve her purse and keys, and as she turned, she ran right into Greg. She stumbled back and pulled her purse up to her chest. The look on his face was distraught as he reached for her. She jumped back at his touch. How dare he try to touch her?

Greg's arms dropped. "Aly, I never meant for this to happen."

"You're married?!" Aly's tears made their way to the brim of her eyes. She looked over to see the door to his office closed.

"I am, but I love you." His tone was hushed. "I was going to leave her. I don't love her anymore."

Aly couldn't even see straight. Her anger was about to blow. "You have children?! You have a family! How could you?!"

"Aly, please," Greg begged.

Angie appeared in the doorway of his office. "Greg, what's going on?"

Aly couldn't look at either of them. She couldn't believe that Greg had lied to her for years, that she had been so gullible. Taking a deep breath and straightening her shoulders, Aly glared at Greg. "Don't *ever* speak to me again." She ran toward the elevator and didn't even pause when Greg called her name.

Once she was in the parking garage, Aly's legs crumbled. Her knees hit the pavement along with her heart, her hopes, and her dreams. How could this be happening? Everything she believed about their relationship was a lie. Her reason for not pursuing a different career after college had been for him, and she didn't date anyone else because she was holding out for him. He led her to believe he wanted to be with her. She even felt like she loved him and that he could one day love her enough to be with her forever. It was all a lie.

He had a family!

The tears carved trails down her cheeks. What would everyone think? How could she show up on Monday and continue working for him? The answer was simple: she couldn't. Now that his wife probably overheard her yelling, everyone would know. There was only one place she could go and receive no judgement. A place with no reminder of Greg and the relationship she thought they shared. Aly pulled out her cell phone and dialed the first number that came to mind.

"Jade? Something's happened. I can't stay in Dallas any longer. I need your help."

Chapter 1

Present Day

The upbeat party song finally came to an end bringing a much-needed rest to Aly's screaming feet. Wedding shoes, though pretty, were never practical. She was no stranger to three inch heels, in fact her closet was full of them. But wearing them in grass wasn't for the faint of heart. She wouldn't dare admit they were uncomfortable to her cousin, Melissa, and wanted to support her on her special day. The field was gorgeous and music filled the air. Friends and family were celebrating Melissa, Blake, and Wyatt becoming a new family. Though her feet hurt, there was nowhere else she'd rather be.

Since moving back to Shaw Creek, Texas three weeks ago, Aly had been settling into her new life quite well. She moved in with one of her best friends, Jade McBride, and was trying to get her life back together. She had thought she knew where her life was headed but that had all been shattered. So, she returned to her childhood hometown instead. Her parents and brother had already moved away but Aly still had some family here. She hadn't spent a lot of time with her Gram, Aunt Julie, cousin Melissa, and son Wyatt over the past few years. With Blake and Melissa getting married, Aly was thankful for the distraction from the heartbreak she left in Dallas.

After college, Aly chose to stay in Dallas when she got a promising job at a up-and-coming insurance company. She hoped it would look good to have some form of administrative management experience on her resume. Getting a degree in business seemed to be a safe choice and gave her lots of options for a career. A career that was slammed shut with the force of a fifty mile an hour straight-line wind.

Aly didn't want to worry about that right now. She was at a wedding on a beautiful evening, surrounded by family and close friends. Everything else could wait.

"Here's some punch." Jade placed a cup on the table in front of Aly. Jade's hair was cut in a short bob haircut, stylish with an edge. It was so different from Aly's long blonde hair, but paired with the mint green bridesmaid dress, Jade looked gorgeous.

"Thanks," Aly said and took a drink. "Are your feet killing you like mine are?"

Jade shrugged. "They aren't too bad. I'm on my feet all day long at the diner. That's something you're going to have to get used to as well. Just wait until Monday night."

Jade had given Aly a job waitressing at her diner, Jade's Gem. She would be eternally grateful to Jade. Not only did she taken Aly into her apartment but she gave Aly a way to help pay rent. It got her out of Dallas and away from her boss. The sickening pit in her stomach began to ache. Aly took a deep breath, willing it to stay down so not to feel strangled. She'd done nothing but sulk for the past few weeks and she was tired of it. Her life was worth more than suffering for someone who lied and cheated. She didn't want to think about Greg. Not now. Not ever again.

A loud crash came from the food tables. Jade stood to see what was happening. "I guess I better make sure my guys are okay." Jade paused before walking over. "Do you want to come? It'll give you some insight on the catering side of the business."

Aly nodded and followed Jade over to the tables. One of the young women dressed in all black was frantically trying to pick up the lost appetizers on the grass. Aly bent down to help her collect the last few pieces.

"Is everything alright?" Jade asked once the girl stood.

"So sorry, Jade. T-The serving tray got off balance and I tried to catch it, but…"

Aly felt for her as the tears formed in the poor girl's eyes.

Jade filled another tray with bruschetta. "Don't worry about it, Crystal. Accidents happen." She extended the now filled tray. "Calm your nerves and take your time."

"Yes, Jade." Crystal took the tray and walked toward the tables with seated guests.

Jade wiped her hands and sighed. "I don't ever want my employees to stress out about making mistakes. We all make them."

"Weddings can be stressful," Aly said.

"Oh sure. But no matter what the event, I don't want Jade's Gem to be a stressful place to work."

Aly squeezed Jades arm. "I'm sure that's not the case."

"Thanks." Jade's voice was sincere and Aly could tell that she cared a lot about her staff.

"Can I help in anyway?"

Jade assessed the serving tables. "I hate to ask but do you mind taking these dishes to the catering van while I prep the next round of appetizers?"

"Not a problem." Aly picked up the dishes and walked out toward Shasten Lane where the van was parked.

After placing the dishes in the back, she dropped the keys and bent to pick them up. Before she realized what was happening, she bumped into something. Someone. "I'm so sorry."

Aly regained her balance and stood up to find the sexiest smile she'd ever seen. It was slightly off center with dimples framing the corners. She swallowed the sudden lump in her throat. He towered over her five foot three frame by almost a foot, if she had to guess. His amber eyes bore into her with a hint of amusement. He ran his hand through his dark brown hair, cut short on the sides and messy on top. The pearl snap shirt he wore fit him perfectly and his dark blue jeans fell on top of black cowboy boots. He was hot. Really hot.

"I'm sorry, ma'am," he said. His voice was deep with a smooth southern drawl.

Aly took a step back. "It's no problem. Thank you," she said, accepting the keys.

"You're awfully dressed up to be catering a wedding." He looked over her mint green strapless tea-length dress in a slow appreciation. Aly felt goosebumps rise on her arms as the corners of his mouth seemed to spread even wider. It was nice to have a guy admire her looks but that had gotten her in trouble before. She looked down at her dress. "I'm actually in the wedding party."

She walked back toward the reception area and he followed, with an ease in how he carried himself. She couldn't help but notice his amazing cologne that swirled around them with the breeze. Just one more thing to make him tempting.

"Are you a friend of the bride?" he asked.

"No, actually she's my cousin." They came to a stop outside the crowd of people on the dance floor. "Thanks for walking me back."

"My pleasure," he said and offered his hand to her. "Colt Teel."

She reached to shake his hand and pulled it to his lips. *Bold.* She inhaled slowly to tame her butterflies as a result of this stranger's soft kiss. He was confident yet... comfortable. She was surprised she felt that way with him. She was still trying to heal the wound that made her everyday life anything but comfortable.

She cleared her throat and said, "Uh, it was nice to meet you. Have a good night."

As she turned to leave, he called to her, "Ma'am?"

She looked over her shoulder.

"Perhaps you'll save me a dance?" He took a step toward her.

It would be wonderful to get lost in the arms of a gorgeous man, but she wasn't looking for that right now. The reason she was back in Shaw Creek was to separate herself from a relationship. It was probably best to keep distance from someone like Colt. His southern drawl, tight shirt, cowboy boots, and crooked smile were a deadly combination. Though she wasn't into his type, he seemed like the kind of guy who was hard to resist. He could cause her more heartache than she wanted.

"We'll see." She couldn't keep from smiling as she turned away.

"Do you mind if I ask for your name?" he asked, and she stopped again.

He would probably find out anyway in this small town. He seemed to be the type of guy who didn't give up easily. "Aly. Aly Meyers."

With that she left him and headed back to find Jade sitting at the table across the field. She hoped it wouldn't be obvious that she'd just had her emotions rocked by a sexy cowboy. How was that even possible when she just met him? *A cowboy?*

"Thank you so much for helping," Jade said as Aly took her seat.

"Not a problem." A few strands of hair blew across Aly's face and she tucked them behind her ear.

"I see you met Colt."

It looked like she wasn't going to be so lucky in avoiding talking about him. Her heart fluttered at the sound of his name. That's not what she wanted. Was it? "Yeah. I ran into him by the van."

"He kissed your hand." Jade cocked an eyebrow.

"I know. He just pulled it up to his lips when I went to shake his hand."

Jade smirked at her.

"Don't say a word. I'm not looking for a relationship." It had taken a lot out of her to escape from Dallas, her job, and her boss. Jade knew the basics, but she hadn't told anyone the real reason for her return. It was shameful. She just wanted to forget it all.

"You know there are a lot of eligible guys around here. I can introduce you?" Jade asked.

"No." Aly was *very* single and still adjusting to that. She didn't feel like having this conversation.

"You can still have fun even though things didn't work out with Greg."

"That's an understatement," Aly chided.

"You don't have to get into anything serious. I'd love to introduce you to some people and help you get comfortable with new friends here."

It would be nice to build new friendships. Depending on Jade for companionship wouldn't be logical or fair to her. She downed the rest of her punch. "Thanks. I'm sure you're right. I'm going to get some more." She got up before Jade could comment.

Aly made her way back to the serving tables and decided to forgo the small cup of punch. It would be best to go for a whole bottle of water on this hot summer night. Though it was the perfect night for a wedding, the heat still cut through when the wind died down. Aly roamed around slowly watching everyone have a good time. Blake and Melissa were having a private moment by the pond. Aly smiled to herself. It would be so amazing to have the chance at a relationship like that. She wanted to have faith that God would bring that man into her life. She wanted to trust that his heart was only for her. She wanted to know what it felt like to truly love someone with all her heart. She'd been down that road, but it turned out she was wrong. Very wrong. She wasn't so sure she knew what love was anyway.

Aly's eyes caught sight of Colt. His crooked smile was so intoxicating and Aly liked it more than she should, until she saw where it was directed. His eyes were focused on a beautiful—okay hot—brunette who pulled him onto the dance floor. Her tea length black dress looked like it could be painted on and she had legs for days. They looked good together. Of course, he would have someone like that on his arm.

Aly sighed. She didn't want to just be someone's dirty little secret. She wanted to believe that she had value and worth. To be the woman a man was proud to show off. Then perhaps she could take a chance and risk her heart again.

Chapter 2

Colt Teel inhaled deeply as he entered the horse barn. The smell of hay and horse filled his senses, instantly relaxing him. After church, Colt wanted to have a moment alone and this was the perfect place. It was Sunday and the ranch hands weren't coming in until after lunch. This gave them time for worship and family.

It was so nice being home and joining his family at church instead of traveling on the rodeo circuit, riding bulls. He had grown up going to church every week with his parents and brothers, but once he graduated high school fourteen years ago, he was gone most every weekend. Making church a priority fell by the way side. He didn't have anything against religion, but his rather colorful lifestyle made listening to the preacher's message uncomfortable. In the past six months, Colt had felt convicted that he should make it a bigger priority.

Colt inhaled the clean crisp air. There was no place like Big T Ranch. He grew up on and was destined to take it over in the wake of his father's desire to finally retire. He loved it and couldn't picture himself doing anything else, but he wasn't done on the circuit just yet.

The south side of the barn had an office, bathroom, and several storage rooms. Along the north wall of the barn there were eight stalls but only seven of them were full. Having one of the largest cattle ranches in the Dallas area, the Teels needed a good number of horses to work the cattle and maintain the fence lines. He stopped at the second stall. On cue the large chestnut lifted his head outside the stall, most likely in hopes for a treat.

"Hey, Duke," Colt said rubbing the horse's long nose. The horse greedily searched Colt's hands. Pulling out some sugar cubes, Colt offered them over to the big guy. "Are these what you're looking for?" They disappeared in an instant. Colt ran his hand down Duke's neck enjoying the feel of the silk coat on his calloused hands.

"There you are."

He turned to see his dad, George Teel, enter the barn. "Hey. I wanted to come out before we ate."

His dad nodded in understanding. "I think your mom has roast and potatoes in the crockpot. It smells awfully tasty in there." He leaned against the stall next to Colt. "I was wondering if you wanted to head over to the horse sale this week. I've heard there are several roping horses that look promising. You think you might want to get a new one for yourself?"

Colt's shoulders sagged at the thought. "You know there's no point, Dad. Duke's the best roping and work horse we've got." Which was true, at least after Jake, Colt's first horse. Replacing Jake wasn't an easy task. Perhaps that's why he'd been horseless for over a decade. Well, that and one other reason Colt did his best to *never* think about.

"Duke is the best but he's getting older. It'd be good to find another one. Just because you'll be here running the ranch doesn't mean that you can't rope as a hobby."

"Because it's time for me to settle down, right?" Colt asked.

George sighed. "You know your mother and I would like to see you slow down and maybe start a family. There's a time for wild antics and a time to take on your responsibilities."

"I know you don't like that I ride bulls, but I'm not going to rope again. No matter how many times we have this conversation." Colt had hung up his roping hat after losing Jake. Though Duke was great, it just didn't feel the same. And just because they were ready for him to take things over, didn't mean he was ready right that minute. "Bull riding's in my blood now."

"I know you like bull riding, but you were the best. You only pick up a rope a few times a year now." His dad's voice held a bit of sadness.

Colt had been the best but that was a long time ago. Bull riding didn't give him the same amount of pleasure that roping had. However, it did give him something he craved now: adrenaline and danger. He enjoyed the prep before sitting on top of 1,700 pounds of pure terror. As the bull breathed, there was a pull on his glove under the strain of the bull rope in anticipation of the opening gate. The following eight seconds were all that mattered. Such a short time, and yet it seemed like an eternity. It was a rush so exhilarating, it's hard to describe to those who'd never experienced it. The high was addictive. But like other addictions, there was often a sharper fall when it came to an end.

Colt looked back at the big chestnut in front of him. Duke *was* getting older. In his prime, he had been a great roping horse. There was no need for a roping horse because their purpose was to work cattle. Colt did miss the bond that came with having his own horse. Perhaps he could think about getting another one. Maybe. "I'll think about it."

His dad gave him a pat on the shoulder and smiled. "Good. I'm going to head back to see if I can help your mother get ready before your brothers get here."

"I'll be in after a while."

His dad exited the barn, and Colt's shoulders relaxed. He hated having that conversation with his dad. Roping had been his first love. One moment he was chasing a dream and the next it was all taken away from him. Remembering things from so long ago wasn't easy for him. It brought pain, heartache, and guilt. It was best to just leave well enough alone.

After feeding all the horses, Colt headed home to get cleaned up for dinner. He lived in one of the ranch hand cabins on the property about five hundred yards away from his parents' house. As the assistant ranch manager, it was convenient living there. He wasn't home on a consistent basis depending on the time of year, but he did work hard to maintain everything with the long-time ranch manager Frank White.

The cabin wasn't anything fancy but Colt had everything he needed. He washed his hands and re-fixed his hair so his mother wouldn't complain. She prided herself in having her children groomed and presentable. Even raising three boys on a cattle ranch, it wouldn't suit a woman of her class to have dirty men at her table.

Taking one last look in the mirror, Colt felt like he was suitable for the meal. It wouldn't be surprising if his mother found something to complain about, especially when it came to him.

He turned off the lights and made his trek across the yard to the main house. There were two extra vehicles in the driveway meaning his two younger brothers, their wives, and five nieces had already arrived. Not a single nephew. They had opened his world up to dresses, the color pink, bows, dolls, and drama, but he wouldn't trade them for anything.

He took the steps up to the front door. The large wrap-around deck brought back pleasant memories of swinging and playing as a young kid. Colt and his brothers used to spend hours with their toy trucks and tractors out there. It was a wonder there weren't worn paths on the wooden planks. Life was simpler back then. The seven foot double wood front doors definitely gave one heck of a first impression. The whole house screamed grandeur and money. Which is what Colt figured his mother was going for.

He could hear the adults in the dining room and the kids in the kitchen, meaning dinner must be getting ready to start. Colt stuck his tongue out at his nieces sitting at the designated "kid table" in the breakfast nook. The girls giggled and returned the gesture. Gosh, he loved them. He paused at the threshold of the dining room, listening to his youngest brother, Scott, talk about some business deal he was working on in Dallas.

"Colt, finally." His mother interrupted Scott. Her voice was tight. "We can start now."

Colt felt his irritation prickle his skin and it seeped through his voice. "I'm not late, Mom. Right on time actually, like always. No need to be upset." He took the only empty seat to the right of his father.

The tension at the table increased immediately. Of course, Linda Teel wasn't about to let her oldest son make her loose composure, even in front of just family. She straightened her back and placed her napkin in her lap. She didn't look back at Colt. "George, can you say grace?"

"Yes, dear," Colt's dad answered.

After grace they began passing the food around the table in relative silence. Colt figured it was best to keep his mouth shut unless spoken too. Scott continued talking about his job and everyone began to eat. The tension eased and light conversation filled the dining room.

"What's up with you, bro?" Matt said from next to him.

"Not much. Just been busy." Colt took a drink of his sweet tea.

"I saw you dancing a lot with some cute brunette at the wedding yesterday."

Colt didn't want to go there. Matt had been the first to get married out of the brothers. He was also aware about how their mom felt that Colt hadn't settled down yet.

"Yeah, I danced with several women."

"Oh come on, Colt. She was tall, had dark hair, and wore a black dress."

"I remember. We had a good time. That's all." Colt took another bite of potatoes. What was her name? Mara? Sara? Who knows. She was pretty but if he couldn't even remember her name it was probably a sign. He did get her number and maybe he'd call her sometime this week.

"If that's it then too bad. She looked like she was really into you." Matt took a drink. "Why don't you open up and consider a relationship with someone? With anyone?"

Glancing around the table Colt noticed everyone was wrapped up in some kind of discussion about a fundraiser or something in the city. He was relieved they weren't paying attention to what Matt was saying. He stabbed a piece of his roast irritated. "You know that's not my thing."

He didn't do serious and he made sure every woman knew that up front. Fun, easy, and fast, that was his motto. Matt would just have to get over himself and realize Colt wasn't looking for something steady.

"You don't let anyone get close to you. We've all dealt with hurt in our pasts and have moved past it. When are you going to grow up and do that too?"

The table fell silent. Colt sensed everyone's eyes on him. His fingers pulled into a fist and it took everything he had not to punch Matt right then. His family should support him and understand that he'd settle down when the time was right. But in that moment, support was the farthest thing from what he felt. They loved him, he believed that. He knew it was odd being the oldest and not having had a serious relationship in years, and everyone at that table knew why that was.

Anger. Hurt. Sadness. Regret. Bitterness.

The Past. The Present.

It all hit Colt with the force of a bull's kick. He didn't want to hear about how he was wasting his life. That he was disappointing them by not living the life they wanted.

He quickly pushed away from the table not feeling hungry anymore. "Thank you for dinner, Mom. It looks great. Excuse me."

Before anyone else could say a word, Colt bolted from the house. When he reached the bottom of the porch steps, the front door opened.

"Colt, wait."

He wasn't stopping until he was inside his cabin. Matt's hand jerked his shoulder around, causing Colt to stumble.

"I'm sorry. I shouldn't have said that back there."

"Why not? It's not like I'm oblivious to the disappointment I am. Mom wants me to get married. Dad wants me to quit the circuit. They're ready for me to take over the ranch and since I won't right this second, they think I'm selfish and irresponsible. It wouldn't surprise me if you and Scott thought the same thing."

Matt's shoulders sagged. "That's not it. We just want what's best for you."

"What's best for me? How would you know what that is? I *am* doing what's best for me, living life and working hard. I enjoy the way things are now. It's my life but it seems like everyone has to keep reminding me that I'm not capable to decide for myself. I don't have the time to worry about crap that happened a lifetime ago."

"I didn't mean to bring up Emily." His voice was laced with remorse.

Hearing her name sucked the air from Colt's lungs. Emily was his high school sweetheart. His first love. His only love. Heat consumed him and he took a deep breath. "You have no right to judge me about what happened that night no matter of how long ago it was. You weren't there. You didn't lose everything. *Everything.*" He took a shaky breath. "When you've lost your whole world, then you can have an opinion."

Matt's face dropped. Colt turned on his heels and ran the rest of the way to his cabin. He slammed the door and raked his hand through his hair. He'd become very good at compartmentalizing his feelings. If he didn't let people into the darkest part of his heart then there was no need to revisit it.

Colt pulled open the fridge and cracked open a can of Bud Light. His family didn't understand. He didn't want to feel like a failure but it never seemed to escape him. He could win every competition and become one of the best bull riders on his circuit, but it wouldn't matter to them. His parents and brothers could say they wanted what's best for him but it didn't change how they made him feel. Matt's words were empty in the reflection of their actions.

Maybe it was time to call up that brunette and get lost in meaningless passion and a drunken haze. It had been a while. He knew it wasn't the cure all to the failure and discouragement weighing him down, but he'd take a few hours of pleasure no matter how he felt in the morning. He typed a quick message on his phone and hit send.

******

Colt rolled his shoulders back and felt the pull of silk sheets fall down his torso. Blinking several times, he tried to get his eyes to adjust to the morning sun slicing through the window shades. He realized he wasn't in his cabin. Glancing to his left he saw a long bare back topped with dark brown hair. Then it all came back to him. The fight with Matt and sending a message to the girl from the wedding. She was alluring and more than willing to partake in anything Colt wanted. It had felt good, but as he stared at the ceiling all the pleasure was gone and he felt cheap. He had just shared one of the most intimate parts of himself with a basic stranger, again. And all he could take from it was shame.

She began to stir and Colt took that as his cue to leave. He was going to be late to meet the ranch hands and was sure to hear about it from his dad. He quickly slid his jeans up over his hips and tossed on his shirt.

"You're in a hurry."

Colt looked over at the woman and couldn't even recall her name. "Yeah. I've gotta get to work." He found his shoes and slid one on each foot.

"Thanks for last night." Her voice was sultry and made his skin crawl.

He turned to her as he reached for the door knob. He didn't like the awkward conversations about when they could see each other again. That's not what this was. Just leave and not look back. "Sure. I'll see ya around."

He headed out of the apartment and down to his truck parked on the curb. He settled in the driver's seat and pulled out onto Main Street. His mind was empty and he liked it that way. So, why did he feel horrible? His shoulders were tense and he hated the guilt that rested over them. In the past, he would've been fine to drive off and even brag about his one night stands to his rodeo buddies. But that was the farthest thing from his mind. He wasn't sure this was the best way to live, but he didn't know if he could escape it.

Chapter 3

Aly wiped her hands on the towel and tucked it into the side of her waitress apron. It had been a smooth first day at Jade's Gem. She had never worked in food service before and found it relatively pleasant. The people in Shaw Creek were so nice, something she'd missed since growing up here. There was something special about a small town: community, love, friendship. All things she'd recently lost in Dallas. Aly felt a pain in her chest at the memory and man not far from her mind.

Married. It still seemed like a bad dream. He hid it from everyone. Once word got out that Greg not only had a wife but also two kids, the office exploded with gossip of Aly and Greg's "affair". Her closest coworkers had filled her in on what was being said since she'd left. Aly was heartbroken and humiliated.

She finished cleaning off another table and took the dishes to the kitchen. She stretched her back and tucked the loose pieces of hair behind her ear.

She took a pitcher of water out to the dining room and filled a couple of glasses. One man, probably in his mid-forties smiled and thanked her. He had a gold band on his left finger, and the woman across from him wore a beautiful diamond solitaire. They were honest about their commitment to each other and everyone could see it. She turned and headed back behind the bar.

Of course, Greg never wore his wedding ring and didn't have anything personal in his office. But that didn't change the fact that she had been the mistress. The mistress that took part in hurting a family, regardless of not knowing about them. The only person she told about the break up was Jade. Thankfully Jade didn't press for more details and had been supportive. It would be best to leave the specifics in Dallas.

Crystal tapped on Aly's shoulder, pulling her out of her thoughts. She had a new table with two men, one in a cowboy hat and the other in a baseball cap. It was time to quit thinking about the past and start looking toward the future. She grabbed two menus and headed toward them. "Good afternoon, what can I get you gentlemen to drink?"

The man with the baseball cap lifted his head and she felt the butterflies erupt in her stomach again. It was the guy from Blake and Melissa's wedding. The guy she had done her best not to think about the past few days.

Colt.

His solid grey t-shirt and faded blue jeans looked like he'd been rolling around in the dirt. She could make out defined arms with what appeared to be a barbed wire tattoo around his bicep. It had been hidden under his shirt at the wedding. Even in the old clothes, he still looked as gorgeous as ever, perhaps even more so. His eyes widened as they took her in and the stubble on his face brought depth to the sharp angle of his chin. She took a deep breath hoping the flush on her face didn't scream of her attraction to him. A slow crooked smile spread across his face.

"Hello," she smiled back.

He nodded and said, "Ma'am."

Oh, that drawl. She was in trouble. She swallowed and turned to look at the other man with the cowboy hat. "What can I start you guys out with?"

After taking their drink orders, she turned and headed back to the drink station behind the bar. She had done her best not to think about him, though unsuccessful. She quickly took their drinks back to the table. "Alright, are you guys ready to order or do you need a few more minutes?"

"I believe we're ready," said the older gentleman with the cowboy hat. "I'll have the bacon cheeseburger and a side of cheese fries."

She wrote the order on her tab and looked at Colt. "For you, sir?"

He smiled at her for a moment and the silence lingering. Why was he looking at her like that? Was there something on her face? She couldn't look away from the unexplainable pull his eyes had on her. She bit her bottom lip, a nervous habit. Colt's eyes dropped to her lips and then back up. Her heart picked up its pace and she wasn't sure what to say.

Finally, he broke the silence. "I'll have the same."

Colt's irises were a yummy caramel color that made her want to dip an apple in them. He had a warmth that made her sense a depth to him. Though it would be easy to stare into his eyes forever, she forced herself to look down to her notepad. "I'll put this in for you."

Aly rushed into the kitchen and tore off the carbon copy of the ticket and hung it up for Jade and her cook. She pressed the palms of her hands into the stainless-steel counter and released a deep breath. She was being ridiculous. She didn't want to like the ruggedly handsome guy. Though she couldn't deny that he was the best part of her day so far.

She closed her eyes and could remember the feel of his callouses, the look in his eyes when he kissed her hand, and the smell of his cologne in the air. She liked it… a lot.

Stop it. Stop thinking about him.

That was easier said than done. Aly flipped through her notepad to check if her previous table's order was up.

"Everything okay?" Jade asked.

Aly shook off the intense affect Colt seemed to have and looked up at her friend. "Yeah. It's been busy."

"Well, you're doing great for your first day. I told you it was pretty straight forward." Jade began prepping a plate to serve. "Keep it up and ask questions if you need."

"Thanks," Aly said. It had been pretty good. She'd only had to ask a few questions and had managed to only make one mistake. Not bad. With two more hours to go, her feet were already sore. They'd be screaming by the time she got to Jade's apartment; something she'd have to get used to. But seeing Colt on occasion would defiantly make the exhaustion worth it.

Aly noticed Crystal putting in a new order next to her and remembered how flustered Crystal had been when she dropped the tray at Melissa's wedding. Overall, Aly liked her. She'd been a big help today, answering Aly's questions. Her thoughts drifted back to Colt and she wondered how often he came into the diner. She had no idea who he really was or what he did for a living but she hoped he'd come in often.

"Is that smile as a result of the sexy cowboy at table five?" The smirk on Crystal's face told Aly she'd been caught. *Deny.*

"No. I was just thinking that my first day is going okay." Which was true, partly.

Crystal shrugged and glanced out into the dining room. "Colt Teel always gives me a reason to smile."

Aly couldn't see Colt because he was facing away from her. Crystal raised an eyebrow at her. "What?" Aly asked. Dang, caught again.

"Don't get your hopes up about Colt."

Aly hesitated. "I don't know what you mean."

Crystal shot a glance toward the dining room. "Let's just say that he has a past that involves a lot of women."

Aly wasn't too surprised by that. A guy like him probably had a long line of women after him. "Don't we all have a past?"

"Sure, but Colt's is tarnished more than others. Women. Parties. Booze. He isn't one for commitment," Crystal answered.

"Who's the older guy with him?"

"That's his mentor, Frank White. They come in together a couple of times a week. Colt's big into rodeos and gone most weekends." Crystal picked up her table's plate before continuing. "Colt comes in almost every day alone if not with Frank, usually for lunch. I just hate to see you get your hopes up because Colt's not someone you would want to waste your time with." She turned to head back out but paused. "By the way, I love your earrings. A little fancy for a diner but super cute."

"Thanks." Aly fingered one of her earrings. She may not be wearing professional office attire but she always found a way to dress up a little. Her eyes moved over to where Colt was sitting. It was unfortunate that Colt had a reputation like that, but she wasn't one to judge quickly. That's what happened to her and she wanted to offer everyone the common curtesy of an honest chance at respect.

"Aly," Jade called. "Don't stress too much about what Crystal said. She's been burned by Colt in the past. They used to date. What she says is true. Colt does have a colorful reputation but he's a nice guy. His family goes to church with us."

Aly grabbed the plates for Frank and Colt. "Well, I'm not looking for a relationship anyway, remember?" It was amazing how efficient Jade was at getting food prepared quickly. Aly smiled and headed to deliver the meals.

"Enjoy," she told the men and turned quickly so she didn't have to look at Colt for long. She couldn't afford to get involved. Her heart still bore some fresh cuts from Greg and now was her chance to focus on herself. It wasn't wrong to enjoy looking at Colt as long as that was all she let happen.

Chapter 4

Colt took the last drink of his water. The burger had been amazing, as always. If he could've been focused enough to enjoy it, that is. Frank had talked a lot but Colt wasn't sure he'd be able to recount most of the conversation. All he could think about was their cute blonde waitress. *Aly.*

When he met Aly at the Knoll-Adair wedding two days ago, he hadn't thought he would ever see her again. He figured she had come to town for the wedding only. She had captured his attention in that bridesmaid dress. Her blonde hair fell like a waterfall over her shoulders and her sky-blue eyes pierced through his. He did sneak several peeks at her throughout the rest of the reception but something kept him from following up on getting that dance.

Frankly, he hadn't thought about Aly after he got home. Then she reappeared working at Jade's Gem, the best little place in town. She seemed to recognize him and blushed when he looked at her. She was definitely something to appreciate, that's for sure. When she bit her lip, he couldn't help himself but stare. If Frank hadn't been there, he probably would've been more forward with her. She kept her shoulders back and held eye contact as long as him did. She was coy in how she answered him at the wedding and spoke her mind. He would bet she could give any guy a run for his money.

Aly removed their plates and placed a piece of pecan pie down in front of Frank. "Can I get you anything else?"

Several things came to mind and Colt quickly pushed them back. Not in front of Frank. He shook his head and said, "No. Thank you."

She smiled and turned toward another table, the blue stones in her earrings matched her eyes. The painted on blue jeans had some type of jewels on the back pockets that were hard to miss. Her red polo clung to her in all the right places and made all sorts of things flash in his mind. Colt looked up to see a smug expression on Frank's face. Reluctantly he asked, "What?"

"You have a thing for her, huh?" Frank asked.

"She's nice."

"Sure seems to be." Frank nodded. "I can tell you guys know each other. Where from?"

"I just met her briefly at the wedding this weekend. She was in the wedding party. The bride's cousin, I believe." Colt smiled when he thought about her in that green dress. Her blonde hair sure looked amazing against it.

"Just be careful there, son."

Colt liked that Frank called him that. Colt loved his own father and had a pretty good relationship with him. However, Frank had become like a second dad to Colt, especially after high school. Frank knew about a lot of Colt's struggles and what he had to overcome. Colt sighed and said, "I know."

Frank's smile was kind. "You're not one to always consider a woman's feelings and I know I've told you this a thousand times, but most women don't want that kind of relationship."

Colt knew Frank was right. Playing the field with woman after woman was a habit he wouldn't mind breaking. But the thought that he deserved an honest and pure relationship seemed impossible. He wasn't worthy of it and might not ever be. It would be nice to have a relationship like his two younger brothers, but that's all Colt was willing to risk.

Frank cut through his thoughts and said, "If she's close with Melissa and Blake, then she's bound to be a good girl."

Colt nodded in understanding. Aly didn't fall for his typical play at winning a girl over at the wedding. In fact, she had turned away and didn't give him a second look. Her eyes dilated when they first met and again just a minute ago. He hoped that meant she was interested. It was something Colt would love to discover.

Aly came back by to refill their drink but kept silent. She moved to the table behind Frank and Colt loved her smile as she helped the customers. When she started toward the kitchen, he thought she would look at him, but she didn't. It disappointed him a little.

Once Frank finished his desert—something that was always a must—they went to the front counter to pay for their food. Jade McBride, the owner, appeared next to them with a bright smile. "Colt. Frank. It's so good to see you."

"Hello," Frank and Colt said in unison.

"I hope you enjoyed your lunch," Jade said as one of her employees received their payment.

"Always is. Thank you." They turned to leave, but Jade grabbed Colt's arm to stop him.

"Colt, can I talk to you for a second?"

Frank gave him a wave. "I'll wait for you in the truck."

Once Frank left, Colt turned toward Jade. "What can I do for you?"

She guided him off to the side away from the counter. "I see you've met Aly."

Colt nodded and glanced back out to the dining room, where Aly was cleaning their table. "Yeah, she seems great."

"She's amazing really." Jade raised an eyebrow.

He had known Jade since they were kids. She was spunky and a go-getter. Colt felt like he knew Jade well enough to know that she had more to say. He simply nodded waiting for her to continue.

"We've been friends for a long time so I wanted to talk freely with you. If that's ok?"

"Sure."

Jade straightened her shoulders and took a deep breath. "We can both agree that you don't do relationships."

Colt knew exactly where she was going. He didn't do commitment and therefore broke a lot of hearts. Girls talk and so most of them knew what his former relationships had consisted of. If you could even call them relationships. "True."

She took a deep breath. "You know I love you. But I'm asking you to not pursue Aly. At least, not right now."

His shoulders dropped a fraction. "I understand."

"When Aly falls in love, she falls hard. She's trying to start over here and a relationship isn't what she wants right now."

"Well, you know I'm not looking for one."

"I'm just saying I'd love for you to be her friend. You've been a great friend to me and that's what Aly needs. Can you do that for me?"

Jade wanted the best for Aly, and with his track record he understood her concern. But for some reason, it stung a little. "I can do that."

Jade grinned. "Thank you. I've got to get back in there, but I'm glad I caught you."

Colt made his way toward the ranch truck but paused, looking back through the window to see Aly cleaning off another table. He heard Jade loud and clear but something about Aly just pulled at him. He didn't know what it was but he had a feeling sooner or later he'd be finding out.

Chapter 5

The next morning, Aly cleaned off the counter and placed the mixing bowl in the sink to rinse. The smell of cinnamon and dough began to fill the apartment. Jade was still in her room and she figured it would be a nice treat to have homemade cinnamon rolls for breakfast. Her feet were feeling much better but her back seemed a little tight after working three long days. But she needed to work the extra hours to save money. If Jade needed the extra help she would do her best to fill in.

"What smells so good in here?" Jade asked taking a seat at the bar.

"Cinnamon rolls." Aly finished whisking the homemade icing in a bowl, pulled the rolls out of the oven, and sat them in front of Jade.

"These look amazing!" Jade took a deep inhale. "You know, I remember you always helping Gram in the kitchen."

Aly began spreading the icing over the top of the hot rolls and smiled at the memory. "Yeah, she was a great teacher. Still is. She'd be so proud of anything I made no matter how messy the kitchen got. When I was living in Dallas, I baked a lot too." She licked her fingers and placed the now empty bowl in the sink.

"Well, you're not going to hear me complain! Bake as much as you want." Jade took a huge bite of a roll and gushed over the taste.

It made Aly so happy to see people enjoying her food. "I'm glad you like it."

Jade nodded quickly, her mouth full. Aly took a roll for herself and sat down with some milk. Jade poured herself a glass and took a big drink. "Man, you're amazing! I wish I was a better baker. Be careful or I might put you to work at the diner here pretty soon."

"Oh, I don't bake for other people. Just family and close friends."

Jade finished her last bite. "I might have to change that."

Aly smiled but she wasn't so sure. She loved baking and everyone had always told her she was great at it. But the thought of making it for the diner was a little scary. Surely, Jade wasn't serious.

"Hey, would you like to go dancing? Ladies night is tomorrow. Maybe Melissa would go with us!"

"That sounds like fun. Though I'm not much of a line dancer."

Jade waved her hand. "The steps are so easy you'll get it. And don't worry about your fancy clothes, I've got something you can wear. We just have to get you to trade those stilettos in your closet for some cowboy boots."

That would be interesting. The only pair of cowboy boots Aly ever owned were from when she was a little girl. In fact, she had no idea what to wear to a country dance hall.

"There's a rodeo this weekend too, Friday and Saturday. We should go."

"Rodeo? I don't know about that." It wasn't really her scene.

"When's the last time you went to one?" Jade asked.

Aly shrugged. "I don't know. Probably my sophomore or junior year in high school."

"Well then, I'm taking you this weekend. There's a dance afterwards at The Wrangler. There's bound to be some cute guys available for dancing."

"Is Andrew ok with you going out dancing?" Aly was surprised that Jade was mentioning going out to scout guys.

"Changing the subject I see."

Aly shrugged a shoulder.

Jade wiped her hands on a napkin. "He's fine with it. Our relationship is casual. I'm not going out to find a guy. It's you I'm helping meet people."

"You seem determined to get me out there."

"Dancing doesn't mean you're headed to the alter. It's just some fun."

"When's Andrew coming back?"

"I'm not sure. I think he's hoping next week. They've got some big deal they're trying to close." Jade washed her hands in the sink.

Since moving in with Jade, Aly had seen a change in Jade's response to conversation about Andrew. Usually, Jade was pretty informative about what was going on in Andrew's life, but now she seemed nonchalant about it all.

"He's always gone and I'm always at the diner. We talk throughout the week: calls, texts, and Facetime. But that's all our relationship seems to be anymore."

Aly had only met Andrew a few times and got the impression that he was committed to his career. They must not see each other as often as Aly thought. Jade was just as committed to her job but maybe she needed more out of the relationship. "Are you still happy?"

Jade was silent for a little while as she placed Aly's dirty dishes in the dishwasher. She turned to face Aly and leaned her back against the counter. Aly could see the conflict in Jade's eyes.

"I don't mean to pry. I just thought since you've been dating for what, three years, that you were serious." Aly felt bad for bringing it up. Maybe she'd read their relationship wrong. Then again she had been in Dallas the whole-time Jade was with Andrew.

Jade rung her hands in a towel. "I'm not sure. We care about each other but not in the way we used to. It's like we're living two different lives. Things have never been *serious*. Maybe love isn't for the two of us, at least the two of us together."

"I'm sorry to hear that."

Jade pushed off the counter. "It's not that big of a deal. We're both busy and we have a great time together when he's home. That's enough right now."

Aly watched Jade disappear into her bedroom. She was sad that Jade didn't have a better relationship with Andrew. Although, Jade didn't seem too upset about it. She seemed to be taking it all in stride. Maybe she was right. How did any of them know when they were in love? Aly knew she had missed the mark on that big time.

She took the rest of the cinnamon rolls and placed them in an air tight container for storage. Then went to her room and finished getting ready. She was hoping her body would adjust to the long hours and physical push of waitressing. She never expected it to be this demanding. One last check in the mirror and she grabbed her apron, purse, and phone.

"Are you ready?" Jade asked from the kitchen.

"Yep."

They jumped into Jade's car and head across town to the diner. Aly's phone rang and she pulled it out of her purse to check it. The moment she saw Greg's name across the top of her screen her heart stopped. Why would he be calling her? There was no reason for him to be calling. She sent the call to voicemail and quickly stuffed it back in her purse.

"Someone you don't want to talk to?" Jade asked.

She still wasn't ready to tell Jade every sordid detail about Greg. "Uh, it was a number I didn't recognize."

Jade smiled at Aly and turned to watch the road. Thank goodness Jade wasn't the prying type.

Her mind wandered back to Greg. She had been doing good at keeping him at bay in her thoughts, at least while at work. The ache in her stomach expanded and she pressed her eyes closed. She didn't want to miss what they had. She didn't want to remember the times that were amazing. She sent up a silent prayer. *God help me. I don't want to feel these things.*

They made it to the diner and began prepping for the breakfast rush in an hour. Aly was thankful to be busy but unfortunately it didn't keep her mind from running wild.

Chapter 6

Aly smiled at her reflection in the mirror. Jade told her that line dancing was about being comfortable and cute. Comfortable because Jade planned on keeping Aly on the dance floor for most of the night. Cute because what girl didn't want to look good for a night out. She had on a light pair of jeans, a form fitting white blouse and a pair of Jade's cowboy boots. Of course, Aly couldn't help but add some type of flare. She paired her turquoise earrings with the matching two string necklace and bracelet. She wasn't sure if jewelry was a big thing at a place like this, but she liked them with the color in the boots. Her hair was loosely curled and it made Aly feel good to be dressed up a little. Granted, tight jeans and boots weren't her typical attire for a night out in the city, but she loved the way she felt. Being in a waitress uniform every day made her desperate for a night out.

There was a knock on the door and Aly rushed out to answer it. "Mel!"

Melissa embraced Aly and gave her a beautiful smile. "Aly, I'm so glad we're going out."

"Me too. I'm sorry you guys didn't get to go on much of a honeymoon."

Melissa sighed. "Well, it doesn't make sense with school starting in two weeks. We did have an unbelievable three days in Dallas. We'll take a longer trip on one of my breaks."

"You just got back yesterday. Are you sure you're up to going out?"

"Most definitely! We've not done anything just the three of us in ages. The grown up world doesn't allow that too often."

"Are you ready to get back in the classroom?" Aly asked following Melissa into the living room. There was a beautiful glow about her. She and her son, Wyatt, had finally found happiness with her high school sweetheart, Blake. Aly was so happy to see Melissa find her happily ever after.

"I miss the kids but I'm not really ready yet. This has been a great summer and I don't want it to end." Melissa sat down on the sofa. "Then again, I love teaching so I'm torn."

Jade came out from her room dressed in dark jeans and a black tank top. Her green eyes were stunning against her short cropped black hair. "You spent the whole summer volunteering for the tutoring program. You definitely need a night out."

Aly grabbed her ID, money, and phone then followed the other two out. Melissa unlocked her car. "I'll drive tonight. You ladies work so hard at the diner you need to both let loose."

Aly wasn't about to object and hopped into the back seat. Tonight was about new beginnings and really living. She was going to relax and enjoy herself. When she went out with friends in Dallas, they would usually eat at a nice restaurant and then head out to a piano bar. They wore either dresses or skirts, never jeans. She was looking forward to the more relaxed scene.

The Wrangler was a popular place in Shaw Creek and drew big crowds from neighboring towns with country concerts. The wood floor was polished and lights flashed throughout the center dance floor. Tables for sitting or standing surrounded the exterior walls in dimmed light and a large bar ran the length of the far wall. They quickly made their way over to the bar to order a round of drinks.

They staked claim on a table near the dance floor. There were several people already dancing. "You going to dance?" Melissa asked Aly.

Line dancing was a little intimidating and she was nervous she'd fall out of sync with everyone. But she wasn't going to let fear hinder her fun. "I think so."

"You're going to have a blast. It's easy once you get started. Especially two-stepping." Jade wagged her eyebrows.

"Oh, I can definitely help with that," Melissa teased and began scanning the room.

Aly wasn't the type to hook up but she didn't mind a dance or two. "Yeah yeah. Here's to a night out with my two favorite people!"

"Cheers!" They all three clinked their glasses together.

The crowd began to pick up and Aly finished off her glass. "Another?" she asked. Jade and Melissa both said yes and Aly headed to the bar. One more round and then it would be time to dance. When a broad back bumped her, Aly stumbled into the bar. Glancing over her shoulder she saw some guy kissing down the neck of a slinky dressed blonde. Ugh. She shifted to the side. Public displays of affection were not her thing. She paid and picked up the three glasses just as the guy turned to place his own order. *Colt.* Their eyes locked and her heart rate skyrocketed through the roof. Why did he have to be so handsome and yet *so* not good for her? His eyes dropped to appraise her.

"Excuse me." Aly held her breath as she zigzagged back to her table.

"Thanks, girl. After this we dance," Jade said.

Aly sat in relative silence, nursing her drink and listening to Melissa talk about Wyatt and Blake. She glanced over her shoulder and saw that Colt and his friend weren't at the bar anymore. With a quick scan around the room, her eyes found him. He was swaying back and forth as the girl was grinding in front of him. When he looked up their eyes met again. The smile on his face fell and he slowed his movements. The blonde tilted her head back against his shoulder and she kissed his neck. Aly pulled her eyes away from them and downed the rest of her glass. She brushed away the feeling of disappointment, knowing she had no reason to want anything from him.

The music changed and Jade clapped her hands. "Aly, you ready to give the Electric Slide a try?"

Aly took a deep breath and hoped that she wouldn't trip and fall. "Let's do it."

All three of them made their way to the dance floor and Aly was placed in the middle. Once the music began, Jade called out a few steps and then they were off. Luckily, this one was easy to follow along to. Everyone around her was hopping and scuffing their boots on the hardwood floor. Aly relaxed as she stepped to the music like everyone else. When they turned, Aly looked for Colt and was relieved and disappointed he wasn't there. She didn't want to see Colt dancing with that hot chick again. Regardless, there was a pang of jealousy behind the thought.

After the fourth song they headed back to their table. Weaving through the packed bar didn't stop her for scanning for Colt. She came up empty.

"That was a lot of fun!" Aly said.

Jade beamed. "I knew you'd love it! We're going to turn you country before you know it."

Melissa laughed. "I'm not so sure that's possible, Jade."

Aly always wanted to escape the country life, but now that she was back, she found herself enjoying it. Being worried about what had happened in Dallas wasn't helping anything and she needed to focus on settling in at Shaw Creek.

"I think I'm going to get some water. Do you guys need anything?" Aly fanned her flushed face. Line dancing was good cardio. At the bar, she ordered three waters and leaned forward against the bar.

A deep voice said, "I haven't seen you around here before, sugar."

Aly turned to see a tall cowboy slide in next to her. His black hat was tipped down on his forehead and button down shirt was freshly pressed. He seemed to be over doing it on the cowboy façade. She offered him a smile. "Hi."

"You here alone?" His speech was slurred.

"I'm here with friends. You?"

He tipped his hat back slightly and she got a good look at his dark brown eyes. They were red and starting to gloss over. He was definitely drunk. "Same. Single?"

She shifted her weight to create a little space between them. "I'm enjoying a girls' night."

"So, there's no boyfriend in the wings." The guy leaned closer to her and rubbed his hand down her arm. "A pretty little thing like you should never be left alone."

Aly grabbed his hand and shoved it away. "I didn't ask you to touch me, which means you don't."

He leaned his face close to hers. She didn't dare fall back. He was going to find out she was no pushover. "I'm everything you could ever need and I don't ever disappoint."

Before she could respond a warm arm wrapped around her waist and pulled her away from him. "She's with me."

Her senses were filled with leather, sandalwood, and earth. *Colt.* The drunk guy snarled at them before mumbling and walking away. The arm around her didn't loosen once the cowboy left and she didn't want to step out of it, but she did. The bartender pushed the waters her way, and she shot a sideways glance at Colt as she picked them up. His smile was so sexy and his amber eyes were swimming with... desire? No. She was not going to be one of his conquests. She wanted to mean more to someone than that.

"Aly." Her name on his lips made everything inside her tingle.

"Thank you," she said and started to walk around him but he stepped in front cutting her off. She took a deep breath and looked up at him. "Yes?"

He leaned down near her ear and said, "I loved watching you line dance. Save a two-step for me. You won't regret it." He tucked a piece of hair behind her ear and smiled. There was no mistaking his confidence and it only made him more attractive to her. Without a word, she returned to the table.

Melissa and Jade continued talking about Wyatt and school starting soon. Aly sat in silence trying her best not to think about Colt. She failed. A boisterous laugh drew her attention to the dance floor. Colt had the blonde she'd seen him with at the bar dipped backward on the dance floor. Colt raised her back up and kept spinning her around the floor. He was clearly enjoying himself by the grin on his face. He wasn't letting much space get between him and his partner. Aly sighed and looked back at Jade and Melissa, who were both watching her. "What?" she asked.

They glanced at each other and then Jade spoke. "We need to find you a cowboy. Fast."

Aly shook her head. "No, no. I'm not interested in anything like that. It's girls' night."

Jade raised an eyebrow. "So you weren't just checking out Colt Teel?"

Aly took a drink of her water. She wanted to deny it but she couldn't. "I was watching all the guys on the dance floor."

"Give her a break, Jade," Melissa said. "She needs this night out and if she wants to appreciate a fine-looking man, then let her."

"Thanks, Mel."

They spent the next hour on the dance floor. Aly was proud that she didn't fall one time. She was glad Jade had convinced her to come.

"I say we go get ice cream! Blake and Wyatt always want to make a late-night ice cream run, so it's our turn." Melissa signaled to the exit.

Aly loved the idea. "Perfect!"

The three women wove their way back to the exit and Aly couldn't help but sneak a peek. Colt was still snuggled close to his dance partner. Yep, she needed her attraction to him to stay buried deep inside. She just prayed it wouldn't end up being easier said than done.

Chapter 7

Aly's first week at Jade's Gem had flown by. She always worked the mornings through late afternoon. If someone called-in then she would work through dinner to get the extra hours. Every day was a whirlwind of people but she was getting to know the regulars. Over all, Aly was pretty happy with her job. It was work and the money wasn't amazing by any means but it gave her purpose and she was making connections. None of these people had heard of her time in Dallas. They knew her from high school and of course through Gram Meyers. Gram was active in their church and whole community. She was best known for her large sunflower field just outside of town, where Blake and Melissa had gotten married. The whole town loved and respected her family. Aly hoped they wouldn't find out about Greg and she wouldn't be the disappointment she believed herself to be.

Colt came in every day for lunch, like Crystal had said, but the two times she'd waited on him, Frank had been with him too. Aly couldn't help but notice the way Crystal laughed when she was around Colt. *Ugh.* She didn't need to be worried about who flirted with Colt. They had only had a few interactions, the last had been a week ago at the Wrangler.

She glanced at the clock and noticed it was past Colt's normal arrival time. Perhaps he wasn't coming in. Why did she have to know that? *Because you're thinking about him too much.*

She walked into the kitchen. "I've got another one for you, Jade."

"How are you doing?" Jade asked over the plating counter.

"I'm doing great. It's been way busier than yesterday but I'm keeping up." Aly wiped her hands on a cloth and stuffed her notepad back into her apron.

"Yeah, that's Friday for ya. There's also a rodeo tonight and tomorrow." Jade slid another plate ready to serve. "Remember me telling you about it?"

"That's right. Is that the reason for the flow of people?" Aly retrieved the two plates for her table.

"Yep. I say we go tomorrow. Justin and I take turns on who's head chef those nights. That way we can each go out if we want on the weekend."

"Sounds like it could be fun." Aly wasn't sure she would fit in with the rodeo crowd but she figured it would be worth a try. She had a really great time line dancing, maybe she would like the rodeo too. She might as well dive in head first.

Aly delivered the meal to table three and picked up the dirty dishes from table two. She turned to head back to the kitchen and ran straight into Colt Teel's chest, causing mashed potatoes and green beans to spill all over the front of her shirt. Aly looked over Colt and saw that he had been spared any of the mess. "I'm so sorry!"

"It's no problem. Here allow me." Colt bent down with her to pick up the broken glass plates.

"Oh, you don't need to do that." Of all the times to drop plates it had to be right in front of Colt. "I can't believe I did that."

Colt offered his hand to assist her to standing. "Let me help you take this to the back."

Aly nodded. Colt followed her and they dropped the broken plates into a tub to be disposed of. Jade stepped out from around the serving counter and said, "Oh no. Are you okay?" She stopped when she noticed Colt.

"Yes. Colt was nice enough to help me pick everything up," Aly said nodding toward Colt. She prayed her face wasn't as red as the ketchup bottle on the counter.

Jade handed Colt a clean towel and said, "Thank you, Colt." She looked at Aly. "How about you go to the restroom and take one of the extra shirts from the break room. I don't want you to worry about this, they're just plates."

Aly nodded and looked at Colt. "Thank you. I'll be out in a second." Aly retreated to the bathroom. She looked at herself in the mirror to see some gravy was smeared on her chin and in her loose hair. *Fan-freaking-tastic.* Colt probably thought she was a wreck. She didn't know if there was anything more embarrassing. What frustrated her even more was that she cared about what he thought. She slipped the new shirt over her head and smoothed it down the front. She tucked some loose hairs back into her pony tail. *No big deal. He doesn't matter.* Time to face Colt again.

Aly scrubbed her apron clean and wrapped it around her waist and checked the dining room. Colt sat at one of her tables and was looking out the window. She got him a large glass of sweet tea and made her way to his table. She placed the glass in front of him and smiled. "Sweet tea?"

"Always. My mamma raised me right." Colt smiled.

"I'm surprised you waited to eat. Crystal or one of the other girls could've gotten your order." Aly felt bad that he had been sitting there without anything while she cleaned up.

Colt adjusted his baseball hat and the left side of his mouth kicked up. "I wanted to wait for you. I didn't get that dance."

Aly felt the butterflies in her stomach start to take flight again. "We left for ice cream. The perfect way to end girls' night."

Colt nodded. "I know we didn't get that dance but maybe we could find another chance to get to know each other."

Aly knew this was probably not a good idea. Okay, no, it was defiantly not a good idea. "I'll think about it."

Colt took a drink of his tea. "I'll have my usual."

After turning in Colt's order, Aly checked on her other tables. Once everyone was taken care of, she paused in the kitchen to take a small break but her mind didn't stray far from Colt. He wanted to get to know her. She shouldn't but she wanted that too. Who wouldn't want to have someone like Colt Teel pay attention to them? Aly's excitement dimmed slightly at the reminder of the girl he danced with last night and then how he flirted back at Crystal. *Don't get your hopes up.* Colt wasn't the type of guy she would usually go after romantically but there was nothing wrong with trying to be his friend. She could have guy friends and nothing happen between them.

When Aly took Colt's order out to him the diner was starting to thin out after the lunch rush. Everyone was probably getting ready for the first night of the rodeo. "Here you go. Can I get you anything else?"

That sexy crooked grin spread across his face. "Sit with me for a minute."

Aly glanced around the room and noticed that her only other table was headed to checkout. What could it hurt to talk to him for a second? "Okay."

******

Colt couldn't keep himself from smiling at Aly. She was so cute when she got flustered and he could tell he had an effect on her. He didn't want to be too pushy about spending time together because it was clear she wasn't that type of girl. He was impressed at how she handled that guy hitting on her in the bar. He couldn't blame the guy for trying to make a move but Colt could tell by her stance she wasn't okay with it. When he first saw her at the bar with Chelsea all over him, it surprised him. Then the expression on her face shifted from surprise to disgust. He usually wouldn't care because he was out to have a good time. But that night, it bothered him. Aly was different and he couldn't help but want to change the way she saw him.

As she took a seat across from him, he appraised her. She'd cleaned the gravy out of her hair and off her face. She looked real good, beautiful really. This close, he could see there were dark flakes throughout her sky-blue eyes. They were amazing. Her long blonde hair was streaked in different shades of blonde and a little color in her cheeks. Her nails were painted a light pink color, nothing flashy. Even in her waitress uniform he could tell she enjoyed her jewelry. Every time he came in she had a different pair of earrings on. Today she wore hoops that looked like someone beat the metal with a hammer. He knew from the wedding that she looked amazing when she dressed up too, but she definitely didn't need it. She was stunning just the way she was with her hair pulled back, minimal makeup, and waitress apron.

"So, tell me something. You're related to Melissa Adair and now live here. Where are you from?" Colt took a bite of his burger.

Aly sat back and said, "Well, originally I'm from here. My dad's family is from here, obviously. I went to high school here."

"What year did you graduate?" Colt asked in between bites.

"Are you trying to find out how old I am?" Aly asked with a bit of tease.

"Perhaps."

"I'm twenty-nine. I graduated in 2007. What about you?"

She's more than four years younger. She was the same age as his youngest brother Scott. Colt took a drink to wash down his bite. "I'm thirty-four. I graduated in 2002." He watched her to see if the age difference mattered to her. He didn't necessarily care much.

She nodded and pulled her bottom lip into her mouth. Maybe she's not as comfortable with the age difference as him. He'd have to remember that so he could prove that it really made no difference to him. "What brings you back to Shaw Creek then?"

Aly's shoulders dropped a little and her eyes flashed a bit of uncertainty. *Interesting.* "I needed a change. Since I've been gone for so long, I decided this was the place for me." Aly fiddled with her apron.

He wanted to find out more but he decided to back off some. "Well, I'm glad you chose to come back here." His phone went off. "Excuse me." It was Frank's text to remind him they had one hour until he was due at the rodeo. He replied and shoved it back in his pocket. "I'm going to have to head out but I definitely want to see you again. Preferably when you're not on the clock."

Aly stood and glanced toward the kitchen. "Well, I'm here pretty much nonstop. I'm sure you have more important things to do than stopping by here to talk to me. You're a popular guy."

"I'm not sure what you mean?" Even though he did know.

"I'm not into flings or anything like that." A girl he didn't recognize walked by and gave him a flirty smile. When he looked back at Aly, she cocked an eyebrow. "You seem to have plenty of ladies interested."

"I'm only interested in the one right in front of me and I think she's interested too."

"You're not used to women telling you no, are you?" She crossed her arms across her chest.

Maintain eye contact. "They don't usually."

She nodded. "I thought so."

"I'm sure you've heard a lot about me considering some of the people you work with." The opinions were mostly true and he didn't blame her for being reluctant. The wild days of partying, drinking, and women in every city should've been behind him years ago. "Sure, I enjoy a good time but it might be time to slow down."

The corners of Aly's mouth curved into a grin. "Well, good for you. I made the same decision and it's working out real nice for me now."

Another clue. "Then we're not that different, are we? What do you say to hanging out as friends?"

She glanced back at the kitchen and bit her bottom lip. He loved when she did that. "Okay. As friends."

Well, at least it wasn't a total rejection. "I'm in the rodeo tonight and tomorrow. You should come. Maybe we can talk after."

Her eyebrows shot up. "You're in the rodeo?"

"I ride bulls."

Aly watched him for a second and he wished he could see inside her brain. Finally, she said, "Jade actually asked me to go with her tomorrow night."

"So tomorrow?" Colt asked. He couldn't help but smile that she wasn't brushing him off.

She nodded and her smile reached her eyes. "Tomorrow." Then she headed back to the kitchen.

After paying for his meal, Colt walked out to his truck. It was time to get ready for his ride tonight. In the past, if a girl didn't give him the attention he desired, he moved on to the next. He didn't know what it was about Aly but he was intrigued with the chase. He never thought he would be pursuing a girl who didn't do flings. But as Colt pulled out of the parking lot, he wanted to be worthy of someone like Aly. Being her friend, like Jade suggested, might be the first step in doing that.

Chapter 8

Aly stood in front of her closet wondering what she had that would work for the rodeo. She thumbed through her dress slacks, pencil skirts, and silk blouses. She was going to stick out like a sore thumb. Perhaps her work jeans and a comfy t-shirt would do. She'd at least be comfortable, but Colt was going to be there and she wasn't sure comfortable was what she wanted to show him. Aly sighed and sat down on her bed.

"Hey girlie! Are you about re—" Jade stopped when she saw Aly sitting on her bed in her bath towel. "What's wrong?"

Aly pointed to her closet. "I have no idea what to wear."

Jade smiled and looked through Aly's clothes. "I have the perfect idea. Wear these dark blue jeans and I've got the shirt for you." Jade left the room.

Aly slipped into her jeans and a white tank top. Her hair was still damp and she figured that a side braid would do the trick. It was bound to be hot and she loved braids. As she placed the hairband around the end of her hair Jade re-appeared. "Here we go!" Jade held up a dark green flowy off the shoulder top and a pair of brown cowboy boots. They'd go great with your silver pendant and hoop earrings."

"That's such a cute top," Aly said as she took the shirt from Jade and slipped it over her head. "I guess I can do the boots again."

"You're going to look amazing in this!" Jade handed the boots and a pair of socks to Aly. She sat down to slip them on. When she was ready, Jade clapped her hands and said, "Gorgeous! The braid is perfect too. You are a head turner for sure."

Aly rolled her eyes and went into the bathroom to check herself in the mirror. She had to admit she looked the part. The dark green shirt was surprisingly slimming. The short layers of hair that didn't fit in the braid framed her face just the way she liked. She put on a little lip gloss and silver dangling earrings to feel a little dressier. Looking over herself, Aly smiled. She felt sexy and it was comfortable too. She grabbed her phone and headed out to the living room.

Jade was waiting by the door texting on her phone. "Let's head out." Jade was dressed similar to Aly with jeans and a red loose top. Her short hair was loosely curled around her chin.

"You look great, Jade." Aly said following her out the front door.

Jade slipped into the driver's seat. "I like dressing up sometimes. Working in a kitchen every day hinders that some."

The rodeo arena was just outside of Shaw Creek and made for a quick drive from Jade's. Once they entered the gates, Aly and Jade helped themselves to getting a drink and chatting with several people they went to high school with. It was good to reconnect with people Aly hadn't seen in years.

The rodeo grounds were packed. She saw a little boy following his father trying to keep the cowboy hat on his head. He was so cute and she wondered if Wyatt would like a cowboy hat. It seemed like a great place that blended singles and families together. There were lots of guys with large belt buckles and cowboy hats and young women in their cut-off shorts. She definitely didn't fit in with them, but she was glad to be there.

"These are going to be great seats, close to the action," Jade said as they found a spot.

Aly waved in front of her face to clear the air. "It's kinda dusty."

"It'll get better once everyone settles down. Did you see all the cute guys?" Jade nodded toward the section just past them.

Aly had noticed the group of what appeared to be friends laughing with a bunch of girls. She figured if Colt was in the rodeo he would be up there doing just that. "I told you, Jade, I'm not looking for anything like that."

"You can still look... with respectable appreciation."

Aly shook her head. She was in trouble if Jade was on the hunt for her.

It looked like there were several events scheduled for the night according to the advertising she'd seen online. When she went to rodeos as a kid she was more concerned with hanging out with her friends than really watching the rodeo. She was looking forward to actually watching everything.

The stands started to fill up and it was clear that Shaw Creek loved their rodeos. Each row was full and people were standing along the edge of the arena. Along the north wall there were advertising signs for sponsors, including Jade's Gem. The school district had lots of booths hosted by different school clubs. Their agriculture program had the longest line, of course. It was great to see the community supporting each other.

"So, what's the favorite event?" Aly asked.

"Bull riding for sure." Jade waved at someone walking by. "It's usually the last event. My personal favorite is the mutton busting."

"That's with the kids, right?" Aly asked.

"Yep." Jade pointed over to a group of little boys all decked out in helmets, vests, and chaps. "Those kids will ride on the backs of sheep. It's the best thing to watch them try so hard to hold on to the wool. It's so fun! It will probably be during the intermission."

Aly vaguely remembered watching kids ride when she was in high school. "I bet—"

"Jade!"

They both turned to see a woman standing in front of them on the walkway. Her long denim jeans were topped with a sparkly belt that accentuated her thin waist. Her floral button-down blouse seemed to be really nice for a dusty rodeo. She ran her well-manicured nails through her shoulder length blonde hair. The gray streaks the only thing showing any sign of aging.

"Mrs. Teel." Jade stood to greet the woman. "How are you doing?"

Teel? Aly looked at the woman again.

"We're doing well. I wanted to check in with you about catering the dinner at Big T Ranch."

"Everything is good to go. I have the food ordered for the menu you approved. It will be *just* lovely." Jade seemed a little over zealous. Why?

"Great. I'll be in touch as we get closer. Thank you." With that Mrs. Teel walked toward the center of the stands.

Jade took her seat again and sighed. "That woman can sure stress me out. She does some big parties out at their ranch which is great for my business. However, her standards are almost impossible to meet."

Aly chewed on this inside of her cheek. That could make catering stressful. "So, Teel?"

Jade shot Aly a knowing smile. "Yes, she's Colt's mom. You know, Colt is in the rodeo tonight."

"Oh, really?" Aly tried to sound surprised but to no avail.

"Don't even try. They're a good family and go to church with us. It's just they're really wealthy and sometimes flaunt it." Jade's tone was flat.

Aly knew plenty of people who were like that in Dallas. She wasn't a fan of it either. From what she knew of Colt, he didn't seem to flaunt money.

The announcer came on over the loud speaker welcoming everyone and started to kick off the rodeo. The opening ceremony was a lot of fun to watch and ended with a single horse and rider holding an American flag circling the arena while the national anthem played.

"The finals for all three events are tonight. They have the leader board up on the marque over there." Jade motioned to the opposite side of the stands where a small digital screen would read the times for each competitor.

The announcer came over the speaker and began the first event, barrel racing. Aly enjoyed watching the riders bolt out across the arena making tight turns around three different barrels in a cloverleaf pattern. She loved horses, though she'd never ridden one before. They were amazing to watch. Jade and Aly cheered with the rest of the crowd through each rider and into the next event, roping.

"I love this event too," Jade said. "There's no way I could loop the horns, jump off, and then hog-tie the steer."

"What's a hog tie?" Aly asked.

"It's where you tie all four legs together with a knot."

"Hmm. I guess I don't really remember this." Aly felt like she should know all these things but she had no real memory of it.

When the timer was set, the steer ran out into the arena breaking some type of string that opened the horse shoot. In a matter of a few seconds the rider had lassoed the steer, jumped off his horse, and tied the legs together. Wow. Aly was amazed at how fast they were. Everyone erupted in a loud cheer.

Even with the excitement, Aly thought the first two events went by slowly. Perhaps it was because she was anxious to see Colt ride a bull. She wondered if she'd get the chance to talk to him tonight. No matter how she tried to hide it, she had her fingers crossed.

The intermission started and lots of people got up to get refreshments. Jade and Aly decided to forgo getting refills right away so they could watch the mutton busting. Aly loved it! The cute little boys were all decked out dressed like miniature cowboys. The cowboy hats they wore when Aly first arrived, were replaced by helmets. When the shoots opened, the sheep took off like their tails were on fire. Aly couldn't believe how long some of the boys held on.

The announcer's voice came over the loud speaker. "We're getting a look at the future bull riders, folks!"

Aly leaned toward Jade and asked, "Has Melissa ever had Wyatt try the mutton busting?"

"Melissa's not into rodeos. Blake is rather indifferent so they don't come very often." Jade said.

"Well, I loved it! It's been my favorite part so far."

Jade looked at her with a cheeky smile. "You're about to change your mind in a minute."

Aly rolled her eyes and did her best to not let Jade see the heat creeping up her neck. She was excited to see Colt. She spotted Mr. and Mrs. Teel in their section talking with several other couples. The men had a clean cut George Strait look with pressed shirts and wranglers. The women had dressy tops and lots of jewelry. She wasn't sure if that was normal attire but as she scanned the crowd it seemed to be over the top. Colt didn't seem like the kind to dress up super fancy and put on a show. In fact, other than the at the wedding, Colt had always been dressed casually. He seemed far more relaxed. The difference between him and his parents made him more intriguing to her. She had a strong desire to try to unmask him and discover who he really was.

It was time for the finals in the bull riding event after the night before.

"We have the top ten bull riders from last night's event ready to compete for the grand price tonight, a whopping $5,000," the announcer said.

"$5000?!" Aly exclaimed.

Jade nodded. "Yeah. The top five will each get something for tonight. The highest is $5000. Depending on what circuit and what time of year it is, the cowboys can make a lot of money. In fact, Colt has done really well in bull riding. He may not be riding for much longer, though. I hear his parents are grooming him to take over the ranch so they can retire. Be glad you came so you get the chance to watch him."

Aly searched the line of bull riders standing near the shoots. It was hard to see their faces because they weren't looking in her direction. As they announced each riders' name in order of ride, they stepped forward and waved their black Stetson hats at the cheering crowd.

Then the announcer said, "Last to ride tonight: Colt Teel. Currently in second place."

The crowd cheered and Colt took a step out and waved. She secretly hoped he would see her but instead he nodded toward his parents. A few women hoot and howl and Colt tipped his hat to them. It wasn't hard to see his cheesy smile and the wink he shot in their direction. Aly felt the excitement she felt in seeing him fade. She had been told Colt was a womanizer and she'd seen him chummy with more than one girl before. However, she couldn't help but be slightly discouraged.

The men turned and made their way out of the arena to get ready for the bulls. Aly suddenly felt the need to move so she turned to Jade, who was talking to a cute guy about the diner. "I'm going to get something to drink. Do you need anything?"

"No, I'm good," Jade answered.

"I just need to stretch my legs." *And stop looking at the ridiculously pretty women Colt winked at.* Aly made her way down to the long lines at the concession stand. She hoped it wouldn't take to terribly long. She settled in her place in line and found herself people watching. In Dallas, Aly spent a lot of time in the park near her apartment and did the same thing. It was more entertaining than sitting in front of the TV sometimes.

The rides seemed to be moving along at a fairly good clip. She hoped that things would slow down long enough so she could get back to her seat before Colt's turn.

The women in front of her had on barley-there shirts and cutoff jeans. Their hair was curled and the makeup seemed a little heavy. They seemed preoccupied by the guys around them and got giddy when one of them looked their way. She didn't have anything against it. Heck, she enjoyed looking at a nice guy but she could do it without making a fool of herself.

"Hey."

Aly turned to see a friendly face standing behind her. He was at least six foot and had sandy blonde hair with grey eyes. His pearl snap shirt fit him like a glove and definitely made him easy of the eyes. "Hello."

"This line's crazy, huh?" he asked.

"Yeah." She looked around them. "It's crazy how many people there are. This town loves their rodeos."

"True. Is this your first time?"

"No. But I haven't been to anything like this in a really long." They moved forward in the line.

"Well, there's an after party tonight. Perhaps you'd be interested in saving me a dance or let me buy you a drink?" He gave her his best smile. He seemed genuinely nice and it felt good to be flirted with.

"We'll see." Her phone buzzed with a text message. "Sorry. It's probably my friend wondering where I am."

"No problem."

When she glanced at her screen it wasn't Jade but Greg. Her heart stopped at seeing his face across her screen. It didn't make sense. She wanted nothing to do with him. She quickly tucked her phone back in her pocket and then stepped up to order her drink.

When she made it back to her seat. It looked like there were two more riders before Colt. She exhaled with relief. Though she didn't want to flaunt that she was here just to see Colt, Aly was excited to see him in action.

The next two riders didn't hold on for the full eight seconds, meaning they were out of the running for the $5000. Aly fiddled with the end of her braid nervously as she realized Colt would be up next. She looked at the shoots trying to pick him out from the group of men.

A guy crawled over the gate and onto the top of a red colored bull. That must be him. The guy she'd met in line walked in front of her cutting her line of sight from Colt. He paused and gave her a killer grin that made her almost blush.

"Don't forget about me tonight," he said and moved down the stands.

Jade wagged her eyes at Aly but before she could comment the announcer cut in.

The announcer's voice cut through the air. "And now it's time for our last rider of the night! He currently sits in second place from last night's event and now it's time to see if he can change that. Colt has been a part of the rodeo community since he was in high school. He started out as a roper and had great success before changing over to bull riding. There has been talk that he may be thinking about stepping away from the rodeo and settling down some. No official statement has been made but we sure do like seeing Colt Teel out here. Let's hear it for our hometown rider!"

Aly was surprised to hear that he did something else other than bull riding. She wondered what made him change events. The bull slammed around in the shoot while Colt tried to get settled. She sent a prayer up that everything would work out, it wasn't just for the ride.

Chapter 9

Colt flexed his hand under the bull rope. He had been looking forward to this ride all day. It was probably one of his last rides in Shaw Creek. He hadn't made that announcement just yet about leaving the circuit because he still didn't know when that would happen. With that knowledge came a great sense of competition. He had to beat this bull, Flame Thrower. He was focused and felt like he had this ride in the bag. Now to just get it done. The roar of the crowd gave him confidence in the support of his home town.

After his hand had the grip he wanted, he tugged on the bull rope and readjusted his hips. Taking one deep breath, he nodded and the shoot opened. Everything around him faded. It was just him and the bull. Flame Thrower bolted from the gate and immediately leapt high in the air. Colt did his best to stay in sync with the flow of the bull's movement. His fingers gripped as tight as he could and his chest was lifted, using his right arm for balance. The bull turned and jolted, doing its best to get him off but Colt countered perfectly. He could do this. *Just a little bit longer.* He squeezed his thighs together and felt the taunt bull's muscles flex against him. The bull spun in the other direction causing Colt to slip slightly but he refused to let go. After what felt like an eternity, the buzzer went off. He dropped his arm to free his left hand from the bull rope. His knees hit the dirt and he looked over his shoulder for the bull. It turned and headed toward Colt with the bullfighters doing their best to block him. Colt shot to his feet and jumped onto the arena pipe. The bull rushed past him and then ran to the back pens.

Colt sat down on the top pipe trying to catch his breath and waved to the crowd who were cheering for him. Then he noticed the very face he'd hoped to see. *Aly.* She sat with Jade and they both were clapping. Her eyes were wide and her smile the biggest he'd ever seen it. She was gorgeous. Her long blonde braid and green shirt made her even more so. Their eyes locked for a few seconds before one of the bull fighters slapped his leg. He hopped down to the dirt and turned back to get one more look at her. She was still watching him and he waved at her. She waved back.

His night just got better.

Colt was the last rider which meant it was time for the judges to combine the scores from last night with tonight's. He found his mentor Frank standing out to the side behind the shoots. "You did good, son."

"Thanks. I felt good before the ride and it just worked out. Maybe it'll be enough to take first place." Colt started to take off his chaps and get ready for the award ceremony. "I'll be right back. I'm just going to put this in the truck real quick." Colt ran out to the truck parked next to the bull pens and put his chaps and spurs in the back. He raked his fingers through his hair and then returned his black Stetson to the top of his head. He was excited to see if things had worked in his favor tonight. He made his way back to Frank and where all the other riders from the event were waiting.

The announcer called Colt's name as winner, and he gave Frank a big hug and ran out onto the stage. The crowd cheered and raised their hats to him. It felt amazing to know that he had such a great support system from his community. He shook some hands and then posed for some pictures with the flood of people who came to greet him and offer their congratulations. His parents came around and he excused himself to say hello.

"You did great out there, Colt." His mother embarrassed him in a stiff hug. Not the warm kind of hug you'd hope to get. She probably didn't want to get her clothes dirty. There was lots of networking to do.

Colt shook his dad's hand. "Thanks for coming, Dad."

George gave him a warm smile. "Of course. I'm so proud of you."

Colt loved to hear that from his dad. He often felt like he didn't measure up to his parents' expectations however, this wasn't one of those times. "I think I'm going to head to the after party for a while."

"Alright. We'll see you at church in the morning?"

"I'll be there." He spoke with several people who were waiting for him and then to a group of women standing off to the side. In the past, he always made his way around to each of them giving them a little attention and a kiss on the cheek. It was somewhat selfish on his part and made him feel good. What red blooded man wouldn't want to have women fawning over him? But tonight, there was one girl in particular that he had his eye on and she wasn't there.

He made his rounds and got caught by all the women and some other young guys who were headed to the after party. One very busty girl, who had them barely covered, threw herself at Colt and kissed him square on the lips. His eyes shot past her shoulder to see Jade and Aly standing at the bottom of the stands. His eyes met Aly's and she quickly looked away from him. *Dang.* Colt gently pushed past the girl and pried her hands off him. He quickly excused himself to head toward Jade and Aly, but they were already exiting to the parking lot. He paused at the gate and watched them jump into Jade's car. *Please be going to the after party.*

Colt ran back to his truck and laid his black Stetson in the back seat where it wouldn't get messed up. He ran his fingers through his hair before placing his old baseball cap on his head – which he preferred over the fancy cowboy hat any day. He hopped in and pulled out onto the road. He was frustrated that Aly had seen him with those women. He wanted her to know that he was serious about developing a friendship… maybe more. The thought surprised him. A week ago he wouldn't have considered having an actual relationship with someone, but now he was. She was getting to him and oddly it wasn't making him push her away but rather he wanted to get closer.

He pulled into the dance saloon's parking lot and scanned for Jade's car. He spotted it out on the opposite side, so he turned his truck to try and park next to them. It was clear the saloon was going to be crazy judging by the cars. Hopefully, he could find them quickly and get the chance to talk Aly.

Once inside, Colt scanned the crowd of people sitting at the tables, around the bar, and on the dance floor. Then he spotted Jade at the bar getting two drinks. He quickly followed her to the back wall and found Aly sitting at one of the tables with a good view of the people dancing. He took a deep breath and hoped Aly wouldn't completely reject him. When he reached their table, he said, "Hey, ladies."

They both turned toward him and grinned. Aly's wasn't as bright as it had been when he first spotted her in the stands.

"Hey, Colt. Nice ride tonight." Jade raised her glass to him.

"Thanks." He looked at Aly. "Do you mind if I join you?"

Jade glanced at Aly for the answer. Aly shook her head and said, "No."

Yes! It was a small win. He pulled out his chair and sat down. Jade was giving him the eye. He needed a safe topic. "So, Aly, what did you think of the rodeo?"

She took a drink of her mojito. "It was fun. I must say my favorite part was the mutton busting. I'm going to have to see if Melissa and Blake will let Wyatt try that."

"Yeah, me and my younger brothers did that. It was something we all enjoyed. It gets you hooked as a young kid and you only want to do more, for me at least."

A silence settled over them and Jade stood. "I'm going to talk to some of those people over there. Just holler if you need me," she said to Aly, who didn't look too pleased.

Once they were alone, Colt knew it was his chance to talk to her about what she saw, but she spoke first. "How many brothers do you have?"

Colt rubbed his hands on his thighs and decided small talk might be best. "Two. They're not into the rodeo anymore. Both are married with kids."

"So, you're the only single one left?"

"Yep."

"Does that make you Mr. Casanova?" Her tone had a slight tease to it but was also seriousness.

Colt felt bad and decided now was his chance. "Look, Aly. I wanted to explain about the girls at the—"

"COLT!!!"

Colt jumped at the sound of his name and turned to see Jessica rushing him. She landed in his lap and hugged him tight. Jessica was one of his many conquests over the years and he wasn't proud of how he'd handled her. She had been perfect for his life because she was just like him, no strings attached. Just what Colt wanted – a hit it and quit it kind of thing. The thought of his time with her made him feel sick. He looked at Aly, who's eyes were wide and lips tight. She looked from him to Jessica before dropping her eyes to her glass. He was the worst person on the planet. She could do much better, but for some reason he still wanted to get close to her. He set Jessica on her feet and she stumbled back. "Jessica, look…"

"You did amazing tonight! If you don't have anyone to celebrate with I'm always available. It's been months, baby." Jessica tried to slide her arms around his waist but he stopped her.

"Jessica. I'm sorry but I'm not interested in that kinda thing anymore." He glanced at Aly who was watching him out of the corner of her eye. "It's a no and it won't be happening ever again."

Jessica looked down at Aly. "Well, if you feel like exploring something vanilla be my guest. When you get bored, just give me a call." She spun on her heel and walked off.

Colt closed his eyes and took a deep breath before turning to see Aly looking down at her glass again. He took his seat and moved closer to her but her back straightened some. "Aly."

"Colt, it's okay. We're friends, right?" she questioned.

Yes, but he wanted to try to be more. "I want to be but that's not all—"

"Look. It seems like there's a good guy underneath your reputation but I'm not wanting to be a challenge for someone. Been there, done that." She stood up and said, "See you around."

"Aly, wait." Colt shoved away from the table but she was already disappearing through the crowd of people. He dropped back down into his seat and stared after her. He didn't want to make Aly feel cheap. The thing was, that's all he'd ever made a woman feel. Well, with the exception of one.

Aly made him want better, which was crazy since he'd only just met her a week ago. How could he be the biggest winner tonight and still feel lower than the floor?

Chapter 10

Aly walked away from Colt trying her best to not let her emotions get the better of her. She was upset, maybe even a little hurt. Though she wasn't quite sure why. She barely knew him and yet she had liked him. Even though she didn't want to, she'd gotten her hopes up regardless of the warnings signs. She pushed through the crowd toward the bar and found Jade talking to some girls. Jade saw her and her eyes got wide. "What happened?"

"It's nothing. Let's just say I quite possibly am the worst judge in character of men. Apparently, I'm too *vanilla* for someone like Colt."

Jade pulled Aly away from the others. "Okay, slow down. Tell me where this is coming from and what happened with Colt."

Aly downed the rest of her glass and then swiped some of her loose hair from her eyes. It was just her luck that someone who had been close to Colt would show up, just as she was starting to feel good about him. Vanilla? Just because she didn't have a super short skirt and her chest hanging out didn't mean she was boring. She was nothing like Jessica and Aly wouldn't apologize for that. But perhaps that was Colt's type and which would mean they could only ever be friends. Of course, she wanted someone she shouldn't. "Did you see the girls all over him after he got his award?"

Jade nodded. "Yeah."

"Well, after you left us at the table, another girl came up and threw herself at Colt. By threw herself I mean literally fell in his lap."

"What did Colt do?"

"He pushed her off and told her he wasn't into that anymore. Which makes me wonder what in the world that really means?! I mean, almost every time I've seen him outside of the diner he has been with a different girl. Then she looked at me like I was trash and called me VANILLA!"

Aly felt a pressure in her temples and pressed the side of her head. Colt wasn't worth all this frustration. She barely knew him and wanted to be fair and give him the benefit of the doubt, but now she didn't know how she could ever see herself being much more than an acquaintance with him.

Jade finished her margarita and said, "Okay, first of all you don't really believe that, do you? You're so much fun and there's nothing plain or boring about you. She was probably just jealous that he was giving you attention and not her."

"I don't know that it matters. I didn't want to judge him based on rumors but it's pretty clear after tonight that I don't belong in Colt's world. He's the type of guy that could get me into a lot of trouble with his casual relationships, smooth drawl, and sexy smile. I would hope I've learned my lesson. Especially after Greg." Aly leaned against the wall behind her.

"I understand that your ex hurt you. Colt is just one guy. There are a million more out there."

Aly rolled her eyes. She didn't want to hear this speech but Jade continued, "Perhaps him pushing that girl away is proof that he is changing, taking things more seriously. I've known him a long time and I can tell you I've never seen him sluff off any girl who was interested in him."

Aly glanced toward their former table but he wasn't sitting there anymore. She sighed. She didn't want to admit there was something about Colt that made her care. She cared about who he was as a person. She cared if he came into the diner for lunch. She cared that girls apparently flocked to him. Ugh.

Someone tapped on her shoulder and a familiar deep voice said, "Excuse me."

She and Jade both look up to see the guy from the concession line. His grey eyes pulled her in and she returned his smile. "Hi."

"I was wondering if you remembered to save me a dance?"

Jade's eye brows raised. "You know each other?"

Aly cleared her throat and said, "Well, we met in the concession line earlier."

"Lincoln Weber," he extended a hand to Aly. "I never got your name."

Aly shook his hand. "Aly Meyers and this is Jade." His hands were fairly smooth and soft. She remembered feeling the hard callouses on Colt's hand but dismissed the memory.

"Nice to meet you, Lincoln," Jade said.

Lincoln turned toward Aly and said, "Care to take that dance?"

Aly hesitated for just a moment. After the encounter with Colt and his female conquests she could use some fun. She took his open hand and said, "Sure."

Lincoln lead her onto the dance floor where other couples were already starting their two step. Aly was relieved when she picked up the steps quickly. Lincoln was charming and nice. He was strong and yet gentle in how he guided her across the dance floor. He laughed when they spun quicker and pulled her in close to help her when she missed a step. She wondered if Colt was watching her. Aly felt a pang in her chest because she didn't want to think about Colt as she danced with someone else. Lincoln was a handsome guy, who smelled amazing!

"My, you're a good dancer," he said.

"I'm just as surprised as you. We didn't two-step in the city." She and Greg never went out, of course, but she did go out with her girlfriends on occasion. However, there was no slow or line dancing in those places. The lights were always dim and music was so loud you almost couldn't have a conversation. She found she preferred this place more.

They took another turn around the floor and then he said, "So, tell me. How does a pretty girl like you not have a date tonight?"

Aly looked over his shoulder into the room. "I don't know. I guess I haven't found a guy worth keeping around yet." *Or that's trustworthy enough.* "I'm okay with it though. I enjoy going out with Jade." She hoped she sounded more confident than her wounded spirit felt.

"I get that. Perhaps someone will change that for you." Lincoln smiled.

That sounded good but Aly still wasn't sure she was ready. Especially after getting her hopes up about Colt. She focused on the song as Lincoln twirled her around the floor. Then when the music came to an end, he kissed her hand. "Can I buy you a drink?" he asked.

"Oh, no. I limit myself to only a couple when I go out. I'm going to go find Jade. Thank you for the dance."

"Anytime. I hope to see you again, Aly." He tipped his hat to her.

"See you around." She turned and started maneuvering between the crowd, but someone slipped their rough hand into her smooth one, pulling her back toward the dance floor. She knew instantly it was Colt, and she couldn't stop herself from following his lead. He pulled her close to him as a slow song came on over the sound system. *Great.* She was doing her best to not let her ego be to terribly damaged and now she was going to slow dance with him, smell him, and look into his amber eyes.

"Aren't you going to ask me to dance? Or do you just expect every woman to do it without question?" Apparently, a snarky attitude was how she was going to hide her hurt.

The edges of his mouth only hitched up slightly. He looked torn and desperate all at the same time. "If I'd asked, you would've said no."

True. She would've ignored him. Now she was slowly swaying to the music, pressed against his chest.

"If you'll let me explain, I really would like a chance. If you don't like what I have to say, then you can go on being a friendly acquaintance that takes my lunch order every day."

Aly wished she could say that she didn't care but she did. All she could muster was a soft, "Okay."

Colt took a big breath and began, "I'm sure you've heard things about me, especially since you work with Crystal. I need to tell you that those things are true. I'm not going to deny it or act like that wasn't a part of my life."

Aly nodded but didn't say anything. She felt relieved that he didn't try to butter her up.

"I've been involved in the rodeo since high school and with that I've had great losses and also great success. With that success came fame, money, and girls." Colt cleared his throat. "I have my reasons for why I turned toward all of that and maybe one day we'll talk about that. Those girls today at the rodeo and then Jessica, they're all a part of who I am... who I was. I'm sorry you had to see it."

Aly was happy to hear that he wanted it to be in his past.

He took another deep breath and continued. "I don't know what it is but I can't seem to break whatever spell you've got on me. There's just something about you, Aly. You make me think about things I haven't thought of in a really long time. I didn't think a meaningful relationship was in the cards for me anymore. But you make it seem valuable again." He pulled her closer and she felt herself relax into him.

Aly was surprised by his honesty but thankful just the same. "Thanks for telling me."

Colt's fingers gripped her a little tighter around the waist. "I would like to ask you to go on a date with me. It can be anything you want."

Aly felt her heart kick up. She believed in second chances and desperately wanted one for herself. "Are we going as new friends?"

His eyes filled with mischief. "Absolutely not. I don't want to just be your friend."

Aly swallowed the lump in her throat. She didn't plan on a relationship but she liked the idea of it. "You don't?"

Colt slowly shook his head. "No. I don't want the kind of relationships I've had my whole adult life." He slowed their dance to a stop. "Will you give me a chance to prove it to you?"

He wanted a chance and she wanted to believe she could have one too. "Okay."

Colt's sexy crooked smile brightened his whole face. Aly felt that if he let her go she'd melt to the floor. He was never someone she thought she'd be interested in, but he was just too irresistible. She was definitely not country and she probably had more shoes than he had cows. She worked as a waitress and baked on her down time. He famously rode bulls and traveled to do so. She had no idea where her feet were going to land and his future was completely mapped out for him. What did she really have to offer someone like Colt Teel?

"You're thinking too much." Colt's voice cut through her thoughts.

Aly looked up at his eyes. "Probably."

"What about?" He spun her out and back in to him.

"Just that I'm surprised that you'd be interested in a girl like me. I mean, you clearly have plenty throwing themselves at you. It doesn't really make sense." She turned to look around the room at all the girls who were watching them dance. She saw Jessica roll her eyes as they went by her.

Gently, Colt took a single finger and turned her chin back to face him. When she met his amber eyes, she didn't see any kind of judgement in them. "Aly, I don't want you to believe anything that Jessica said tonight. I want to be honest. I like you. Nothing that she says influences my personal beliefs or desires. Okay?"

"Okay." She still had her doubts that they could make a relationship work and she knew it would take some time for her to open up to him, if they even lasted that long. The song came to an end and Aly felt awkward because she didn't know where they went from here. "Thank you for the dance. I guess I need to get back to Jade."

"Sure. Let me walk you over and we can exchange numbers." Colt offered his elbow and she took it. It felt good to be on a man's arm again. They stopped next to Jade, who was engaged in a lively conversation. Once they exchanged numbers, Colt looked directly into her eyes and said, "Thanks for giving me a chance."

Aly's heart squeezed at how vulnerable he seemed. She understood the need to be heard. "I believe we all deserve second chances."

"That *is* why you said you returned to Shaw Creek. If we're lucky, we'll both find it." He dipped the tip of his baseball cap and winked. "Have a good evenin'." With that he turned and headed toward the exit.

Aly released a deep breath she hadn't realized she was holding. She could smell Colt's cologne hanging in the air. Closing her eyes, she sent a silent prayer up that she wouldn't let her heart fall to fast this time. Colt Teel was the kind of man that could take hold of it quickly and that was something Aly wasn't sure she should do ever again.

Chapter 11

Sunday morning broke with a wonderful cool breeze that cut through the Texas summer. Fall was just around the corner and Aly couldn't wait for it. Even just the slightest change in temperature would make life more enjoyable. She sat on Jade's balcony drinking her coffee and munching on some of her freshly baked croissants. Aly slept great last night for the first time since she arrived back in Shaw Creek. Greg still kept texting her, but she refused to give him the pleasure of knowing that she thought about him. He couldn't possibly be serious about trying to continue their relationship especially after his wife found out. No way.

She leaned her head back against her chair and closed her eyes. She sent up a silent prayer for peace about the steps she was making with her move, her emotions, and Colt.

The door opened and Jade stepped out taking the seat next to Aly. "Girl, if you don't stop baking every morning I'm going to double my current weight."

Aly smiled. "I highly doubt you'll be putting on weight. You're so active and busy you burn it off before you take a bite."

Jade scoffed. "We'll see." She handed over Aly's phone, which was tucked into her robe pocket. "Your phone was ringing on the counter."

Aly glanced at the missed call. Greg. She turned it upside down and placed it on the table in front of her.

After a few beats Jade asked, "Do you mind if I ask you something?"

"No. What it is?"

"I've been noticing that the past week or so you've been getting a lot of phone calls and you're not answering. I'm not one to pry but I want to make sure you're okay."

Jade was such a great friend, the best really. Maybe opening up about things a little wouldn't be a bad thing. Aly looked down at her cup of coffee sitting in her lap and sighed. The cream swirled in circles, which was exactly how she felt about Greg's continued contact. "I told you about my boyfriend and I splitting up. Well, it wasn't that simple. It was a clash between my personal life and…" she hesitated. "My job. It was really bad and I had no other choice but to leave."

Jade took a drink of her coffee and remained quiet.

"I'm embarrassed and would prefer if it stayed in Dallas. That's why I didn't tell you everything."

"The phone calls have to do with what happened? Is it Greg?" Jade asked. Aly swallowed the vile that was working its way up her throat and simply nodded. "Why don't you tell him to stop calling?"

Aly would love to yell at Greg and tell him to leave her alone, but what good would that do? The damage was done and she had nothing else to say to him. "It wouldn't matter."

"You can't work it out?"

Aly laughed bitterly. "No. Never." *Understatement of the century.*

Jade leaned forward. "You don't have to tell me everything if you don't want to, but I don't want you to be dealing with this alone. If you believe things will never work out then you definitely need to move on. Speaking of…" Jade bobbed her eyebrows. "You've got a hot date with Colt Teel sometime."

Aly's spirits were instantly lifted.

"You'll see him today at church and possibly the luncheon after."

"Like I told you last night, I'm going to give him a chance and see if I'm ready as well." Aly was still cautious about getting attached to Colt. Her hope was that he was really able to change and she was ready to open up to him.

Jade stood and stretched. "I'm going to head inside and get ready for church. I can't wait for everyone to taste your amazing croissants at the luncheon. You're going to become the best kept secret of Shaw Creek if you're not careful."

"I'm looking forward to it." Aly followed Jade and headed into her room to get ready as well. Aly had only gone to service once since moving in with Jade and she enjoyed the worship and teaching. It was something she felt gave her a chance at a weekly reset. When she lived in Dallas, she never went to church. Maybe going with her family now would help give her clarity.

Once they were both dressed and ready, they hopped into Jade's car and headed across town. The church parking lot was full. Aly and Jade took seats next to Gram, Aunt Julie, and her cousin Cami and husband James. Blake, Melissa, and Wyatt were in the row just in front of them. Aly had missed having them a part of her life. Guilt twisted her stomach because she hadn't made much time for them since being back. She needed to change that. Gram squeezed Aly's arm and offered her a warm smile.

"Cami, you look beautiful," Aly said.

"Please. I'm swollen like a balloon and about to pop. Praying the next month pass quickly." Cami rubbed her baby bump.

"That's not true, Cam. You're beautiful," James kissed her cheek.

Aly was so excited for them to be having their first child. She loved that she was going to be close when Cami had her baby.

She glanced around the room hoping to catch a glimpse of Colt but to her disappointment she couldn't find him. When it was time for the sermon, Pastor Robert shared about how God is offering us an extended hand of forgiveness but that we must also forgive ourselves. Who we were in the past doesn't have to define our future. Aly felt the weight of all the hurt, pain, anger, and sadness descend on her. She knew the pastor was right but what Greg did to her and what she did to his family didn't seem like something she could forgive herself for. She was the *mistress.* Aly's throat burned at the word, but that's exactly what she was. How could God forgive her for the affair in the first place? Aly's mind became a fog for the rest of the service and she was ready to get out of there.

With the concluding prayer, Pastor Robert dismissed the congregation. Aly followed Gram out into the center aisle. "I've got to get the food out of the car for the luncheon," Aly said and she excused herself.

Everyone was starting to make their way around the back side of the church, where the tables were set up outside. It was a beautiful day and Aly was looking forward to getting to know more people in the church. Though she grew up going to church there, the congregation had grown significantly and she didn't recognize many faces. She knew Gram would be excited to introduce her. She grabbed the container from the back seat of Jade's car.

When she crossed back across the parking lot she spotted Mr. and Mrs. Teel. She quickly scanned for Colt, hoping he came with them. She placed her food on the buffet table and then turned to look over the crowd. Her family and Jade had found a table near one of the maple trees. She looked around the open yard as she walked toward them. When she arrived at the long rectangle table and she took a seat next to Jade.

"You're looking for Colt, aren't you?" Jade asked.

Aly sighed. "Is it that obvious?"

"Only to me. I'm sure he's here."

They didn't specify when they would go on a date last night at the party. She was busy and so was he, but she wished that it would be sooner rather than later. Some people were laughing behind her and she turned to see who it was. To her relief, it was just the person she was missing. Colt was laughing with a couple of older men. He wore a dark green polo t-shirt and khaki pants. She could see a slight dimple in his cheek when he laughed. The moment he looked in her direction, his features softened. His eyes were kind and warm. Aly sighed. *I'm in trouble.*

"I'm going to get some more of your croissants. Do you need anything?" Jade asked as she stood.

"I'm good. Thanks."

As Jade headed toward the serving tables, Colt excused himself from the men and met her at the table. Aly loved the flex in his shirt as he hugged Jade. His smile was to die for as well and she was especially glad when it was directed at her.

"Aly, dear."

Aly turned to see Gram standing next to her with none other than Mr. and Mrs. Teel. She quickly stood up and smoothed her skirt. Gram rested her hand on Aly's back as she introduced them. "Mr. and Mrs. Teel this is my granddaughter, Aly Meyers. She's my son Mark's youngest. She's recently moved here from Dallas."

Mr. Teel extended his hand to her and shook it kindly. "It's a pleasure to meet you."

Aly could see a familiar pair of amber eyes and dimple in Mr. Teel's cheek. Mrs. Teel's eyes ran the length of Aly and ended on her face. Though she was smiling, Mrs. Teel didn't appear to be very impressed but she nodded hello to Aly anyway. "It's a pleasure to make your acquaintance. Ms. Meyers, your grandmother has spoken very highly of you."

Aly ducked her chin slightly. "Gram is a bit partial."

"Not at all." Gram squeezed Aly's arm. "Mrs. Teel, how did Colt do this weekend?"

Mrs. Teel's grin dimmed some. "He did very well. He got first place, in fact."

Aly could hear the pride in her voice but yet there was also a displeasure too. As if she wasn't excited about it.

"That's wonderful. How many events does he have this year?" Gram asked.

"We're not sure, but hopefully not many. He'll be leaving the circuit to take over the ranch. The official date hasn't been set as of yet." Mrs. Teel glanced at her husband before answering. The tension in her jaw evident. "We're anxious to retire and see him finally settle down to start a family."

Aly felt her heart speed up.

Mrs. Teel looked over at the table where Blake, Melissa, and Wyatt were eating. "The newlyweds appear to be settling into married life well."

"They are. It's wonderful to see two people who are meant to be together end up together," Gram said.

"And what about you, Ms. Meyers?" Mrs. Teel asked looking at Aly. "What are your plans now that you've moved back?"

Aly looked at Gram hoping her unease wasn't apparent. Gram saved her by saying, "Our Aly is an amazing baker and actually made the croissants for today's luncheon. She's helping Jade at the diner for now."

"How lovely," Mrs. Teel responded but it was anything but. Aly felt like she was about two feet tall. This was Colt's mother? Regardless of how confident Colt came off, there was something warm about him. Mr. Teel appeared nice and friendly as well, but his wife seemed to be stiff and critical. As the Teels excused themselves, Aly's eyes landed back on Colt across the yard still talking to Jade. She had a sinking feeling that made her hope for him diminish slightly. Not only was she not comfortable in cowboy boots but she could tell his mother wasn't her biggest fan. Aly pulled her eyes away from him and sat back down at the long table.

All the affirming words Colt had said last night seemed so far away now. The hope that they could maybe build a relationship in spite of both of their pasts seemed almost impossible. Aly squeezed her eyes closed as she felt their differences close in on her heart tighter than before.

Chapter 12

Colt stepped out of the church feeling content for the first time in a long time. He had sure missed the people, the message, and the worship. When he did decide to quit the circuit, he'd get the chance to go to church every weekend. Usually, he would be so uncomfortable because of his actions the previous night that it almost wasn't worth going. Today was different. He was able to relax and actually take in everything the pastor said.

He had been running late and sat at the back of the sanctuary. He immediately found Aly sitting with her family. She was beautiful in her floral dress and her hair fell past her shoulders in beautiful waves. By what he had learned about Aly, through Jade and his own time with her, it appeared that she had some things in her past that weren't positive. However, she believed that everyone deserved a chance to rise above it. He respected her for that and was grateful she was willing to give him a chance.

It had been eight days since he first laid eyes on her and he felt out of sorts about how much he wanted to see her. In the past, he would've been quick to score a physical release and nothing more. Sure, he was attracted to her but his motives for getting to know her weren't for a short term pleasure.

The preacher spoke strongly about forgiving yourself. It was important to try to move beyond who he was. He wasn't proud of the things he had done or how he handled the darkest time in his life. Heck, last week he called up someone who didn't mean anything to him just because he was angry that Matt had accused him of not getting over Emily. How was that respectable? If he was ever going to be worthy of something valuable he would have to change.

No more selfish ambitions.

No more shallow relationships.

Relationships.

He looked over his shoulder and saw Jade headed to the food table. He excused himself and met her there. "Hey, Jade."

She embraced him. "Hey, yourself. You doing ok this morning?"

"I am. I feel real good actually." His eyes darted over to Aly.

"We've been friends for almost a decade, Colt."

He raised an eyebrow at Jade. Where was this going?

"Don't look at me like that." She glanced over to Aly at a table with her family. "She likes you."

"She does?" he asked. Maybe a little too excitedly.

Jade laughed. "Yes. I can tell you like her too."

"And you're not ok with it?"

"It's not that." She sat down her plate and gripped both of his arms. "You are an amazing guy. Have you messed up? Yes. Will you mess up? Yes. But I really believe that if you'd commit to one person it would surprise everyone, including you. A shock to the heart if you will."

"You make it sound so romantic," he said sarcastically.

"You can call it whatever you want. But I've been watching you around Aly. You're different."

He steadied his feet and slid his hands in his front pockets. "How so?"

"You're pursuing her, like really pursuing her. Before you'd get bored if a women seemed complicated or like she'd be too much work. This is the first time I've seen you like this."

It was true. He'd noticed that about himself some. Aly was different and therefore he was different. "So, what? Are you saying you're ok with me pursuing more than just a friendship?"

Jade took a deep breath. "I'm saying that I love you. Both of you. You've both been hurt and broken in past relationships. You more than any of us."

Colt swallowed the lump that sprung to his throat. He didn't want to remember the most painful time in his life.

"I want you to be happy. The sparks that are shooting between you two can be seen from a mile away. Maybe God is bringing you together because you're the only ones that can help each other heal."

He hadn't thought of it that way before. He couldn't explain why he was so drawn to Aly. "Maybe you're right."

"The only thing I will say is…" Jade paused and picked up her plate. "Just tread lightly. You'll benefit more if you keep doing things different from what you're used to." She winked at him and walked away.

He looked back over to where Aly was now talking to his parents. *His parents!* Colt instantly felt nervous about her meeting them. Just as fast as the nerves came on, he questioned the concern. He had never cared much about what his parents thought about a woman he was seeing. *Whoa, wait. Seeing?* They were just friends right now, hopefully more soon.

His father dipped his hat to Aly and Mrs. Meyers, cordial and respectful as always. His mother's shoulders were straight, proper, and poised as always, nodding politely. But she had a tendency of analyzing everything about a person and would talk his father's ear off later. He didn't believe his mother would be able to find a fault in Aly anywhere. It pained him to think back to when Jessica had said those horrible things to her because it wasn't true.

Aly took her seat at the long rectangular table and his parents walked away. He filled a plate and headed straight for her. She was listening to something Jade was saying when she noticed him. Her smile was warm but not near as bright as he knew she was capable. He wanted to see that smile he loved. "Hello, ladies. Do you mind if I join you?"

"Oh, Colt! Your parents were just over here. They told me you won last night at the rodeo," Aly's grandmother said cheerfully.

"I did. It was a good night." He shot a quick glance at Aly who didn't look at him. There was an uneasy feeling that came over Colt.

"Please join us." Mrs. Meyers motioned to the empty spot across from Aly.

He placed his plate and took a seat. "Thanks, ma'am."

Jade nodded to Colt's plate and said, "I see you got a couple croissants on your plate. I'll have you know that those were made this morning in my kitchen by none other than Aly Meyers."

Colt looked at Aly and saw the blush in her cheeks. "Really?" He took a bite of one and loved how it melted in his mouth. There was a hint of cheese and honey in them. "These are amazing. Another surprise I'm learning about you."

"Aly is full of surprises, Colt. All good of course." Jade nudged Aly, who rolled her eyes.

"It's no big deal, really. Anyone can make them," Aly said.

He made a mental note to remember that she didn't like to be bragged on, or the attention maybe. Then again he thought he noticed a hint of regret maybe in her eyes before she blinked it away. Maybe he was wrong.

The table fell into easy conversation as everyone ate their lunch. Colt couldn't take his eyes off Aly. She was so beautiful with her long blonde hair curled and her eyes were the purest blue he'd ever seen. She had a few bracelets on each wrist and another pair of earrings he hadn't seen before. He had looked forward to seeing her today and discussing when he could take her out to dinner. However, she had only offered him a slight smile and now silence. He needed to find out what had changed in a matter of hours. When everyone else at the table was engaged in conversation, he saw his opportunity to talk to her. "You look beautiful today."

She didn't look up at first and finished taking the bite on her fork. He could see the slight tension in her shoulders. "Thank you."

"I like the jewelry. You've worn a lot of different kinds."

She dipped one shoulder. "What can I say? A city girl likes pretty things."

"I'm gathering that." And he liked it.

"Did you enjoy the service?" she asked.

"I did. I came in during worship and had to sit in the back. It seemed like it was written just for me. I needed it." He took a drink of sweet tea.

She nodded. "Yeah, I needed it too."

They were quiet for a second and Colt figured it was as good a time as any to ask about taking her out.

"Would you like to go to dinner tonight? There's a great Mexican restaurant that has an outdoor area with a live band. It's one of my favorite places to eat."

Her eyes flashed with hesitation and she bit her bottom lip.

"Is something wrong?" he asked.

She sighed and shook her head. "No. I've just been thinking and I don't know if I'm the kind of girl for you. I don't think I'm in the place for a relationship right now." Her eyes darted past him. He turned and found his mother watching them. Once they made eye contact, she raised an eyebrow at him. Had something happened between her and Aly? He looked back as Aly continued. "It was pretty obvious last night that we're really different. I'd like to be your friend, though."

He leaned towards her and talked in a lower tone. "I thought I made it clear last night that I don't care about what other people think. My life is mine to live and even my parents don't have the final say. I want to be better and I meant every—"

"Colt, dear. Why don't you come sit with us? There are several people who'd like to congratulate you on your win last night," his mother interrupted.

He leaned back and looked up at her. "I'm visiting with the Meyers family. I'll be over there in a little bit."

His mom looked across to Aly, who was watching her carefully. Aly's shoulders were slumped slightly, hands in her lap, and arms tight at her side. Before he could say something else his mom continued, "Well, I also have someone I want you to meet. Amanda Smith is here with her parents and I know you two would hit it off."

He looked at Aly who quickly averted her eyes from his. *Great.* He was trying to prove to her that he could be better and his mother had perfect timing to try and set him up. Of course, the women she introduced him to were wealthy and had connections that would benefit his family's business. He had no interest in being set up, especially knowing his mom. He stood and stepped toward his mom. "I appreciate the effort. I'm sure she's lovely. However, I'm visiting with Aly right now and will not be interested in Ms. Smith. If I get the chance to say hello I will."

He could see his mother bristle at his words and her face started to flush with anger, but Linda Teel would not be seen off kilter. She straitened her shoulders and regained her composure. "Very well."

He nodded to her and said, "Thank you, Mom. I'll be over there in a little bit." He leaned in to give her a kiss on the cheek, which she stiffly accepted. Then she glided back across the lawn to where his father was talking with the Smiths. It was never his intent to be disrespectful to his mother but he needed to prove two points in where he stood, one with the mom and the other with Aly. He took his seat again and noticed that Aly's whole family looking at him. He lifted his tea glass to them and they all returned to their conversations.

Colt looked across to Aly. Her eyes were warmer and her smile a little brighter. *Good.* "Sorry you had to see that."

"Not a problem. Your mom seems… nice."

"She is. There are just a few things she likes to get too involved in. My love life would be one of them." He sighed.

"I think all parents like to know about that. They just want their kids to be happy." The corners of her mouth slowly curved up. She leaned back in her chair.

"And I'm glad they care. She's just pushy with me. Like I told you before, I'm the only one still single." He was happy to see Aly's body relax again.

"Well, neither my brother or I are married, so I'm sure my parents will get that way too." She paused and then said, "I'm sorry I was a little stiff. I didn't mean to be rude when you came over."

Colt nodded slightly. "I saw my mom was over here earlier. Did she say something to you?"

Aly's body shifted slightly but she held eye contact with him. He wished he could see inside her head.

"She didn't say anything hurtful to me. Honest." The wind picked up for a moment and her hair got tossed in the breeze. She quickly tucked it behind her ear and smiled at him. She took his breath away.

"Okay. I love my parents and we are very blessed but I'm not naïve to the fact that they can be critical, my mother in particular." He reached across to take her hand. Luckily, she didn't pull away. "I really would like to take you out tonight."

Those big blue eyes sparkled. "I would love to go out with you, Colt."

Maybe he wasn't worthy of someone like Aly but he was relieved she agreed. He hoped she wouldn't see how tainted he really was and run away before he had the chance to show her he wanted to change. He'd finally been given the chance and he wasn't going to mess it up.

Chapter 13

Aly ran a comb through her hair one last time. The girl she saw looking back at her looked good. The stress was gone from her face and she looked at ease. She was excited to be going out with Colt. He said to wear pants and comfortable shoes. She traded her church clothes for jean capris, a sleeveless black blouse, and a pair of Toms. She hoped that outfit would work. Since he said he noticed she had a lot of different jewelry, she decided to wear the same jewelry she wore to church. The doorbell rang and she heard Jade answer the door. Aly hurried out her room with a cheesy grin on her face but it fell when she found Melissa and Wyatt instead of Colt.

"Well, don't look so happy to see me, cousin," Melissa said putting her hand on her hip.

Aly gave Wyatt a hug and then Melissa. "I'm always happy to see you. How are you doing?"

Melissa rolled her eyes. "Just getting ready for school to start."

"I guess it's that time again. Fall is almost here." Aly ruffled the top of Wyatt's hair. "I bet you're ready for school."

"Ewe, no." Wyatt scooted past her and took the chocolate chip cookie Jade was waving at him. "Thanks, Jade!"

"That boy sure loves sugar." Melissa shook her head. Jade winked at Wyatt.

"Aly's got a date tonight," Jade said.

Melissa cocked her head to the side. "Oh really? Who might the lucky guy be?"

Aly didn't want to make a big deal about the date. She wasn't sure it would become anything other than friendship. After the encounter with his mom and the way Colt had responded to the situation, Aly's hopes for getting to know him better were slightly restored. She may still think they are too different, but she was happy he wanted to get to know her.

"Earth, to Aly." Jade said waving her hand in front of Aly's face.

"Oh, sorry. I was just thinking."

"I'm sure it was about Colt," Jade teased.

Melissa straightened her shoulders. "Wait, Colt *Teel*?"

"Yes," Aly answered.

"Aly is going on a date with a *very* hot cowboy, Mel. A cowboy! Who would've thought?"

"I know. That is a surprise, but a good one," Melissa answered. "He's a nice guy and I know Blake has gotten to know him more through the men's ministry at church. His dad leads the group and Colt's been helping more over the past few months when he's home. I think it's great that you're going out with him, getting back out there."

"I'm not a spinster," Aly said defensively.

Melissa smiled. "I know you're not, but I'm really happy to see you thinking about someone other than Greg."

Before Aly could respond, her phone signaled a text message.

"I bet that's Colt," Jade said.

Aly headed over to the counter to check her phone. Greg. He was still trying to contact her. There were at least a five text messages and one phone call every day now. He clearly wasn't getting the hint and it confused her more than ever. She opened the message and read it.

Aly, please, I'm begging you. I love you and need to speak to you. I never meant for any of this to happen. Please, it's important. I'm not going to lose you.

Aly squeezed her eyes shut as she locked her phone. Why is he still doing this? He's married! He has children! He lied to all of them! Even in her anger, Aly felt a slow ache form in the pit of her stomach. She didn't want to but she missed him.

No.

She missed what they had. She missed the way he made her feel. She missed his touch. She missed it all. Her fingers clenched the phone. She felt disgusted with herself that she did. There was no way she could see him again. Ever. All the guilt and shame wrapped its cold fingers around her heart, trying to squeeze all the joy and happiness she was daring to feel to death.

She deleted the text. She was not going to let Greg win here. He'd done enough and it wasn't worth wasting her time dwelling on it. There was a guy who wanted to take her out and regardless of her insecurities, she was going to enjoy him while she had him. She stuffed her phone in her purse and turned back to Jade and Melissa.

"Well, was it who you wanted?" Melissa asked.

"No, it wasn't Colt. He should be here any second I think." She ran her fingers through her hair. Her eyes connected with Jade and she gave her a wry smile. Luckily, Jade didn't say anything.

The doorbell rang, and Aly was thankful it didn't allow for more questions. Colt had on the most amazing blue and grey plaid pearl snap shirt paired with dark blue jeans that fit him perfectly. No cowboy hat or baseball cap but that was just fine. Aly loved that she could see his face clearly, no shadow. He nodded to Melissa and Jade then locked eyes with Aly. She wasn't sure how a guy like him would be interested in someone like her, but she wasn't going to complain.

Aly turned to give Jade a hug, who held onto her a little longer before whispering in Aly's ear. "I don't want you to think about Dallas or Greg. You have a good guy who wants to treat you, let him. You deserve this."

Aly nodded and said, "Thank you. I'll be home later tonight." She said goodbye to Melissa and Wyatt before stepping out onto the landing with Colt. Once the door was closed he revealed the bouquet of wild flowers he must've picked for her. They were a mixture of white, yellow, purple, and pink. She'd never received anything like them but she loved it! "These are very pretty. Thank you."

He took her other hand. "I had to do a few chores at the ranch and saw them out in the field not far from my cabin. I'm glad you like them."

He opened the door to his four-door F150 and helped her in. As he walked around the front of the truck, Aly let out a deep breath. She didn't want to worry about anything but Colt. She was determined to enjoy every second with him.

He hopped in and started the engine. The radio came on rather loud and he quickly turned it down. "Sorry. I like my country music."

"Not a problem. I like country music too." Good, there was something they had in common.

"I don't know how you can be from Texas and not love it." He winked at her and pulled out onto the road. "So, tell me about what life was like for you when you lived here as a kid?"

"I bet our lives were pretty similar, with school and church at least."

He shrugged one shoulder. "True. But we do have a little bit of an age gap, so I'm sure you experienced different things than me."

Their six year age difference had given her a little pause at first. He didn't seem bothered by it and so she figured it wasn't worth the worry. "Well, I enjoyed living here. My older brother, Luke, and I were pretty lucky. Until my parents' got divorced when I was in high school, it was pretty ideal."

"I bet that was hard."

"My grandparents babysat us a lot. They were a huge part of our lives. That's where I fell in love with baking. Gram is an amazing cook."

"If you ever need a taste tester, I'm your guy," he said.

"Alright." She liked the idea of him enjoying her food. She felt confident and most like herself when she baked.

They parked the car and he came around to open her door, ever the gentleman. He even pulled out her chair at the table. It was a fairly newer restaurant that felt like you were walking into someone's home. They ordered their drinks and she began to skim over the menu.

"You really do look beautiful tonight."

"Thank you." She glanced at her clothes. "I hope this is appropriate for what you had in mind. Since you still haven't told me what we're doing after dinner."

His eyes washed her for a moment and then he leaned back in his seat. "It's good. I'm not saying just yet. I like surprises."

"How do you know I do?" she teased.

One eyebrow rose and he countered, "I have a hunch. And I'm pretty good about knowing these things."

Aly couldn't help but smile. He really was Casanova. No wonder all the girls fawn over him. She didn't mind surprises, and lately she was the one who fell for them. She realized she hadn't felt in control of her life in years. Then after things got more serious with Greg and she chose to deviate from her plan. She had thought the safe route to a good career would be to branch out and try different companies. But her world became more dependent rather than independent. She wanted to make Greg happy because he made her happy. Now that she looked back on it, she felt awful about herself. She thought he was worth giving up those plans. Now her life was spinning and just seemed to be stuck in a holding pattern. She missed having a tight grip on her life. That's where the new walls came in. The walls gave her a buffer and helped her hold the pieces together. She didn't want people to know about her mistake. If she kept it secret, people wouldn't be able to see how broken she really was.

"Aly?" Colt asked.

She refocused her eyes and shook her head. "Sorry. I just spaced out for a second. Umm, I do like surprises." She gave him her best smile.

"Good. I hope you'll like it."

They ate their dinner and enjoyed pleasant conversation. His childhood was very similar to her own, until her parents divorced.

"When we were younger our home was always full of laughter no matter what seemed to be happening. With three rowdy boys, who loved to roughhouse and play in the dirt, it's a wonder we didn't end up in the hospital more often. Perhaps that's what ended up making my mom so uptight." He laughed flatly.

Aly couldn't help but feel bad that his relationship with his mother seemed to be strained, but she kept quiet. She listened to him discuss his job on the ranch. They talked a little about the rodeo circuit and bull riding. She learned about his brothers and their wives. But she saw the most joy when he talked about his nieces. His eyes lit up and he laughed as he told stories about them. He was very proud of them and it was clear he loved them dearly. It warmed her heart to see a softer side to him. The conversation never fell flat or awkward. They laughed in shared humor.

Colt finished paying the bill. "What did you think?"

Aly placed her napkin next to plate. "It was great. I'll be back for sure."

Colt stood and offered her a hand, that she gladly took. She felt the calluses pull across her smooth skin and it sent goose bumps up her arm. How could a man who was tough enough to ride crazy bulls have such a tenderness about him? She knew there was more to Colt Teel than most people saw. Even though she wasn't sure where their relationship was going, in that moment, Aly would hold Colt's hand anywhere he wanted to go. With the first step, the heaviness she'd been carrying soften some. If she took a look at her heart, the walls would have a small crack with the smallest glimmer of light breaking   through.

Chapter 14

Colt pulled out of the parking lot pleased with how their date was going so far. He'd been nervous that they wouldn't have much in common, but it was quite the opposite. They liked the same music, loved kids, enjoyed their childhood, and were optimistic about the future. Aly seemed to be in limbo a little bit, like him. He knew what he was going to do, it was just a matter of finally letting go of a dream he'd had his whole life. Though she seemed positive minded and content with working with Jade, he wasn't sure what her long term plans were.

"So, where are we headed now?" Aly asked.

"Well, are you ready for a surprise?" He sneaked a peak at her. She was looking at him expectantly. He winked and she pulled her bottom lip in, dropping her eyes. Dang, she had no idea what she did to him. Yep. He was in danger of falling for this girl, fast.

"I guess so." She looked out the windshield.

"Good. You've said you think we're too different. So, I wanted to take you to the place that means the most to me."

To give her a glimpse of the real Colt Teel, not the preconceived idea she had in her mind. Her eyes were filled with surprise and what he would describe as hope. Her smile warmed him to the core.

"Okay," she beamed.

They pulled under the gate of the Big T Ranch. The sun shone perfect across the open fields. He took a quick glance at Aly and saw the delight in her face. She watched with wide eyes, her head whipping around to take it all in. The drive was lined with trees that stopped just as the lane opened to the large front yard of the family home.

"Oh my," Aly said in disbelief. "This is beautiful."

"It's where I grew up. My great-grandparents built it." He followed the drive and curved toward the south side of the house.

"What are those?" she asked pointing to the line of cabins ahead.

"That's where the ranch hands live." He pulled into the first one and put the truck in park. "This is my place."

Aly looked over at him and then back at his cabin. "You live here?"

"I do." He hopped out of the truck and walked around the front of the truck to open her door. Extending his hand, Colt said, "Can I show you something?"

Her smile could've melted him right there in the drive. She was stunning and had something genuine that he couldn't describe. When her fingers wrapped around his, he squeezed them in reassurance. To his delight she didn't release it.

They made their way in the opposite direction to the barn. The giant metal barn was one of the many upgrades his parents had made from the original homestead. Once they entered the east side, all the horses stuck their heads over the stalls. Aly gasped in excitement. "Horses!"

He couldn't keep himself from laughing at her. "Yep. We have seven horses that help on the ranch. They're more valuable than I can even begin to tell you."

She paused in front of Duke's stall and looked over her shoulder at Colt. "Can I pet him?" He nodded. Aly stepped up close to the horse and stroked down the long nose slowly. "He's so soft. What's his name?"

"Duke. He's our oldest horse." Colt took a step closer to her and leaned against the side of the stall. "You like horses?"

Aly shrugged one shoulder. "Yeah. I've never been around them much."

"Would you like to take a ride?" he asked.

Aly's eyes widened and her smile was the brightest he'd ever seen it. "Can we?!"

"I was hoping you'd want to. I have somewhere special to show you." He went into the tact room and brought out Duke's saddle. He opened the stall and began prepping Duke for the ride. Aly watched from the stall door and he could tell she was having a hard time keeping still. When she met his eyes again, she grinned and clapped her hands together. Her excitement was contagious. He finished getting Duke saddled and then went into Lucky's stall. Once both horses were ready to go he grabbed a pair of work boots.

"What are those for?" she asked.

"Well, since you don't have long pants on you'll want these to help protect your calves from rubbing." He sat them down in front of her.

She looked down at her pants and said, "Sorry. I guess I'll know for next time."

He liked the idea of doing this again with her. "Not a problem. These will work for the ride."

She slipped out of her shoes and into the boots. He couldn't help but think she looked cuter with the boots on. Aly stepped into his cupped hands and he raised her onto the back of Duke. She wiggled in the saddle and looked like a kid in a candy store. "Wow. You're good at that. Not scared at all."

She looked down at him. "I'm so excited I don't have room for nerves."

Colt settled onto the back of Lucky and they exited the barn. "Duke is a great horse and he'll do everything you tell him too. You can trust him." *And me.*

Aly nodded. "Great. I'll follow you."

They made their way out through the pasture and toward the woods to the north. Aly stayed pretty close to him. She looked relaxed and at peace on the back of a horse. Her long blonde hair gracefully fell over her shoulders and across the black top she wore. It fit her perfectly and he enjoyed the view. The nice denim capris tucked into the top of the old work boots made him smile. He hoped she loved it as much as he did.

As they weaved through the trees, they began making their way up the only hill on the ranch. "You'll want to lean forward as we incline so you don't fall off."

She did as he said and gripped the saddle horn like her life depended on it. They made it to the top and he pulled Lucky to a stop. Aly brought Duke to rest right next to him. "Wow."

Hundreds of acres stretched out in front of them, the black cows scattered across the grass like ants. The sun cut through the trees creating a wave of motion with the wind. Colt inhaled deeply and dismounted his horse. He took one of Aly's hands to help steady her as she slid off Duke's saddle. Her foot slipped slightly and he wrapped his arms around her to keep her from falling to the ground. Their eyes locked and their faces were only an inch apart. Colt swallowed the sudden lump in his throat and felt his heart rate jump as Aly's eyes dropped to his lips. The look in her eyes mirrored the heat swarming between them. Oh, how it would be amazing to kiss her but he hesitated.

Slowly, he released her and took a generous step back. He rubbed the back of his neck. It was strange that he hadn't just kissed her. Normally, he would've swept her off her feet and found a conformable spot with privacy, but not with Aly.

"Follow me." He tied off the horses on a branch and walked toward the edge of the hill—right where the slope began to descend—and took a seat. Aly joined him but not quite close enough to touch.

"This is my favorite spot in the world." Colt leaned back on his elbows and crossed his legs.

Aly smiled as she looked out over the ranch. "I can see why."

"It's the only place I feel most like myself."

Aly's eyes fell on him. "What do you mean?"

Colt wanted her to know him but wasn't sure how much to share. He was captivated by Aly and didn't want to risk moving too fast.

"I grew up here and have a lot of good memories. I don't know that I could see myself being anywhere else. I'm not George and Lind Teel's son. I'm not a big-time rodeo star. I'm not the one who—*"Killed the love of my life.* He caught himself before revealing too much. He held his breath as he tried to control the unexpected wave of emotion that swept over him. "I'm just me. A guy who loves nature, who loves this ranch, and who wants to be better."

If Aly had noticed the catch in his voice she didn't make it apparent. She tucked a fly-away stand of hair behind her ear.

"I get that." Her eyes dropped to her lap. "That's why I moved away from Dallas. I guess I needed to be reminded of who I really am too."

Colt looked over at her and asked, "And who are you, Aly Meyers?"

She leaned back flat against the grass and stared up at the blue sky. Colt remained on his elbows as he took her in. Her eyes were beautiful but yet held something mysterious, guarded. She inhaled deeply and kept her eyes steady. "I'm just a girl who wants to discover who she really is. I think I lost myself a long time ago and I'm trying to get her back."

He thought he saw her eyes fill with unshed tears but she quickly blinked them dry.

"Do you want to know what I see?" Colt asked. He didn't want to see her hurting or struggling. She turned her head to look at him. Her blonde hair almost glowed against the green grass. "You're tender and care about those around you. They may be strangers but you are welcoming to them. I see a girl who's trying desperately to keep herself guarded but can't help but love others. You have a beautiful heart." Colt reached out and slid his hand across her cheek.

He couldn't help himself. She didn't pull away and her eyes lit with longing. "Aly, I'm going to kiss you now."

A smile crept up her cheeks and she said, "I think I'm going to let you."

Colt released a breath. He slowly leaned in and felt everything inside him explode when his lips touched hers. They were soft and warm with a hint of vanilla. He kissed her slowly gaging her reaction. She reached up and hooked her arm around his neck and pulled him closer. A second burst rushed through him. He hadn't felt this way with a woman in a long time and it was just a kiss. All he wanted was to wrap himself around Aly and take his time to discover every inch of her. He felt his resolve to go slow weakening and he knew that's not what Aly deserved. Reluctantly, he pulled back from her and looked into her eyes, the blue seemed a shade darker with her desire. There were no words for what he felt and it scared him to try and analyze it at this point. He returned her smile and kissed the tip of her nose, then leaned back and laid next to her. Aly wrapped her hand around Colt's and squeezed it at their sides.

After a long time in pleasant silence, Aly said, "Thank you for bringing me here, Colt."

"I hope you'll come out here with me again."

Aly sat up and ran her fingers through her hair. "I'd like that," she said.

Colt took her hand and helped her up but didn't kiss her again, though he wanted to. They mounted the horses and made the trek back to the barn. The sky was dark when they emerged from the barn after putting up the horses. They made their way over to Colt's truck and he helped Aly into the passenger side. The charge between them seemed to have eased some. He didn't want his time with her to end. Usually, it was no big deal to see a woman only once or twice and move on, but he couldn't stand the thought of doing that to Aly. He needed to get his head on straight because it could get serious fast and he wasn't sure how he felt about that. He pulled up in front of Jade's apartment and walked Aly up to the door.

"Thank you again for today, Colt."

"Thank you for agreeing to give me a chance."

There was a slight flush to her cheeks. "I'm really glad I did too."

Colt leaned in to give her a good night kiss and she closed her eyes to accept it. Her phone buzzed in her pocket, and she jumped. She checked it and he saw the light leave her eyes.

"Is everything alright?"

Aly cleared her throat and quickly locked her phone. Colt had an uneasy feeling about it. Aly gave him a strained smile and said, "Oh, yeah. Nothing for you to worry about."

"Are you sure?"

"Yes." She leaned up and kissed his cheek. "Goodnight, Colt." Then she turned and left him on the porch.

Colt hated the sudden change in Aly, but he wasn't going to push her. He hoped that in time she would feel comfortable enough to trust him, but just as the thought came, he felt instant guilt. He couldn't judge her too harshly because he had plenty of secrets of his own.

Chapter 15

Someone called Aly's name, and she saw Crystal walking out from the diner kitchen. She had a homemade cinnamon roll in her hand.

"Good morning, Crystal." Aly kept refilling the salt and pepper shakers before they opened for the day.

Holding up the half eaten cinnamon roll, Crystal said, "These are amazing! I had no idea you were a baker."

Aly was pleased that her coworkers were enjoying the breakfast she made for everyone. "I'm glad you like them."

Jade came in to set up the cash register and Crystal grabbed her arm in excitement. "Jade, tell Aly she needs to open her own bakery. People would love her food!"

Aly shook her head. "Oh, I just bake for friends and family."

"I don't know, Aly. Have you thought about opening a bakery someday?" Jade asked.

Her mindset had always been geared toward working in the corporate world. It seemed the most secure, even though it hadn't worked out so far. "No."

Jade continued counting the money and said, "I think you should consider it. You have a business degree and I could help you look at the numbers to get started."

"I don't know, guys. I don't have any idea where to start on that." Aly took her tray of shakers and began setting them out on the tables. She had to admit the idea of having her own business and doing something she enjoyed sounded appealing. Could she really do that?

"You know." Jade turned to face them. "I have a large section on the back side of this building that has an extra kitchen in it. I've only used it when we had an emergency. That would give you some place to bake. There's already a window and door back there. We could make it a store front."

Aly was surprised at how much the idea appealed to her. She had her doubts and concerns but maybe it wouldn't be such a bad idea to talk to Jade about it, to know her options. She took her now empty tray and turned toward Crystal and Jade. "That's very generous of you. I don't know what to say."

Jade waved her hand in the air. "It's nothing. Let's talk about it tonight and see if it's something you'd be interested in doing."

"Thanks."

"It would be amazing, Aly. Just wait and see!" Crystal clapped her hands together and turned to finish getting ready to open.

The day began and Aly got to work serving breakfast. It was pretty busy but didn't keep her mind far from what Jade had offered. The more she thought about it the more she liked the idea of opening a bakery. She had the business sense in a lot of ways and she loved the idea of baking for a living. It would really give her the new beginning she had been desperate for. When she left Dallas, she hadn't given much thought to what to do with her life. Her plans had been to stay with Greg, hopefully ending in marriage. Even if she hadn't stayed at the insurance agency, she would have Greg. Now, she was only focused on bettering herself. This could be her chance at a real fresh start.

The day seemed to be flying by. Aly checked the clock on the wall and was surprised to see that Colt would be coming in for lunch any minute. He always came in to eat at exactly 12:50pm every day, some with his mentor and the others alone. She preferred the ones alone. She hadn't talked to him since last night's date. When he took her out to the ranch and had opened up with her, she'd been pleasantly surprised. It would make sense that he might ask her more about herself, and she wasn't sure she should answer. She could share about her childhood, time in college, and the friends she had in Dallas. Now the only problem she had was not letting everyone find out exactly who Greg was. With his persistence in contacting her, Jade already knew he wouldn't leave her alone. Now Colt had been present when it happened again and she knew she hadn't hid her displeasure well. Why wasn't he getting the clue that she wasn't going to continue the affair?

Aly placed some dirty plates in the tub and headed to the kitchen to deliver them to the dish washers. She didn't understand why Greg wouldn't just disappear. Even now she was thinking about him when she wanted to do anything but that. She finished wiping down a table when she felt someone standing close behind her. She stood slowly and inhaled the smell of leather, sandalwood, and earth. His breath was near her cheek as he whispered in her ear, "You look amazing today."

A smile broke out across her face and she felt him take a step back. She looked up at Colt and he winked at her.

"Can I sit here?" Colt asked motioning to the table she just cleaned.

"Of course." She saw that he was alone and asked, "Is Frank with you today?"

"No. He's been spending the week with his wife for their anniversary. Forty years." Colt placed his elbows on the table and flashed her his signature grin. "You've just got me."

She could feel the walls around her heart breaking some and it felt good. "Well, congratulations to Frank. Let me get your drink." She turned in his bacon cheeseburger and cheese fries and filled a glass. Placing his glass in front of him, Aly smiled. He looked good, like always. His old work jeans, t-shirt, and worn boots were her favorite look. Cowboys usually wear cowboy hats but Colt's tattered baseball cap suited him better.

"Did you have a good night?" he asked.

"It was ok. I didn't get the best sleep but I made cinnamon rolls for the staff this morning. They seem to have made everyone's day, so that helped me feel better." Aly brushed her hand across her cheek bone hoping that she didn't have bags under her eyes.

"I hope I'll be as lucky to have you cook for me some time," Colt said. "I'm sorry you didn't sleep good. I hope everything's alright."

"Oh, yeah. I just had a hard time falling asleep." *Thanks, Greg.*

He nodded slowly and she could see him assessing her. She suddenly felt self-conscious. "Well, I've got to get back to work. I'll bring your food out shortly."

She went into the kitchen and leaned against the wall in one storage closet. It would be so nice to share personal things with someone. Greg was such a hassle. She didn't want to worry about his calls and messages but it dumbfounded her that he had the nerve to continue to try and contact her. They were almost all the same: a desperate plea to talk to her and about how much he wanted to be with her. She didn't want to miss who he'd been with her, but she did. He had been so sweet and affectionate to her, even when they were in different cities. When he stayed over, he was always holding her hand, rubbing her shoulders, and pulling her close to him. Even though it was all a lie, she had felt like she was falling in love with him.

She tilted her head back against the wall and stared at the ceiling. She didn't want to deceive Colt. How could you have a relationship with secrets? Greg was proof that it couldn't last.

"Aly?" Jade's voice made her jump. Jade peeked into the closet and immediately looked concerned. "Are you okay?"

Aly didn't want to lie but she didn't know how to tell Jade what had happened. "I just need a minute."

Jade pulled her into a hug and squeezed her tight. "We can talk tonight when we get home."

Aly nodded and pulled back to look at Jade. "Sorry."

"When I had to ask Crystal to take Colt out his food and I knew something must've been wrong. Did something happen with him?"

"No. He's been amazing to me. It's just..." Aly couldn't say it. "I just needed time to think about some things."

"If you need to leave early just let me know."

"No. I'm good. I need to work." Aly stepped out of the closet and tightened her ponytail. "Thank you, Jade."

"Of course." Jade headed back into the kitchen.

Aly knew she had to face Colt. She pushed through the door back into the diner and his eyes immediately locked with hers. His lips were thin and eyes crinkled some in the corners. She slapped a smile on her face and walked toward him. "Sorry. I had to take care of something." She cringed at another lie. "Do you need anything else?"

He looked down at his plate and shook his head. "No."

Aly stepped away to tend to a new table when Colt grabbed her hand. She felt a mixture of hope and nerves shoot through her body.

"Aly." Colt almost whispered.

She looked back at him, scared of how exposed she would appear to him. She saw such warmth and longing in his brown eyes. It made the hope she felt fall and drown in her guilt.

Colt looked at their joined hands and then back at her. "I want you to know that I care. I know there is something going on and it may not be good. I saw it last night when I dropped you off." She wanted to jerk her hand from him so he wouldn't be able to see how tainted she felt. He released her hand and said, "I want you to know you can trust me."

How could he be so nice? If he noticed her reaction to Greg, she must not be hiding her feelings as much as she thought. She could see that he meant every word he'd said. "Thank you, Colt. I believe you."

She walked away to check on the other table and didn't say much else to Colt the rest of the time he was there. He left her a very generous tip and a note that said he'd call her later that night. There were so many things that could keep them from a lasting relationship, but Aly wanted to believe that none of those things mattered. He was pursuing her regardless of the secret she had.

You don't have to walk through this alone.

Aly felt those words in her heart and knew that God wanted more for her life than worry, regret, and guilt. She sent up a prayer that she'd find a way to be open with Colt and Jade. And that when they found out, she wouldn't be abandoned all over again.

Chapter 16

A few days later, Aly sat down on the sofa with her bowl of popcorn and picked up a book she'd found on Jade's bookshelf. She was freshly showered and it felt good to get all the diner smell out of her hair. Jade came in with her hair in a towel and in the brightest pajama pants Aly had ever seen. They were a mix of neon pink, yellow, green, and blue. She'd noticed that Jade had a never-ending supply of pajama pants. Jade grabbed a water bottle and plopped down next to Aly.

"Your pants are so crazy." Aly said chuckling. "Do you have a PJ fetish or something?"

Jade shrugged. "I love my PJ pants. They're the most comfortable thing I have to wear. If I could get away with it in the kitchen at the diner I would."

Aly shook her head and began flipping through the book again.

After a minute, Jade broke their silence. "So, I really want you to talk to me. I hate seeing things bother you."

Aly sat the book on the coffee table and knew Jade was right. "I've really enjoyed my time with Colt."

"That's good. He seems to really like you."

"I still have my doubts but he makes me smile and I enjoy being around him."

They sat in silence with the TV playing a rerun of the home improvement show *Fixer Upper*. Aly hesitated knowing she had to tell Jade everything about Greg. There was no telling what would happen once the truth was out about her affair. What if people didn't believe that she had no idea Greg was married and that she continued seeing him anyway? Would they think she went after a married man regardless of the family he already had? Though she shouldn't, she cared what people thought. Then there was the risk it could embarrass her family, especially in a small town. She wanted to make them proud not shamed. She trusted Jade and would never be able to repay the kindness she had shown.

Aly took a deep breath. "When I was in Dallas, you know I didn't date a whole lot. Just a couple of guys."

Jade nodded. "I remember."

"I was busy studying and working, which didn't make a lot of time for dating." She paused. "Then I started seeing Greg, but he wasn't just anyone."

"Who was he?" Jade asked.

"My boss."

Jade's eyebrows shot up. "Greg was your boss?"

"Yes." Aly told Jade about Greg's early advances and how she did her best to keep things professional. Then she admitted how she eventually gave in. She explained that they didn't go out often and about how adamant he was to keep her to himself. He was great at making her feel special on a daily basis. Then she admitted that she'd hoped they were headed for marriage.

"I felt like we were getting serious. Sure, I wondered why he always shied away from talking about it, but I believed it could happen. I wouldn't have stayed in the position that I was in if I hadn't seen a future with him. That is until…" She didn't want to keep going it made her feel dirty and trashy.

"Until what?" Jade asked.

Aly took a deep breath. "Until his wife showed up at our office."

Jade gasped and covered her mouth. "He's married?!"

"He isn't just married but he has two kids too." She rubbed the side of her popcorn bowl. "I had no idea."

Jade shook her head in disbelief. "Wow. I'm so sorry."

"I never saw him wear a ring. He had nothing personal in his office. Then again, Dallas wasn't the headquarters. He wasn't there all the time. His wife had no idea either. She came to surprise him for their anniversary." Aly looked up at Jade. "I called you from the parking garage right after it happened."

Jade linked their arms together and leaned her head against Aly's shoulder. "I'm so sorry. That's horrible." Jade was quite for a moment. "So, he's still trying to talk to you.

Aly nodded.

"What does he want?"

"I'm not sure. He says he wants me back and he won't give me up. It doesn't even make sense. I mean, he's married and has children. He can't possibly think I would continue anything with him after knowing."

"Is he dangerous?" Jade asked flatly.

It hadn't ever crossed her mind to worry about him in that way. He just wanted to continue their affair and she wasn't going to let that happen. "No. I'm not afraid of him."

"Have you told Colt about it?"

"No. I think he knows something happened and he knows that I'm not telling him about it. I feel horrible because he's been so honest with me about the girls he's been with and the life he's been living on the rodeo circuit. What I've done is worse than what he's shared. I just feel like trash when I think about Greg."

Jade sat up straight. "No, Aly. Don't you dare think that. Greg's the trash. He's the cheater. You didn't know."

"But that doesn't change the fact that I'm the reason a family was hurt. Kids, Jade. I've been the kid through a divorce. I saw Melissa's parents get a divorce. I'm the reason. The mistress." She felt the tears threatening to fall. "One of my former coworkers shared what people have said about me. I'm worried about what would happen here. Small towns are horrible with rumors and judgements. I don't even want to think about Gram finding out."

"No matter what people say, it doesn't make it true. You didn't know, Aly. And once you found out you left." Jade squeezed her hand.

Yes, but it didn't change the fact that she'd been in a relationship with a married man. She had given everything to their relationship, but he wasn't hers to have. "I don't want anyone to find out. I haven't even told mom or Luke. They know I was dating a guy named Greg but they don't know anything else."

"I know you're hurting and angry but I can't stand to see you still worrying about this. If we need to change your phone number or have him blocked, we can do it," Jade said.

Aly looked down at her phone sitting on the coffee table. She didn't want to hear from Greg. If she blocked him there would be no way for him to contact her. "That's probably a good idea."

"Just let me know and we'll go take care of it. You don't have to do any of this alone." Jade hadn't judged her or made her feel horrible. Aly was probably crazy for worry about what Jade would think.

"Thank you for listening to me. I do feel better."

"Of course." Jade pat Aly's leg and then stood. "Now, let's get the laptop and we'll talk about the bakery you're opening."

****

Aly lay down on her bed trying to finish the chapter she was reading before going to sleep. It was a good story about a girl on a path of self-discovery. The heroin had to shed all her insecurities and doubts to come through on the other side. Aly could definitely relate and she was having a hard time putting the book down. Then her phone rang and she hesitated to answer it. Praying it wasn't Greg, she looked at the screen. Relief. It was Colt.

"Hey, cowboy."

"Hey, city girl. Sorry it's late. Since Frank is gone there were a lot of extra things on everyone's plate." He sounded tired.

"Don't worry about it." She closed the book and placed it on the night stand. "How was the rest of your day?"

"Oh, good I guess. I've been looking forward to talking to you so it seemed to drag some. How was yours?"

"It was busy. When we got home, Jade and I ate popcorn and had a good talk."

"Oh, yeah? What was it about?"

"Well, we did discuss the possibly of opening a bakery on the back side of Jade's Gem."

"Seriously? Aly, that's amazing!"

She laughed at his excitement and it warmed her heart to know that he was genuine in his happiness for her. "Yeah. There's still some stuff to work out but Jade's going to help me get started. It's a whole new beginning for me."

"That's really great. I'm so happy for you."

"Umm, we also talked about some things that have been going on. It helped me a lot to open up about it and I think things are going to be better going forward."

Colt was quiet and Aly had to look at the phone to make sure he hadn't hung up. "Colt?"

"I'm here. I'm glad you got to talk to Jade," he said. Aly could hear a little disappointment behind it. Before she could say more he continued, "Look, umm, I have a rodeo this weekend, so I'll be leaving Friday morning and won't be back until Sunday afternoon."

She was bummed at the idea of not getting to see Colt over the weekend. "That sounds like fun."

"I would like to take you out tomorrow. Since it's Thursday, I figured it would be easier to get Jade to let you off early."

"I'm sure that can be arranged. I'd love to."

"Great." The silence stretched between them. Aly was torn in needing to say something and wanting to do it in person. Then Colt cleared his throat and said, "I guess I better let you get some rest—"

"Colt, wait," Aly interrupted. "Can I say one more thing?"

"Sure."

Aly pressed her eyes together praying that Colt would understand what she needed to say. "About what you said today at Jade's. I haven't shared this with anyone until Jade tonight. You've been so honest and open with me and I want to do the same with you. It's just… I don't want to do it over the phone. Can we try and talk about it tomorrow?" One beat. Two. Four. Aly held her breath waiting for his response.

"I'd like that. I'll see you tomorrow?"

She released her breath and answered, "Yes."

"Goodnight, Aly."

"Goodnight." Aly lowered her phone to her lap.

Regardless of how the guilt and anger tried to keep themselves at the forefront, she was ready to heal, to move on. She had her family, who loved her unconditionally. She had Jade, who was giving her the chance at a new beginning. And she had Colt, who shared his past with her. Aly snuggled down under her comforter and said a silent prayer of thanks. She had people in her life that cared about her and genuinely wanted the best for her. The hurt and anger hadn't disappeared but she was determined to not let it steal her tomorrow.

Chapter 17

Aly clocked out and turned to Jade in the kitchen. "I'm headed out."

Jade walked around the cooking line. "I'm so glad you're going on a date tonight." Aly looked around quickly to make sure there wasn't anyone else around. Jade waved her hand and said, "Don't worry about anyone hearing."

"I just know that Crystal has a past with Colt and I don't want to make things awkward." Aly untied her apron and tucked it into her purse.

Jade grabbed both of Aly's arms. "Aly, it doesn't matter. He likes you. You like him. You're getting to know each other. Don't worry about Crystal."

"Okay. I'll see you later."

Jade dropped her hands. "Now you better be ready to tell me all about it. Including a rating on Colt's kissability."

"Kissability?" Aly laughed.

"Yes. I need you to rate his kiss."

"Whatever." Aly waved and headed out to her car. She hadn't told Jade that she'd kissed Colt already. She had a feeling there would be a lot to share since she wanted to find a way to kiss Colt as many times as possible.

She arrived home and quickly hopped in the shower. Colt hadn't given her any instructions on what to wear tonight, so she was going to stick with jeans, just in case. She loved riding Duke and getting to see the place that meant the most to Colt. It was refreshing and helped her stop and really think. She'd never been a big nature person but quickly realized that it might be just what she needed.

The doorbell rang and Aly checked the clock thinking she'd run out of time. She hadn't finished straightening her hair so a braid would have to do. She quickly tied off the end and opened the front door. Colt took her breath away. He had on light blue jeans and a nice black polo t-shirt. She would never tire of looking at him. She stepped back and motioned for him to enter. "Come in."

He leaned down and kissed her cheek. "You look beautiful."

"Thank you. Let me grab my purse and I'll be ready." She ran back into her bedroom and checked herself one last time in the mirror. Her braid was nice and her loose layers framed her face just the way she liked. She applied a little more lip gloss and took a deep breath. She wanted to take a chance with Colt, but there was still a small voice that wouldn't fully let go of how different they were. Sliding her purse over her shoulder, Aly pushed aside the doubt. She didn't want to over think. Greg's continued texts did enough of that on their own. She closed her bedroom door. "I'm ready."

He pushed off the wall next to the door and reached for her hand. "Great."

They headed down the steps and he led her to an older classic truck. It was a beautiful royal blue with yellow pin striping down the side. Colt reached for the door and Aly asked, "Where's your truck?"

Colt helped her into the passenger seat. "This is my baby." He ran his hand along the door frame appreciatively. "A 1949 Ford F1. Her name is Dory."

Did he just say Dory? She chuckled and shook her head. He closed the door and walked around the front. The interior was a dark gray with royal blue trim. It was spotless and had a shine that made her believe it was freshly waxed. Clearly he took a lot of pride in it. Colt started the truck up and it purred like a kitten.

"So, Dory?" Aly teased. "She is blue. Are you a secret lover of Disney movies?"

Colt had a cheesy smile on his face. "I have been known to watch one on occasion. However, my nieces named her."

"You let them name your truck?" she asked. "That shocks me."

Colt glanced at her and then took a right turn. "Why is that?"

Aly shrugged. "I guess I didn't have you pegged for a softie. Letting little girls name your baby." Though it was unexpected, she loved it, actually. It was nice to see that he was clearly fond of his nieces to involve them in something that appeared to be so special to him.

"I hope I keep surprising you. I can't risk how helpless I am around little girls to get out on the circuit." He winked at her. "I'm sure a lot of people know me by my past and actions, but they don't know the real me." His tone had turned dejected. Aly felt a little guilty. She never wanted to judge someone. That's what had happened to her in Dallas, and now she did the same thing to Colt.

"I need to apologize to you." Aly fiddled with her bracelet.

Colt reached over and took her hand in his. He placed it on his thigh and squeezed it lightly. "Aly, I'm not mad. I know some of my history may be hard to accept. I've watched you when that past reared its ugly head." Aly felt a little pang in her chest. "I never thought I'd see the day those things didn't appeal to me, but now it all seems so cheap. I want something better and worthy of having." He kissed the back of her hand.

Aly appreciated that Colt was honest. "I'm sorry. You've been nothing but gracious and respectful. I want something better too."

Colt smiled and pulled onto the rural road that lead to Big T Ranch.

"What are your plans for us today?" she asked.

"I want to make you dinner."

Aly's eyebrows shot up in surprise. "You can cook?"

Colt nodded once. "I can. It's not gourmet by any means but I know how to treat a lady."

Another surprise. "I'm honored. I can't wait."

They pulled around the main house and parked in front of Colt's cabin. She was curious how many girls Colt had brought out there. It wasn't a pleasant thought and she quickly pushed it away. He hadn't done anything to make her question his desire to be with her. They walked up the two steps to a small deck on the front of his cabin. There were two chairs with a small table in between them. It looked like the perfect place to rest after a hard day of work. The door was painted a deep blue color, similar to Dory. All the other cabins had white doors.

"Welcome to my place." Colt pushed the door open and stepped aside so she could enter. The cabin was small but seemed perfect for him. A loveseat and chair sat opposite of a small galley kitchen. The walls were covered in a warm wood paneling and nothing but a clock hung on the walls. There wasn't much of a personal touch anywhere. She wondered if his bedroom was just as bare. Colt walked over to the refrigerator and pulled out some steaks and vegetables.

"Do you like living here?"

"It's just me so it works." Colt grabbed some tongs from a drawer and headed toward the door with the steaks. "I'm going to put these on the grill real quick."

"Ok." Aly headed over to the kitchen and saw the zucchini, yellow squash, tomatoes, and onions. Colt came back in and placed the tray in the sink. "Can I help you with anything?" she asked.

"Nope. I'm treating you." He leaned over and gave her a kiss on the cheek.

Aly felt a light warmth from where his lips had been. She rested against the counter creating a little space between them. "Where did you learn to cook?"

"I guess my mom. When we were little we always ate at home and she did everything. She's a great cook." He began cutting the veggies and lining them in a baking dish. "But later on she ended up hiring help more and more. It's not like a full-time thing but with the family business growing, she caters a lot more."

He finished lining the dish and pulled out the shredded cheese, then paused. "You like cheese, right?"

"Of course. You're crazy if you don't."

"Most definitely. I've got to flip the steaks." He quickly tended to them and returned. "Would you like something to drink?"

"Sure."

He pulled two glasses from the cabinet and opened the fridge. "I pretty much only have beer, sweet tea, milk, or water."

"Sweet tea sounds perfect. I can't stand the stuff without the sugar."

"A woman after my own heart." He tossed ice into each glass and followed it with the tea, then handed her one. She took a large drink and Colt did the same.

A second later their eyes met and the heat between them ignited. His gaze dropped to her lips and she desperately wanted to kiss him, so she did. He wrapped one arm around her waist and deepened the kiss. It didn't last long but when they separated their lips were only a breath apart.

"I like when you take the lead," he said.

Aly pecked his lips and stepped out of his embrace. "You're hard to resist."

"You have no idea how hard I have to work not to take that kiss further." He kissed her forehead. Aly knew the feeling. "Let me go get the steaks and we can eat."

Aly pulled the vegetables out of the oven and inhaled at the smell of the rosemary on them. Colt returned and placed one steak on each plate. "You can divvy up your portion of vegetables, if ya' like?"

"Thanks. This looks amazing." She filled her plate and took a seat at the small table. Colt said grace. Aly loved that he was comfortable praying with her. She'd never dated anyone who did that.

The steak was cooked to a perfect medium and melted on her tongue. She couldn't help but moan her approval.

Colt grinned. "I'm glad you like it."

She finished chewing and said, "I more than like it. I'll have to make you cook for me more often." She took another bite.

"I think I can make that happen." His amber eyes seemed to lighten even more. She was learning that they were lighter when he was happy. It appeared they would be the window to his emotions.

Aly wanted to know more about him, mainly how no other woman had snatched him up yet. "So, you're somewhat domesticated and still single. How does that happen?"

Colt stiffened slightly. *Hmm.* Why did he have that response? Nothing came to mind from what he'd shared with her that would cause him to hesitate. Maybe he hadn't shared everything with her yet. "I mean, you're a bull rider, your family is well off, you're easy on the eyes, and seem like a genuinely nice guy. I'm just curious is all."

Colt finished chewing his bite and took a drink of his tea. When he looked up, she noticed his eyes had lost the sparkle from earlier. What did that mean? Was he upset or angry?

Colt cleared his throat and sat back in his chair. "I guess I just haven't been the settling down type."

"I don't know if I believe that."

Colt watched her for a moment and finally his features soften. "I've been on the rodeo circuit since I was in high school. I thought I had found someone but—" His features twisted and pain flashed across his face before he recovered. "Then I got busy out here and life kept going."

"I can understand that." She watched him carefully wondering what he was about to say. "So, was she the only girl you felt strongly for?"

"She was." Colt picked at his food and wouldn't look at her. It was clear he wasn't going to reveal any more right now. She hoped that one day he would share whatever he wasn't now, but she wasn't going to judge since she still had some sharing to do too.

During the rest of dinner, they fell into easy conversation about the bakery. She was happy it was natural to talk to Colt. She didn't want to worry about the deep stuff. It was her plan to tell him about Greg so that they could move forward with no secrets. But his hesitancy made her wonder what had happened with that girl? Maybe it was too soon and eventually they would both feel comfortable enough to share more about their past. However, she was nervous about what he'd think after hers was revealed.

Chapter 18

Colt was glad that he'd done something simple with Aly today. It was nice to stay in the cabin instead of a busy restaurant. Seeing her was the best part of his day and what he looked forward to the most.

"That was wonderful, Colt. Thank you." Aly said as he took their dirty plates. "You could give Jade a run for her money."

Colt laughed. "I don't know about that, but I am sure glad you liked it."

"Oh, I wanted to tell you that I'll be helping Jade cater the party your parents' are having Sunday."

Colt paused while wiping down the counter. "You are?"

"Yeah. I told Jade I'd help her with catering and maybe once the bakery is up I can help supply all the desserts for her. Will you be at the party?"

Colt sagged against the counter. His mother wouldn't consider it acceptable for the heir to the Big T Ranch to not make an appearance for networking purposes, regardless of the long drive home from Austin. He had to make them look good. Colt nodded and said, "I will."

Aly's face broke out into a gorgeous smile. "That's great! Then I won't have to wait until Monday to see you."

He hated that he wasn't excited about it. Aly was too sweet and good to be put under his mother's microscope. He would do what he had to in order to protect Aly from that scrutiny. Granted, his mother didn't know they were dating, but she would certainly have her eyes on him. He wouldn't just give Aly the cold shoulder, in order to keep their relationship a secret. He cringed at the thought. She didn't deserve that.

"Let's go outside." He reached for her hand, grabbed a blanket that was sitting on the back of the living room chair, and they walked out to Dory. He dropped the tail gate and hopped up inside to spread the blanket out. "Care to join me?" He asked motioning to the truck bed as he climbed out.

"Sure." She put her hands on his shoulders bracing for him to lift her into the back. The space between them electrified. A gorgeous smile crept across her face and he knew she was feeling the same thing he was. There was just something about the two of them together that was different than anything he'd ever had. His desire quickly rose in his chest. He hated breaking their connection but he did, and lifted her to rest on the edge of the tailgate. He stepped around her legs and hopped up. Aly lay flat on her back and looked up at the stars. Colt mimicked her and laid down close enough that their arms were touching.

After a few beats, Aly broke the silence. "It's been a long time since I did anything like this."

"I'm glad I get to share it with you then."

Aly looked over at him with a pleasant smile. "Me too. You can't see the stars like this in the city."

Colt pulled his eyes away from her and looked back at the sky. He couldn't imagine himself living anywhere else. Even in all his travels with the rodeo circuit, he always felt the best in Shaw Creek. "Do you like being back here?" he asked.

"I do." There was a smile in her answer and that made him smile too. She continued, "I'm enjoying getting to see a life I've never known before. That's thanks to you. I can see why you love the country life so much."

He wanted to ask if she could see herself loving it to... with him. *Wait! Where did that comes from?!* They were nowhere near that conversation. He never let himself think like that.

"Like I told you the other day, I've never pictured myself anywhere else." He wanted her to talk more about her time in Dallas and why she left but didn't want to seem pushy. So, he chose a more casual question. "What was it like being away?"

"College was great. It took some adjustment, coming from a small town and going to a big city. There were more kids in one of my business classes than were in my whole senior class. I did some partying with my roommates but it didn't do much for me. I had fun but I spent most of my time working and studying. Once Jade went to culinary school, it wasn't the same. But overall, I enjoyed my time there."

"Sometimes I wish I'd gone to college, but it never crossed my mind back then. Things happened after high school that took priority." *Like losing Emily.* "I just didn't picture myself doing anything other than rodeo." He didn't want to talk about the plans he had right out of high school, he wasn't ready to bring her into that. So, he changed it before she could ask. "What did you do after college?"

Aly shifted slightly and Colt couldn't help but notice the distance she was trying to create between them. She linked her fingers and rested her hands on her stomach.

"I got a job at an insurance office while I was in college. It was the perfect job for me because it was flexible with my school schedule and I learned a lot about business too. After I graduated, I felt strongly about staying there. It was great at the time and I decided not to look for other jobs right away." Her voice was distant.

"Why'd you leave then?" Silence was her only answer. He looked at her but she kept looking up into the stars. "You can tell me." His voice a soft plea. Aly turned her head and looked at him. There was longing and sadness in her eyes. It sliced at his gut.

"I've not told anyone about what happened, except for Jade." Aly's voice was soft and broken.

Colt reached for one of the hands resting on her stomach and pressed it to his chest. He fought the urge to roll over on his side and hold her. They stared at each other. Colt wanted to give her every reassurance his heart could possibly offer. It may be broken, bruised and battered but in that moment, he wanted to give it to her. "Aly," her name only a whisper on his lips.

She pulled her hand away and sat up, running her fingers through her hair. Colt quickly joined her, afraid that he'd pushed too much. There were no tears in her eyes, but there was something else. He wasn't sure what.

Aly took a deep breath. "I've never had a problem trusting people, men mainly. I dated some in high school and in college. It was fun. There was never anything to worry about. Granted, they weren't serious by any means, but something happened just before I came here that has made it hard for me. I don't want to tell people because I just wanted to leave it in Dallas. I haven't even told my parents or brother. I know Luke will react like a crazy over protective brother, even though we're not that close anymore. I'm not ready to tell them yet. I needed to center myself and start over." She turned and looked at him. "I did have a relationship that became serious. I shouldn't have let it happen, but I did. Then it ended in the worst way I could ever imagine. I was embarrassed and humiliated."

Colt sat silent for a moment. "I understand not letting people in. I'm the poster boy for uncommitted relationships. We're just getting to know each other. I know I'm trying my best to trust you and I want you to trust me too."

"I don't know if you'll like what you hear."

Colt hopped down from the tail gate and stood in front of her. "We've both been through so much. Probably more than the other realizes. I, for one, can't judge anything that has happened in anyone's past, but I want you to feel safe with me." He meant every word.

She looked down and wrung her hands anxiously. "Thank you, Colt. I didn't mean to mess up your beautiful evening. You've made my time back in Shaw Creek very special."

He took a finger and lifted her chin. "This may sound cheesy, but I'm going to say it anyway. You could never mess it up. You're what made my night. I enjoy spending time with you." He loved the sweet smile that graced her face. "Hey, you're pretty lucky to get to sit in the back of Dory. I'm very protective of her."

That got a soft laugh out of Aly, and Colt's heart soared.

"What? You don't bring all your girlfriends out to star gaze?" she teased.

Colt shifted closer, his stomach pressed against her knees. "I've never let any girl in the back of Dory. Ever."

Aly rolled her eyes. "Right."

He leaned in closer to her and he didn't miss the small gasp. "I haven't, Aly. Little girls sure, but I've never let any *woman* near Dory. Just you." It was true. His truck was something he kept just for himself, but now it was something he wanted to share with Aly. He was surprised at how happy that made him. "I'm not interested in anyone but you."

She bit down on her bottom lip and Colt felt the air around them charge again. He gently pushed himself between her knees and leaned his belt into the edge of the tailgate. There was no doubt that Aly was meant to be kissed. Her eyes were wide with anticipation and her full pink lips parted slightly. He couldn't help himself. One hand slid around her neck and into her hair as he dipped to meet her mouth. Her hands gripped the shirt at his sides. He used his other hand and pressed the small of her back so they were flush against each other.

He kissed her lips slowly allowing her to discover him as well. He wanted her to know that he was willing to let her lead and that he enjoyed it even. There was longing, passion, tenderness, and respect in their kiss. He hoped she felt everything he wanted to convey. Possibility. Hope. Acceptance. Desire. Her head tipped back and he kissed along her jaw to just below her ear. She shuddered and Colt loved that he had that effect on her. Slowly, he worked back up her jaw and captured her lips for another long lingering kiss.

When they came up for air, Colt looked at Aly and she had the most beautiful content smile. Her eyes slowly opened to meet his. He slid his hands down her sides and settled at her waist. He gripped her slightly and helped her down to the ground.

Aly tugged at her shirt. "I should probably get going. I've got to get up early and bake in the morning."

Colt nodded. "Let's get you home."

The drive back across town was pleasantly quiet. Colt was glad Aly didn't need to fill the blank space. She was comfortable with silence just like him. He pulled in next to her car and hopped out to open her door. They ascended the steps hand in hand, then paused under the porch light. Aly wrapped her arms around Colt. He hugged her back and loved how her head came to the center of his chest. He dipped down to kiss her cheek and inhaled. "You smell like cucumber."

"It's my body wash. I may be out of the city but I still want to feel like I've gone to the spa." She nuzzled closer to his chest.

Colt inhaled again and kissed the top of her head. "Well, I like it." She leaned back to look up at him. "Thanks for going out with me tonight, my sweet little thing."

Aly raised one eyebrow. "Is that a knock at my height?"

"No. I love how you seem to fit just perfectly against me."

"I do too." She went up on her toes to give him a quick peck but he held her in place. He poured himself into the kiss and she met him just as passionately. She pulled back slowly and looked up at him from under her eyelashes. He had to suppress a groan. He was putty in her hands.

"You have no idea what you do to me." His voice was gruff.'

She tilted her head slightly. "I have a pretty good idea because I feel the same about you. I'll see you Sunday night?"

"Yes, ma'ma." He kissed her forehead. "Sleep well."

"Safe travels." She took a step back, resting her hand on the door knob. "Goodnight, cowboy." Then winked at him before slipping inside.

Yep, Aly Meyers was the potter and he was just clay in her hands. He couldn't wait to see what they'd become together.

Chapter 19

The Teel family had an unbelievably gorgeous home and Aly couldn't wait to see what it would look like when the leaves changed in a few months. She followed Jade around the house to the back yard where a large tent was set up for the party. A small band was setting up on the stage next to a wooden dance floor. Gorgeous crystal vases filled with different floral arrangements of twigs, crystals, and flowers of all colors rested on the round tables covered with white table cloths. Several long tables stretched the length of the tent on the edge for the buffet. Aly began prepping the trays with all her sweets. The presentation of pastries, puddings, cakes, and cookies looked good.

Jade stepped next to Aly. "It looks like the bartender Mrs. Teel reserved is starting to set up. I've got Justin working the two dinner tables. Brittany and Crystal are going to refill drinks and clear plates. How are things at the dessert table?"

Aly appraised the table. "It's good. I'm nervous about the food."

"Don't be." Jade squeezed Aly's forearm. "This is like your debut!"

"I guess. I've never had any of my food out for a party like this. These people are important and I just don't want this to be a bust." Aly looked across the room. More than that, it was Colt's family. She wasn't sure his mother would approve that they were in a relationship, especially after meeting her at the church luncheon. Then if her desserts ended up being mediocre, everything between her and Colt could become strained.

"Mrs. Teel picked the menu." Jade turned Aly to face her and gripped her shoulders. "You're an amazing baker and this is just to prove to the world that you are. It's a great way to get some opinions before we open the bakery."

Aly nodded. "Thank you. I can never repay you for this."

"You don't need to. Just put on that smile and be excited. Your man is going to be here tonight."

Aly inhaled a deep breath. She was proud of her desserts and had faith that they would be everything she wanted them to be. The best part of the evening was getting to see Colt. She'd missed him more than she thought she would. Seeing him every day in the diner and the few dates they'd gone on had been amazing. Sure, they had text every day while he was gone but it just wasn't the same. She hoped they might get the chance to spend some time together after the party.

Aly finished setting up all the food and noticed more people entering the tent. The men were in pressed jeans and nice button down shirts, some even had dress jackets. The women wore gorgeous evening dresses. They weren't the silk and chiffon she would see at a party in the city, but they were equally as beautiful with lace. Most wore full length gowns but others had shorter cocktail dresses on. Aly spotted Mrs. Teel visiting with a few families and hugging everyone who entered. She was a graceful woman and definitely had an air about her. Aly sent a silent prayer up for peace. She didn't want to feel insecure about anything, her baking or her social status.

She busied herself with serving and taking care of people as they came through the buffet and desserts. A pretty young woman, probably Aly's age, in a tea length royal blue dress, had a warm smile. "This is lovely. I'm not sure I can make a choice."

Aly picked one up to offer to her. "My personal favorite is the bread pudding. It's a family recipe."

The woman accepted the pudding and fork. She took a small bite and her eyes lit up in delight. "Did you make this?"

Aly sighed in relief. "Yes. It's my grandmother's recipe."

"It's amazing. Do you make these at Jade's Gem?"

"Well, I'm actually getting ready to open a bakery on the other side of the diner, but yes, Jade and I are working closely to combine both."

"Wonderful." The woman extended her hand. "My name is Maria. Maria Teel."

Another Teel. "It's a pleasure to meet you. I hope you'll come check out the bakery once we open." As Maria walked off, Aly looked across the tent as people began getting their food. Where was Colt?

"Aly, can you run and get more silverware out of the van?" Jade asked.

"Sure." She left the tent, ducking by guests milling around the entrance. She opened the back of the van and had to climb in to dig through the boxes. Once she found the silverware, she backed out of the van, but when she hopped to the ground she lost her footing. Lucky for her, someone was there to catch her. She looked up and came face to face with her favorite cowboy. He helped her regain her balance and she loved the feeling of his hands gripping her waist. He was dressed in new wranglers and a black pearl snap shirt. He made her weak in the knees and he didn't even have to try.

"Hey, babe," he said. "It seems we keep meeting like this."

Aly loved the pet name. "Hey. Yeah, I'm the lucky one since you're always there to catch me."

"I hope to always be."

She felt her heart flutter at his words. "I wasn't sure you were going to make it."

"I know it's been a long day, but I'm here." He took the box and they began to walk towards the tent. She felt a little bummed that he didn't kiss her. Maybe he was just tired. The music was playing and it filtered around the house. "I've got some people to see but will you save me a dance after?"

Aly looked down at her black pants and shirt. "I don't know since I'm working."

"Well, I need to have a chat with Jade. Surely, you get a break." Colt winked as they entered the tent. He ducked around the group of people talking to his parents. Was he avoiding them? She decided not to ask as they stopped at the first buffet table. "This looks great."

Aly opened the silverware and began laying it out. "Your parents' sure know how to throw a party."

"That they do." His tone was resigned but he shook it off and looked toward the last table. "How are your desserts doing?"

"Great, I think. People seem to really like them. Come see." Aly walked toward the end of the buffet and Colt followed.

"Everything looks amazing. I'm so excited for you." Colt's smile reached his eyes and he looked like he was going to kiss her.

"Colt, dear!" They both jumped. Mrs. Teel and a pretty blonde wearing a red tea length dress and jean jacket were approaching. "I'm so pleased you've arrived. The Franklins are here and..." she stepped back to usher the blonde forward. "So is Olivia."

Aly glanced up at Colt and could see his eyes appraise Olivia. Jealousy clenched her gut. She wished he hadn't looked at all, even if the woman was hard to miss. Colt kissed his mother's cheek then extended his hand and shook Olivia's hand. "It's nice to see you, Olivia."

Olivia batted her eyes and held onto his hand longer than normal for a hand shake. She shifted her weight so that she was closer to him and had a slinky smile. It was obvious that Olivia was a big fan of Colt and she wasn't shy about her flirting. They began a cordial conversation and based on her extensive knowledge of the rodeo, Aly could tell it was something they were both passionate about. She ducked her head and took a step behind the table.

Mrs. Teel jumped into their conversation. "My, you two have so many memories together."

Aly felt stupid for hating that. She'd only been in Colt's life for a month. But she still didn't like that Olivia held parts of Colt's past in her hands.

"Colt, do you remember last year when we got stuck in dad's stock trailer for over an hour?" Olivia laughed a little too obnoxiously.

Colt joined her laugh and it stabbed at Aly's heart. "Yeah. Did he ever get that fixed?"

"Yeah. It's too bad really. I had a good time." Olivia flipped her hair over her shoulder.

"It was unbearably hot in there. It's a wonder we didn't pass out."

"We took good care of each other." Olivia batter her eyes again. Ugh, Aly felt like throwing up.

Colt glanced at Aly and cleared his throat. "Well, that was a while ago."

Aly knew that had been his life back then, but it still sucked having to hear the play by play from the girl herself. She tried to keep her discouragement at bay but she didn't succeed. There were guests approaching her table. It was time to get back to work.

"Colt, I've got several people who are wanting to meet with you," Mrs. Teel said.

"I was going to visit with Aly for a moment." Colt gave her his sexy smile but she couldn't bring herself to match it.

Mrs. Teel glared at Aly before shooting daggers at Colt. "That's nice but she's just here to serve our guests. I'm sure she can understand that you have people to entertain and far more important responsibilities to uphold."

Aly's straightened her shoulders to keep them from sagging. His mother's words stung. She glanced up at Colt and met his eyes. She offered him a half smile and he looked torn. That gave her a little relief that he wanted to spend time with her, but she knew he had a job to do too.

There were people standing in the buffet line and it wasn't any surprise to see them watching the exchange. Though she didn't want to, Aly broke eye contact and said, "Excuse me."

She walked toward the other end of the table to help the next person in line. She didn't dare look back to see if Colt was still standing with Olivia. After a few people came through, Aly finally glanced out into the crowd. There were a few couples dancing and she was relieved to see Colt wasn't out there. She found him making the rounds through the crowd, no doubt networking for the ranch. He was charming and smooth with every person, bringing a smile to their face. It was evident that people loved him.

"How's it going?" Jade asked.

"It seems everyone likes the desserts."

"I think your bread pudding was the favorite. It's all gone!" Jade gave Aly a hug. "I knew you'd be amazing."

"Thanks." Aly felt good about opening the bakery. It was a new dream but it looked like it just might come true.

The music turned slow and Jade looked out toward the dance floor. Her face sobered and Aly followed her line of vision. Her heart seized slightly when she spotted Colt putting his arm around Olivia's waist. Olivia was leaning in close and Colt was smiling at whatever she said. *Why did he have to look like he was enjoying it?* They were a handsome couple. Mrs. Teel was talking to another woman and pointed to Colt and Olivia. They shared an approving smile.

Jade leaned in and asked, "Do you need a break?"

"We're not done yet."

"Dinner is coming to a close. I was going to have Justin keep things up for a little while longer in case anyone else wanted one last plate. The bartender will cover drinks for the rest of the night. Brittany and Crystal are still clearing tables. You can take some of the dirty dishes out to the van and stay out there a while. I'll watch the dessert table."

Aly looked down at the table and saw that everything was mostly empty. She could use some space. "Ok. I think I will."

Jade nodded her understanding. Once again, Aly sent up a silent prayer of thanks for Jade's friendship. She bent down to retrieve one of the tubs full of dirty plates. There was no need to over think things. She didn't want to be the jealous type. She knew this was just for show.

After a few trips to the van, Aly retrieved the last tub and looked back out at the dance floor. The song was coming to a close and Colt kissed the back of Olivia's hand. It was hard to deny the pleased look on his face. She recognized it from the first time they met, when he did the same thing. She squeezed her eyes as she left the tent, not able to look at Colt again. Yeah it may be for show, but it stung. He hadn't shown any affection to her in public, especially with his family around. If he wanted to have a relationship with her, wouldn't he share that with those closest to him? She couldn't help but wonder if she was just the type of girl that men liked to keep hidden. She wasn't the one men carried on their arm to impress people. She hated that it even came to mind, but she felt like a stranger in Colt's world.

Aly continued to help load everything in the van, not wanting to go back inside. She didn't belong in there. Once everything was loaded up, Jade came out and leaned against the van next to Aly. "That's everything. I think it will be a longer night for the bartender but I got everything we need for tonight. Are you ready to head back to the diner to unload?"

Aly knew what Jade was really asking. Was she ready to leave without seeing Colt? No, but she didn't say that out loud. "Yes. Let's head out. I'm ready for a hot shower and my bed."

Aly slid into the passenger seat and Jade behind the wheel. She didn't want to look in the review mirror but as they pulled away from the house, she couldn't help it. To her relief and disappointment, Colt wasn't there. He was still inside fulfilling what his family needed and what he wanted more than anything, the betterment of the ranch. There was no doubt in Aly's mind that he would be amazing at taking over everything for his parents. She was just afraid that their short time together was all they'd ever really have. The real world was calling Colt and she wasn't sure she had a place in it.

Chapter 20

When morning broke, Colt needed to find Aly. It had been a long weekend and he was desperate to see her. His heart must really be changing for him to feel that way. If his buddies on the circuit could see him now they would definitely call him a sap. They'd be shocked really. Colt Teel didn't do commitment and the idea of him "desperate" to see a woman, that was crazy.

He got the ranch hands all assigned to different jobs for the day and he headed into town. There was no way he'd be able to wait until lunch before talking to Aly.

After he finally finished schmoozing everyone his mother introduced him to at the party, Aly was gone. He figured she needed to get back to clean up with Jade but he missed getting to tell her goodnight.

He had to reel in his frustration with his mother interrupting him and Aly, especially with Olivia. She was an attractive woman and they had hooked up in the past, but he wasn't interested in her. He'd seen Aly trying not to look at them dancing, and he would've given anything to be dancing with her instead. Once he got into his cabin at the end of the night, he called and sent a text but she hadn't replied. He couldn't help but be a little worried.

Olivia would make the perfect wife, as far as Colt's mother was concerned. She was well versed in ranch life and familiar with rodeos. She was a great barrel racer, had been since she was a kid. The idea of dating Oliva had crossed his mind on more than one occasion but there was only one girl in the forefront of his mind now. A woman he missed when she wasn't around. A woman he thought about constantly. A woman he couldn't stand to lose. And that woman was Aly.

Colt parked across the street from Jade's Gem. He opened the door and looked around the diner. However, he didn't see Aly anywhere. Jade made eye contact with him from behind the kitchen line and smiled. Surely, that was a good sign. She came out from behind the line to meet him. "Good morning, Colt. You're usually not here for breakfast."

"Yeah, I wanted to come and see Aly this morning. I didn't get to catch her before you guys left last night." Colt flexed his fingers at his side, anxiously.

Jade watched him for a moment. "Yeah, we had to get things back here. She's actually testing recipes in the bakery. The door's on the north side of the diner."

"Great. Thank you." Colt turned and made his way to the unmarked door around the building. He stopped before opening it when he spotted Aly through the window. She was busy at the counter putting the top crust on what looked like a pie. Her hair was in a messy bun with wisps around her face. She had an apron on that said 'Mind your own biscuits, the rest will be gravy'. There was music playing on her phone and she sang along with it, swaying her hips slightly. He could stand and watch her bake all day. She glanced up and did a double take when she noticed someone was there. A slow smile grew across her face. He pushed the door open and said, "Good morning."

"Good morning, cowboy. I usually don't see you this early." She wiped her hands on a towel and put one on her hip. "What can I do for you?"

Colt leaned over the counter his look intent. Aly's cheeks turned a little pink and smile faded slightly. "Well, there's this beautiful woman I didn't get to spend time with this weekend and I just couldn't wait to see her."

"Is that right?" Aly said tilting her head slightly. Colt nodded twice. She raised an eyebrow but her grin didn't brighten like before. "She sounds special."

"She is." Colt slowly walked around the counter. "The most amazing thing is that she doesn't know just how special." Aly eyed him as he closed the distance between them. "Come to think of it, she still owes me a dance."

That made a smile break out across her face and Colt wrapped his arms around her, bringing her close. Aly relaxed against him and said, "Well, she does like to dance."

The music from her phone filled the silence and Colt pulled her out into the center of the room. She resisted for a second before letting herself melt into his chest. He wasn't sure there was a better feeling. Aly fit perfectly with him.

Their feet swayed and spun around the old storefront. Her black strappy heels clicked on the tile drawing his gaze to what she was wearing. Such a contradiction to the cotton button down shirt and skinny jeans. He realized there would always be a little city in everything that was Aly Meyers, and he loved it. She looked beautiful and content. Colt felt the need to talk to her about what happened at the party. "Babe?"

She turned her head up to look at him. "Yeah."

"I'm sorry." It's all he could think to say for last night.

She looked slightly confused. "What for?"

"Last night," he said plainly.

"You have nothing to apologize for." He voice was soft. He could see the sincerity in her eyes but they looked drained as well. "It was a beautiful party—"

"Aly." Colt stopped dancing but kept her close to him. Her expression hardened as if giving herself reinforcements. He hated to think that she was guarding herself from him, but he couldn't blame her. "What my mother said doesn't reflect what I feel in any way. You have to believe me."

Aly's beautiful blue eyes never wavered. She took a step back and his heart dropped. Distance.

"Colt, I'm okay." She squeezed his arms and walked back behind the table to continue baking. More distance. He had to stop it.

"You don't sound like it."

Aly pulled an empty bowl closer to her. "I am. Your mother loves you and loves the ranch. She's just looking out for you and your interests."

"She may think she knows what's best for me." Colt pressed his palms on the counter in front of her. "I meant what I said. You *are* special... to me."

She stared at the bowl in front of her. "I believe that you mean that. I do." There was something behind her tone that made him think otherwise.

"But...?" Colt prompted her to continue.

Her shoulders dropped and she looked up at him. "I like you Colt. I do, but I don't know what this is between us or where it's going. You have a wonderful life, with everything laid out in front of you and I'm just starting to chase a dream." She shrugged one shoulder, like she always did. "Maybe a relationship isn't what either of us needs."

A panic raced through Colt and he walked behind the counter in order to get closer to her. He had to keep her from pushing him away. "Aly, please—"

"Colt," she interrupted and held up one hand to stop him. He was two steps away from touching her and yet it felt like a mile. "We've both got a lot of things going on. We don't need any more pressure than we already have."

He could see the determination in her eyes and it gutted him. "I know we haven't known each other for very long, but the last thing I think we need is to push each other away."

"It's okay. You don't owe me anything and I'm not mad." She turned to start mixing ingredients.

He knew she was upset. Things were bothering her and she was trying not to show it. There was something inside Colt that couldn't imagine not being with Aly. "Don't you want to be happy?"

"Of course, I do," Aly said without looking up. "Friends make me happy."

"I don't want to just be your friend. I never thought I'd feel this way again." Colt took a deep breath.

Emily had meant everything to him and then she was ripped from this world, gone forever. Falling for Aly had been against everything he'd promised never to do again. Feel. Trust. Love. He moved toward her slowly and Aly didn't budge. "I never saw this coming but..." He took another step. "I've felt unexplainably drawn to you." Another step. "I want to be close to you." He was now one step away and he could see her eyes widen as she looked up at him. "And I think you feel the same way too."

"You think so?" she asked. He nodded and Aly raised one eyebrow. He loved when she did that. "You're that confident in yourself, cowboy?"

He nodded again. There was no doubt that it was worth the risk. "I especially like..." he started and dipped his head until their lips were just a breath apart. Her breath hitched slightly. Colt whispered, "Getting to kiss you."

Aly closed her eyes and he kissed her. It was hesitant at first, like she wasn't sure she should drop her guard. He wanted to take his time and prove just how much he wanted to be with her. Whatever she was holding onto gave way. She relaxed into his chest and clung to his shirt as their kiss deepened. There was so much longing and desperation pouring from them both. Though she hadn't spoken the words, Aly's kiss said it all. She wanted him as much as he wanted her. She broke the kiss but didn't let go of his shirt. Colt loosened his grip on her waist and hoped that she wouldn't choose to push him away again.

"Wow." His voice was hoarse. "Aly, I don't want you to doubt anything I just said. We can give this a shot. Believe me?"

She watched him closely, as if searching for the truth behind his words. Her eyes softened and she said, "Okay."

"Thank you." Colt kissed her forehead and hugged her to him. "I'll prove it to you."

When they released each other, she smiled up at him. "Thanks for coming to me, Colt."

"Just promise me that when you have any doubts, you'll come talk to me about it first." He couldn't run the risk of things ending without a word.

"I will."

Colt wished he could spend the whole day removing any doubt she had but he couldn't. "I've got to get to work but I had to come by and see you. It was important that you know how I'm feeling about us."

"I'm glad you did."

"Good luck with the sweets. Remember to call me first when you need a taste tester." Colt winked at her.

"Thanks. I'm getting ready for a booth at the sunflower festival." She handed him a list of desserts. "This is what I'm planning on having samples of. It'll help get my name out there and also associate me with the diner."

"It looks awesome." He handed the paper back. "I guess I'll let you get back to it." He reached for her hand and kissed just above her knuckles. "I'm pretty busy this week. We've got to get things ready to take some heifers to auction, along with a number of projects on the ranch. Can you come out one evening?"

"I'd like that."

"Great. You'll have to wear different shoes, though." He smiled eyeing her feet.

Aly lifted her foot and looked back at her shoes. "What? You don't like my heels?"

"I didn't say that at all, quite the opposite actually."

She dropped her foot. "Well, I don't have any work boots but I do have something that will be easier to walk around out there."

"Perfect. I'll talk to you later." Colt exited the soon-to-be bakery and walked around the building towards his truck. Since he met her, Aly struggled with their differences and the possibility that they could have a real relationship. Thanks to his mother, those doubts hadn't gone away. It was just going to take extra work to prove himself worthy of her. It may take some time but something deep inside told him this would be worth the effort.

Chapter 21

Colt twisted the last t-post clip on the new catch pen. If they were going to support the increase of bucking bulls the Franklins were asking for, he knew they needed at least two more after this one. It would be a lot of extra work and the ranch hands would have to work double time. He needed to stick to his father's plan in order to accommodate the growth.

He took one glove off and ran his hand through his damp hair. Thankfully, it was hump day, the week was half over. He'd worked continually the past two days and he hadn't got to see Aly once. They'd talked both nights on the phone but he missed her. He wanted to kiss her, hold her, and smell the cucumber scent on her skin. In the upcoming months, he knew it would be harder to spend time together with the bakery opening and the ranch getting ready for the expansion. He wasn't looking forward to it.

He slipped his fencing pliers into the saddle back on Duke and was ready to head to the barn for a break. It was the end of August and soon the heat would start to ease up. He settled onto Duke and headed out. When the barn came back into view he noticed someone standing on the wooden fence, big black glasses and blonde hair blowing behind them.

Aly.

She had on a red cardigan and dark skinny jeans tucked into knee high flat brown boots. All sense of exhaustion evaporated from his body. His heart raced at the sight of her. She waved at him and brushed some hair from her face as it tossed around in the breeze. His chest swelled at the thought of seeing her like that every time he came in from working. Yep. He didn't shy away from the idea of her being out on the ranch with him in the future. Regardless of what he still didn't know about her, Colt wanted Aly indefinitely.

"Hey, handsome," Aly called out. Colt walked Duke in line with the fence and stopped right in front of her. "You look good on the back of a horse. I like the rope too. It's like you were made to be there."

Colt loved riding and he loved roping, but that was a lifetime ago. "I must say you've never looked more beautiful than you do right now."

"Thanks. It feels good to be here."

"Do you want to take a ride?" He asked holding out his hand. Aly's face broke out into a smile and he wished he could have someone paint a picture of her in that very moment. Bliss. Excitement. Happiness. All the things Colt wanted to give her. She took his hand and used him for balance as she stepped onto the top rung of the fence. He scooted back in the saddle and helped her settle in front of him. She quickly braided her hair to the side and gripped the saddle horn. He kissed her exposed neck and felt her shiver at his touch. Her side braid was definitely his favorite. "Hold on."

They took off in a gallop toward the hill. She found the rhythm with Duke and they raced across the grass. After they climbed the hill, they dismounted and walked hand in hand over to the edge. "Do you need to tie him up?" Aly asked looking back toward Duke.

"Nah. He won't go far." Colt took a seat and Aly joined him. Colt tapped her clean boot noticing the studs running along the back. "Nice shoes."

Aly beamed. "Thanks. These are my favorite for the fall and winter."

"You're favorite, huh?"

"Yep, they keep my legs warm and still look good. Yes, I am aware that they don't have a heel or strap." Aly stretched her legs out in front of her and crossed her ankles. She was so cute. He couldn't help himself, so he cupped the back of her neck and pulled her toward him. He kissed her deeply, loving the taste of strawberry lip gloss. When he pulled back she smiled pleasantly at him. "What was that for?"

"I just like kissing you." He loved the light blush on her cheeks as she leaned in for another quick kiss. Aly inhaled deeply and closed her eyes to the sky. Colt loved how free she looked.

"Can I ask you something?" Aly asked with her eyes still closed.

"Sure."

"If you could do anything with your life, regardless of what other people wanted, what would you do?"

Her question surprised him. His life had always been defined by his family. His younger brothers made the decision to go out and make their own way; college and family. Colt stayed home. Well, there was a reason for that. He couldn't bring himself to do anything after losing Emily for almost a year. Shaking the dark memories from his mind, he knew the answer to her question even if he'd never told anyone else before. "I'd train roping horses and give lessons to riders."

Aly turned to look at him. "Really?" Colt shrugged trying to keep her from seeing how he really felt about it. "Why don't you do it?"

That was the question wasn't it? In order to answer that Colt would have to bring up the past, and that was something he never did. "I gave that up a long time ago." When she didn't say anything else he continued. "It's not what my family does."

Aly nodded slightly. "I can respect that. The ranch is a wonderful gift to you."

True. The only problem Colt had were his parents' attempt to control his personal life. He wondered if they'd truly give up control of the ranch once he took over. "It is. What about you?"

Aly clicked her shoes together and looked back over the ranch. "I guess I'm doing it. I've always loved baking but never considered it until Jade suggested opening a bakery." She started to pick at the seam of her jeans. "I guess the deeper question for me is what I would change rather than what I want to do next."

"What do you mean?" Colt asked. Aly pulled her legs up and rested her chin on her knees. Colt shifted so he was facing her, pulling her between his legs. He tucked a stray hair behind her ear. "You can tell me. Please."

Aly tilted her head to rest on her knees so she was looking at him. "I was in a relationship with someone I shouldn't have been. He wasn't abusive or anything like that. It was quite the opposite actually. He doted on me and made me feel really special." She paused as if trying to pick her words carefully. She looked past him toward the trees. "You see that hawk flying over there?"

Colt followed her line of site. "Yeah."

"When I see a hawk flying I think powerful, skillful, graceful, and free. All things I believed my ex brought out in me." Her eyes shifted to him then back to the hawk. "But now I realize he only felt that way about me when it was convenient for him. We didn't see each other all the time because of his job. He was split between Austin and Dallas. When he was in Dallas we never went out, just stayed at home and kept things quiet. I thought it was because he wanted me all to himself and it made me feel good." She sighed. "Now I know different."

Colt hated to hear that her ex had made her feel that way. She was good, honest, beautiful, and deserved to feel special. Before he could think of something to say she spoke again. "There were a couple of problems with my relationship with him."

"What were they?"

He could see her wrestling with what to say next as her jaw clenched and released. She took a deep breath. "He just wasn't who I thought he was. I guess I'm not sure my heart has fully recovered."

He had a surge of protectiveness fill him about her. "What if I can help you put it back together?"

Aly didn't say anything for a long time but Colt didn't dare speak. He surprised himself in his question. He wasn't a romantic person, never had been. He didn't need a woman because that meant he was opening his heart again, but here he was wanting to put hers back together. Satisfaction he'd never felt settled over him, he wanted to do just that.

Aly shifted and straightened her back. "Why don't you section off some of this place for roping?" she asked changing the subject.

He tried to hide his disappointment and thought about her question, but didn't. "I don't know that it would be a good idea. My parents' have a deal with the Franklins to build a partnership with the cattle. It will expand a lot of our operation. It would take money, time, and land away from building up the cattle herd." Colt liked the idea of starting a small training place but he knew it wouldn't be the priority.

"If you're in charge, won't you get to make that decision?"

"Yes, but the partnership has already begun. We're building more pens and sectioning off acres for the new steers and heifers." Colt sighed. "It's just not in the cards for me right now."

Aly sat quietly for a moment, looking out over the property. Then she shifted and pushed up off the ground. "I'm getting hungry, cowboy. What do you say we grab a bite to eat?"

He stood up and said, "I've got a few more chores to do in the barn. Do you want to help me first? Then I'll be all yours for the rest of the day."

Her eyes sparkled and her smiled was infectious. "I love the sound of that!"

Colt and Aly saddled up on Duke and headed back to the house. He loved the smell of cucumber as he kissed the skin of her neck. It just felt right having her ride with him and he wanted to do it every day. Now, he just had to get her to agree.

Chapter 22

The rest of the week went by fast for Aly. She spent most of her time working on her baked goods for the festival. Jade had been wonderful in helping her get things organized in the bakery's kitchen. When she wasn't baking, she was waiting tables in the diner. It was exhausting but she knew it would be worth it.

Her feelings for Colt were only getting stronger. After surprising him out at the ranch Wednesday, Colt made sure they were able to Facetime every night. She couldn't wait to have another date. She loved the feel of his arms around her, his breath on her neck, and the taste of his kiss. She couldn't resist him and that scared her. It was eerily similar to how she felt about Greg at the beginning. Falling too fast could prove to be dangerous, especially with Colt's habit of no long-term commitment. Not to mention the apparent disapproval of his mother playing against them too.

"The booth looks ready," Jade said coming to stand next to her. They had a single table booth with all the sweets Aly wanted to showcase. There were several three tier serving trays and rectangle platters, allowing an easy view of everything. A few vases filled with sunflowers and baby's breath sat on the edges. Gram had the best sunflowers around and they were just perfect for the display. Everything was simple and fresh. That's what Aly wanted for her bakery and the booth would give people that feel.

She hoped.

"Thank you so much, Jade. I couldn't have done this without you." Aly gave Jade a hug. "You're the best friend I've ever had."

"You have a great gift and I want to do everything in my power to help you." Jade paused for a moment and then pulled Aly's phone out of her coat pocket. Her voice was flat as she said, "You left this in the van."

Aly took it and instantly saw why Jade's tone changed. Greg had called her once and left a voicemail. It had been six weeks since she'd left Dallas. He'd been persistent for the past three weeks to speak to her.

"Can I ask you something?" Jade asked.

Aly locked her phone and slid it into her back pocket. "Yes."

"Have you talked to him at all?"

"No." She didn't want to talk to Greg. He didn't deserve her time.

"I think you may want to say something to him. He hasn't stopped and it doesn't appear he's going to." Jade looked concerned. "It's getting creepy."

"He's not dangerous, Jade. I swear." He probably just wanted to continue their affair. She felt sick at the truth of what their relationship had been. "His messages are always about how desperate he is to talk to me but he doesn't mention anything else. No word about his wife or his kids. He keeps saying he can't live without me and about how much he still loves me."

Jade didn't look convinced. "Do you believe him?"

"I don't want to even think about what he feels for me. I'm not that girl anymore and I want nothing more than to just move on with my life," Aly said. Jade raised an eye brow. "I'm serious, Jade. At one time, I believed that I could love him, and maybe I did. But none of that matters because he's married."

Jade was silent for a few moments, while Aly straightened the already perfect serving plates. "All I'm saying is you need to do something to get it through his head."

After the festival, she would respond to him and set him straight.

People began filling the park and Aly felt the butterflies in her stomach. She hoped that her baking was good enough to really make it. No matter how many times Jade or Colt told her it was amazing, there was still a whisper of doubt. She wanted to believe she could make something of herself as a baker.

"Hello, Jade. This is a lovely booth."

Aly turned and saw the lady from the Teel party. She was related to Colt; Aly just wasn't sure how. What was her name again?

"Maria, I'm so glad you stopped by. This is actually my roommate Aly Meyers' booth. She'll be opening a bakery on the north side of the diner." Jade stepped back to let Aly shake Maria's hand.

"Oh, yes! Aly, we met last weekend. I'm pleased to see you're baking more. If the bread pudding from the party was any indication, I'm sure you will do very well." Maria scanned the table.

"You're very kind." Aly was glad someone in the Teel family liked her, or her food at least. "I hope to open up in a month."

"Maria is married to Scott Teel," Jade interjected. "Colt's youngest brother."

Aly remembered Scott. "Oh! I went to high school with Scott." He had always been nice to her.

"I may have to pull you aside and get some dirt on him then." Maria winked at her. "So you're a friend of Colt's?"

"Well, I'm actually—"

"Maria, there you are." Linda Teel interrupted before Aly could answer. Aly's neck tensed slightly as Mrs. Teel stopped in front of her. "What fine desserts."

Jade explained what everything was. "Aly is the best baker I know! You had some of her desserts at the party last weekend."

"How lovely," Mrs. Teel sounded indifferent. She and Maria began talking about all the dishes on the table when Aly's phone rang again. When she saw Greg's name, she quickly silenced it.

"Greg?" Jade asked slightly hushed. When Aly shot a sideways look at her Jade continued. "Do you need a minute?" Jade asked.

"No. He can wait. I'll call him later and straighten everything out," Aly answered, but Jade didn't look convinced. "I promise I will. There will be no question about our relationship status." If she ever wanted a chance at something new, she had to talk to Greg. She just prayed that she could make a clean break without everyone finding out about the details.

"Is everything alright, dear?"

Aly looked up and saw that Maria had moved to the next table but Mrs. Teel was still watching her. Was she listening? Aly straightened her shoulders and nodded. "Yes, ma'am. Can I help you with anything?"

Mrs. Teel appraised Aly again. There was judgement and speculation swirling in her eyes. Aly held her smile in place in hopes of at least maintaining her professionalism. Mrs. Teel's expression remained cold. "No. Excuse me."

Mrs. Teel strode away, and followed Maria to the next booth.

"What did you do to her?" Jade asked.

Aly shrugged. "I have no clue."

"Does she know about you and Colt?" Jade asked.

Colt had been very clear with her that he wanted to be with her. But had he done so with his family? What if he hadn't? Why?

No.

She didn't want to let worry dictate her thoughts so she pushed the doubt away. That's not who she wanted to be anymore. She swallowed and took a deep breath. "I'm not sure."

More people began coming by their booth, Aly and Jade spent the next few hours advertising the new logo and information about the bakery. Overall, Aly was getting great feedback and it helped boost her confidence.

A cute little red headed boy was waddling behind his parents with a candy apple. She watched as a father and son were carving a pumpkin at a table across from theirs. People were sitting across the open lawn listening to a small band. A handsome couple walked hand in hand while laughing and eating popcorn. A pang of longing settled in Aly's stomach. It would be amazing to have all those things in her life. The person who came to mind was Colt. *Woah!* She shook her head to clear the thought. They had only known each other for a little over a month. Thinking serious like that wasn't smart, but there was no denying the smile that slipped across her lips at the idea.

Gram approached the booth and gave Aly a big hug. "I'm so proud of you, Aly."

"Thank you, Gram. I really have you to thank!"

Gram scoffed. "Oh, I may have helped peek your interest but you've taken off and gone farther than I ever will."

"Aly!" Wyatt yelled and gave her a big hug. Melissa and Blake walked up behind him. "You're the best baker ever!"

That little boy sure had a way of melting Aly's heart. "Thank you, Wyatt."

"How's everything going?" Blake asked.

"Well, we've only got an hour left and it looks like we'll sell out before then." Jade placed another set of tarts on the table.

"How does your class look this year?" Aly asked Melissa.

"It's only been three days, but I'm optimistic."

Blake squeezed Melissa to his side. "She's modest. Everyone speaks her praise at how good she is with her students." He dipped down to kiss Melissa's nose.

Aly loved how Blake adored Melissa. What girl wouldn't want a guy like that? She was a bit jealous of her cousin but happy for her all the same.

"Mom, can we go carve a pumpkin?!" Wyatt asked tugging Melissa's arm.

"Well, it looks like we're off. Let's do dinner together this week girls." Melissa said before being pulled by Wyatt with Blake in tow.

Gram came up next to Aly and whispered, "Are you alright?"

Crap. Gram was always good at reading people. "For the most part I am."

Gram asked patting Aly's cheek. "I love you so much, Aly. You'll let me know if you need to talk, won't you?"

"I will. Maybe you can come by the bakery and see what we've been doing." Aly was excited to share that with Gram.

"I'd love to. How about you come for Sunday lunch after church tomorrow? You've been living here for over a month and I've hardly seen you. You can bring that young man I hear you've been spending an awful lot of time with." Gram gave her a knowing smile before glancing at Colt. Aly felt a flush fill her cheeks. "I may be eighty-one but I'm not blind."

Aly looked over at Colt, who had just arrived and was visiting with his mentor Frank White. "I'll ask him."

"Wonderful. Tell him I insist." Gram headed off toward the pumpkin carving. Since being home she'd only spent a little time with family and she needed to change that. Sure, working and starting the bakery were important but nothing replaced family.

Her mind quickly went to Colt and she glanced at him nodding to Frank. Since the Teels had family dinners on Sunday night, Colt might be free for lunch.

Aly saw Mrs. Teel and Maria visiting with another ranching family Aly knew from the diner. When Mrs. Teel saw Colt and motioned for him to join them. She rubbed his arm and beamed at him. Colt shook hands with the man and woman his mother nodded to. The coldness that Aly had seen in Mrs. Teel's eyes was replaced with a warm fondness. They looked like a very happy family. She caught Colt's eye and he excused himself. His mother eyed him as he approached Aly.

"It looks like you're baking is a hit," he said looking over the table.

"It sure is," Jade said. "I think the bakery is going to be a huge success."

"I believe so too."

Aly wanted him to come around the booth and kiss her but he didn't. In fact, he didn't even touch her. Though he looked happy to see her, to the rest of the world they were just friends. Why was he acting so different from when they were in private? He was known for public displays of affection. In fact, that was one of her first impressions of him at the Wrangler. She wished he would just pull her into a kiss and let everyone know about their relationship. Was he hiding her?

Colt shook hands with a man who approached him in front of her booth. His mother appeared and joined the conversation. She didn't look Aly's way once. Aly stepped away for a moment to pull another tub of desserts out from behind the table. She sent a silent prayer up that Colt's mom would warm up to her. If they were to have a future, they had to get past his mother's objection.

Chapter 23

Colt could tell that Aly was abnormally quiet on the drive over to her Gram's house the next day. He wasn't the best with women and didn't know much of anything about being in a relationship. He placed his hand over hers and gave it a squeeze. "Did you enjoy church this morning?"

She glanced at him. "Yeah. Worship was wonderful. I needed it."

"Why is that?" he asked.

"I've been tired. It's been a lot of work getting things ready for the bakery to open. Then I need to work at the diner more and more for the extra money, but it'll be worth it." She fiddled with her necklace. "I've only come to Gram's a few times since moving back. I've got to do better at seeing her. Everything just takes up my time."

Colt squeezed her hand again. "You're amazing."

"I'm not so sure about that, but it does feel good to be working toward something."

Colt could hear the pride in her voice and it made him happy for her. She knew what she wanted to do and was going after it. He couldn't help but think about the looming decision he had to make about the ranch. His parents were ready for him to take it over any day.

He broke the silence. "I'm only scheduled for two more rodeos in September. This coming weekend I'm free but the next two I'll be gone."

"Are you ready to be done with it all?" she asked.

That was a good question. He loved the high he got from bull riding but he had missed Aly terribly the last time. His buddies on the road gave him a lot of flak for texting, calling, and Facetiming with her. In fact, he only went out for a drink a few times and left once he finished. Man, how he'd changed in the process of a few months.

"Maybe so. It's hard to wrap my mind around it. You know?" He glanced at her. She nodded in understanding. "I want to take over the ranch but to quit the one passion I've had in my life that was all mine. That's hard. But my dad is getting older and he'd like to retire. I want to give him that opportunity."

"The commitment you have to your family is commendable. Leaving the circuit doesn't mean you're totally removed from it. You can train riders, like you mentioned." She squeezed his hand. "I think you'd be great at that."

Everything she was saying sounded like a dream, but he wasn't sure how practical it was. The business would be his priority, not leaving much time for a hobby. "We'll see."

The drive was about ten minutes, a benefit of a small town. The trees that lined Main Street were a deep green color. Soon they would begin to streak with yellow and orange as fall approached. It made work easier and more pleasant to finally get a break from the relentless Texas heat, but he still had a month to go. He turned down the dead-end road that ended at Gram's sunflower field and pulled over in front of the mailbox. They both got out and when he came around to take her hand, he kissed her cheek. "Thank you for inviting me. I'm looking forward to spending time with your family."

"I'm glad you were able to come."

Instead of going through the front door, they made their way around the side of the house to the back yard. Aly's heels clicked on the pavers. "How in the world do you wear those things all the time?" he asked.

Aly glanced down at her feet and smiled. "Years in the city. Plus, heels always make a girl's butt look good." She winked and pulled him along the path. Colt wasn't going to disagree.

There was a long rectangle table with a cream table cloth stretched across it. Three blue vases filled with sunflowers lined the center, flanked by a blue rectangle place setting. It wasn't near as fancy as his mom's family dinners but it felt comfortable and welcoming. Blake was playing catch with his step-son, Wyatt out in the yard. Gram came out the back door followed by Melissa and a woman he'd never seen before. They were carrying all the dishes for lunch. All three women looked similar and it was clear that they were family.

Gram's face lit up. "Oh, Aly! You made it just in time. We're ready to eat."

"Everyone this is Colt Teel," Aly said. He'd hoped she might say he was her boyfriend but she didn't. "Colt, you know Gram, Melissa, Blake, and Wyatt." She said pointing to each of them. He returned their wave. "This is my aunt Julie."

He shook her hand and said, "It's a pleasure, ma'am."

"Colt, we're honored you could make it," Julie said.

They all took their seats and began passing the dishes around the table. It was much more relaxed and casual than his mother's dinner.

When Melissa started talking about an upcoming women's night at church, Aly leaned into Colt and said, "I'm glad you're here."

"Me too. Your family's great."

She smiled and then began eating again.

Gram set the basket of rolls back in the center of the table. "Colt, I didn't see your parents at church this morning. I hope they're doing alright."

He took a drink of sweet tea and then cleared his throat. "They sat toward the back this morning. We were all running late with the morning chores."

"I can understand that. You're more than welcome to sit with us anytime. Aly can save a seat for you." Gram tilted her head to Aly, who nodded.

Colt hadn't thought much about where he sat during church. It was very common for him to come in after the services had already started. The ranch hands only came in after lunch on Sundays, so he got some extra paperwork done before church. It was always easier to just slide in next to his parents. "Thank you. I'll remember that."

"How are the things on the ranch?" Gram asked.

"I think my parents are ready to retire, but things are good."

"Retirement. That's exciting," Julie interjected. "Do they have anything planed for when they have the time?"

Colt felt Aly shift next to him slightly. "I'm not really sure. They love the ranch but there has been some talk about traveling or moving into town. I don't know if that will happen though."

Aly looked up surprised. He realized he hadn't mentioned that to her.

"What will happen with the ranch?" Gram asked.

Colt swallowed knowing that they were all interested in the future, especially since Aly was in his life now. "I'm going to be taking it over. Not sure when just yet but I think it will be fairly soon. If they're gone then I'll move into the house."

"That's wonderful, Colt," Gram said genuinely happy for him. "Good for you."

Aly smiled at him but didn't say anything. He knew they hadn't really talked much about their future plans. Now that he was sitting with this family next to the girl he couldn't imagine not having in his life, he was starting to feel something he hadn't in a long time. Hope. Hope that he could love someone again despite Emily's death. Hope that he was worthy of someone like Aly.

Blake leaned over to kiss Melissa before going into the house to refill the water pitcher. A pang of jealousy hit Colt in his core, like when he hits the ground after a bull ride, jarring and smashing. In that moment, he wanted something like that more than anything else. He looked at Aly and she turned to meet his eyes. He knew he didn't deserve her but he wanted to be with her. Only her.

They finished their lunch and began cleaning off the table. Colt knew he couldn't stay for very long. There were chores he needed to tend to before the family dinner that night. Aly and Colt said their goodbyes and headed back to her apartment.

"I think they like you," Aly said, breaking the silence in the truck.

"I'm glad. I like them too." Colt squeezed her hand.

The best part about the Meyers family was that everyone genuinely cared and accepted each other whole heartedly. He loved his family and wanted to carry on their legacy, but there was a lot of pressure to do everything they wanted *when* they wanted it. Take over the ranch, now. Quit the rodeo, now. Get married and have children, yesterday. His mother trusted him to take over everything they'd built but didn't trust him with his personal life.

He parked next to her car and got out to open her door. Before she could slip out of her seat, he stepped in to kiss her. She accepted it and melted into him. When they finished, he pressed his forehead to hers. "You have no idea what you do to me," he said. She ran her fingers through his hair, making his eyes roll back. "No idea."

"Hmm. I think we're in the same boat, cowboy." She continued running her fingers through his hair, massaging his scalp.

He opened his eyes and got lost in hers. "You're making me feel things again. You're working your way into this lonely heart." He took a deep breath and spoke from his heart. "I want to give it to you and I don't want it back. It's yours."

Tears formed in her eyes and her voice dropped to almost a whisper. "Be careful saying things like that, cowboy. You're going to make me fall in love with you."

Colt leaned in for another kiss before helping her out of his truck. He was falling for Aly Meyers. By the look in her eyes he knew she was falling too. There were only two things that could ruin it, his mother and Emily.

Chapter 24

Jade sat at a corner booth with Andrew, her boyfriend of three years. There was just something odd about their relationship. He traveled a lot for business and Jade worked continually at the diner. It seemed like their relationship didn't get the chance to grow the way it should after so long. They talked pleasantly and it appeared that there was no tension. Aly just hoped that Jade didn't settle for something that was just comfortable and convenient. A relationship shouldn't feel like a routine. It should grow and stretch with time, not fall into a stalemate between two people who used to be crazy about each other.

Colt never made her feel that way.

Having him over yesterday afternoon with her family was so great. Then the sweet things he said to her at her apartment made her realize she was already falling for him. She knew from previous talks that he wanted to stay on the ranch and she understood that. The news about his parents considering leaving the ranch had given her hope for their future a boost. If they were to get married, space between his parents and them would make things easier. She'd be lying if she said the thought of a future with Colt hadn't crossed her mind. She liked the look of it, even though it was nothing like she thought she'd want. She was starting to enjoy the things he loved because she cared about him. If they were going to make it work, she would have to live on the ranch.

Crystal came up next to Aly and said, "You've got Frank White at table four."

Aly turned hoping to see her favorite set of cowboys but it was just Frank. *Hmm.* Colt hadn't text her that morning but she hadn't worried about it because she'd see him with Frank for lunch. She walked over and placed his drink down in front of him. "It's good to see you Frank. Will you be having your usual?"

Frank tilted his cowboy hat back and smiled warmly. "Yes, ma'am."

She hesitated not knowing if she should ask Frank about Colt or not. She decided not to. "I'll put that in for you."

"Oh, Aly," Frank said before she left. "Colt had a business meeting in Dallas today. I wasn't sure if he told you or not."

"No he didn't. I hope whatever it is goes well for him."

"I hope so, too." Frank took a drink and Aly headed to the kitchen. She turned in his order and leaned against the wall. She pulled her cell phone out and checked to see if there was a text or call. Nothing. However, there was a missed call from Greg. The past few days Greg hadn't tried to contact her, and she'd hoped he finally got the message. She had planned on calling him this weekend but when he didn't contact her, she decided not to.

Sliding the phone back in her pocket, she figured Colt must've been busy this morning and just forgot. Though it didn't set well, she didn't want to get mad or overly upset.

The rest of the day was busy, really busy. She felt like the moment she cleaned a table another customer filled it. At seven o'clock, she clocked out and went over to the bakery. She checked her phone again, still nothing from Colt.

New equipment had been delivered and she couldn't wait to try it out! The walls had been painted a baby powder blue with white trim, and the same cream tiles that were in the diner carried over into the bakery. She ran her hand over the new glass display case, imagining all the delicious treats she'd have for customers. Even the signs with the menu and daily specials were ready to be hung.

One of the few things left to come in were the window decals. Otherwise everything else was coming together perfectly.

She began unpacking and organizing her dishes and baking supplies in the back cabinets. It was really happening. She was going to be a business owner. The dream of starting over was coming to fruition. Now, if only she could hold onto the hope that Colt just might be another dream come true too.

******

Colt stood outside the coffee shop in Dallas, the hustle and bustle of people everywhere made him slightly uneasy. He couldn't imagine living in the city and he was glad that Aly wasn't here either. Though it was clear she wasn't raised as country as him, he was starting to rub off on her and he loved it.

He barley listened to his father and brothers talking on the sidewalk, their voices muffled by the passing traffic. His mother had excused herself about an hour ago because she had a personal matter to attend to. He had no idea what that could be and so they were just wasting time until she was done. Like an idiot, he left early this morning with his parents and forgot his cell phone. He hadn't been able to tell Aly about the spur of the moment meeting with the Franklins. Of course, Olivia was there and his mother insisted that they sit next to each other. His father and Mr. Franklin were good friends and though they were both in the cattle business, they did things differently. It was a good partnership because they helped each other out with networking and promotion.

Colt spotted his mother coming out of an investigator's firm. What in the world was she doing in there? She approached and greeted his two brothers. Nothing was said regarding her personal matter, so Colt let it go. They all went to lunch and returned home soon after.

He sat through lunch only interjecting when things were directed to him. Then they made the forty-minute drive back to Shaw Creek.

When they arrived back at the ranch, Colt quickly excused himself and headed for his cabin. He needed to check a few things in the barn but first he had to call Aly. Before he could pick up his phone there was a knock at his door. He opened it and sighed as his mother stepped inside. "I need to talk to you for a minute."

"Alright." There was no point in trying to tell her he couldn't right now.

She looked over everything in the cabin, he was sure finding that it was too messy. Then her voice was cool when she asked, "How well do you know Aly Meyers?"

Her question threw him because he hadn't ever talked to his parents about Aly. "Where is this coming from?"

She walked over and placed her purse on the counter. Her shoulders and back were stiff. "I know you've been spending time with her."

"And?" He didn't care what his mother had to say about it.

"What do you know about her time before she moved back here?"

"Why are you worried about it?"

"I'm your mother. I can ask."

Aly's previous life wasn't his mother's business. "She worked at an insurance office and got a degree in business."

"Is that all?"

This was getting ridiculous. "I don't know what else you expect me to say."

"You need to be careful, son." She had the most serious look in her eyes and he wasn't sure what to make of it. "She has a past that could taint our image if you let her get too close."

Colt felt anger stir in his chest. "Don't we all have one? What do you think about my past, Mom? I'm sure it can't be worse than mine."

"I've done my best to look beyond the rather distasteful things you've done. You're my son. I worked extra hard to restore your reputation." She straightened her blouse. "The last thing we need is someone else's past coming in and tarnishing our reputation," she said flatly. "Plus, you're better off with someone like Olivia."

The pressure in his temples surged. He was tired of her trying to run his life. He couldn't stand that she thought she knew what was best for him.

"I'm never going to be with Olivia. You need to understand that once and for all." He did his best to keep his tone even. "You don't know what makes me happy. Therefore, it's not your decision."

He could see the anger flash in her eyes but she quickly turned to ice. Picking up her purse she headed front door. "You have a responsibility to this family and to our business. Gallivanting around with the likes of Aly Meyers isn't what we need. You've been warned." With that she left the cabin.

Colt released his fists, his fingers ached from the strain of it. His mother had no right to tell him who he could be with. What did she have against Aly, anyway? Colt dropped down onto the loveseat and stared up to the ceiling. He loved his mother but her constant need to control and meddle in his personal life was going to make him push her away. A rotten feeling settled in his gut. He didn't want to admit the next question that came to mind. What if is his mother had something on Aly?

Instead of calling her, he sent a text.

I left my phone at home this morning. I've got a lot of catch up to do after being gone today. Can I come see you tomorrow night?

She responded after about thirty seconds.

Ok. See you tomorrow!

Colt let his arm fall to his side. He didn't like what his mother had said about Aly but he'd be naïve if he didn't understand they still had a lot to discover about each other. If his mother did have something on Aly, he couldn't be too upset about her not sharing it. He was just as guilty at keeping secrets as she was.

Chapter 25

"So what do you think?" Aly asked excitedly as she lead Gram back out to the front of the bakery. She'd been anxious about showing Gram all she had planned.

"It's perfect, Aly. Just perfect."

"I'm so glad you like it." They took a seat at one of the round tables next to the window. "Jade thinks we're on track to open in just a few weeks. I've got signs made up and will place the 'Grand Opening' notice in the paper and online tomorrow."

"You'll do great. I've been telling all my bridge club ladies and everyone at church too. They're all looking forward to it."

"Thank you. I think people got a good sampling at the sunflower festival and word has been getting around. I can't wait!" It really was a dream come true.

"I wanted to ask you about Colt. How are you two doing?" Gram asked kindly.

Aly ducked her head slightly. "We're good. We agreed to take things slow and see where this all leads."

"You like him a lot, don't you?" Gram asked.

"I do." Aly paused before continuing. "Do you think we're good together?"

"I can tell he really likes you and he fits in well with our family. You seem to smile a lot more than when you first moved back."

After leaving Greg, Aly had been fighting an internal battle of regret, shame, and sadness. Throwing herself into work and now the bakery had definitely helped her. Spending time with Colt is what pushed her into feeling alive again. She laughed more and had someone to day dream about not sulk over.

"Colt has helped a lot with that. I just don't know about his mother. She's not my biggest fan and I worry that she'll never be okay with us together."

"Have you spent any time with his family?"

Colt had never asked her to join in a family function. "No."

"Perhaps he will invite you in a few weeks' time. Your relationship is still new."

"Am I crazy to feel this way after only knowing him for five weeks?"

"I think God created our hearts to love and be loved. Falling in love doesn't come with a guide book. It'll be different for every person, but it's never wrong."

"Even if it doesn't work out?" Aly asked.

"Yes, especially if it doesn't. You were meant to love and care for him at that time. Without that love and loss, you wouldn't be where you are now. How else do you change and grow without those experiences?"

Aly was surprised at how strongly she felt for Colt. He'd made it clear that he was falling for her too. Maybe the hurt she'd experienced hadn't been in vain. She felt stronger and was willing to risk her heart for love again.

Gram reached over and placed her hand over Aly's on the table. "You are beautiful, talented, ambitious, and caring. He's lucky to have you."

"Thanks, Gram." Aly loved that Gram never shied away from making sure her family knew how she felt about them.

"We don't always see the best in who we are because we feel like we're bragging. It's easier to complain than compliment ourselves. I know Colt sees those things in you. Don't worry about his mother. Worry steals the joy from our hearts." She pat Aly's hand. "Now I've got an ice cream date with my favorite great grandson."

Aly gave Gram a hug and opened the door for her. The words Gram said hung on her heart. *Worry steals the joy from our hearts.*

She didn't want to live like that. She waved goodbye as Gram walked to her car.

Aly saw an elderly couple walking across the street. He had her hand tucked into his elbow and they were smiling. How could she ever expect to have something like them when she worried about all the problems that could happen with Colt? Aly headed back to the kitchen and made a promise that she wouldn't let herself worry but to trust in how she was. She was falling for Colt. Fast. Perhaps, that's exactly what should happen.

******

Colt loved the feeling of Aly snuggled into his side as they sat on Jade's sofa watching a movie. It had been a horribly long Friday and he needed some alone time with her. She made him feel at home wherever they were. They could simply just be together and that was enough. When they were apart, something was missing. Yep. He sounded like a sap.

After Aly tried to break it off last week, Colt felt like they'd become more comfortable together. They didn't question things, at least not to each other. He hoped her concern about their differences had been replaced with confidence. That's who he wanted to be, the very best version of himself for her.

"What are you thinking about?" Aly asked and took another bite of popcorn.

Us. Turning down the volume to the TV, Colt answered, "I've been thinking about everything in my life, but mainly you."

"I've been thinking about you too," she said softly.

They sat quietly for a few moments before he spoke again. "I've been really happy and it has everything to do with you."

She looked up at him. "Yeah?"

Colt nodded. "I haven't been like this in years."

"When was the last time?" Aly asked.

They had been going back and forth to see who would open up first. As far as his past, they had only talked about the last ten years. He never went back farther than that. How would she even react to Emily? He wasn't sure they were ready for that. Was he?

Deflect. "That was a lifetime ago. When was yours?" He flipped the question around on her. Yep. He was a coward. There was nothing in the world he avoided more.

Something flashed across her face and he knew she was very aware of what he was doing. However, he was thankful she didn't call him on it. "The guy in Dallas I told you about, Greg." She shifted uncomfortably and created a little space between them. Colt wasn't sure why.

"How long were you together?"

Aly gnawed of the inside of her cheek. "About a year."

She was clearly not going to give up much information and it didn't surprise him because he did the same thing. It would make sense that they would share as time went one but neither were budging. He decided to change the subject. "I'm thinking about quitting the circuit this year."

"Really?" she asked.

"Yeah. My body's getting weaker in my *old* age," he teased.

Aly rolled her eyes. "Right. Like you can complain about how you look."

"You like the way I look?"

"You're decent." She shrugged her shoulders and looked back at the TV.

In a split-second, Colt slid an arm under her legs and tossed her back onto the sofa. He loved the sound of her laugh. He settled his hips on top of hers and ran his fingers into her hair. "Decent? I think you can come up with something better than that."

He felt her fingers fiddle with the bottom of his shirt. "Nah. Decent seems appropriate."

"Liar."

"What makes you say that?"

Colt leaned down and kissed her deeply. She sighed into his mouth and her fingers slid under his shirt. Everywhere she touched caught on fire. When he raised his head, Aly bit her bottom lip. "Because when you're nervous and don't want me to know you bite your bottom lip." She quickly released it and pressed her lips together in a pout. "So there's no need to try and hide who you really are, sweetheart."

"The same goes for you." She held his gaze.

Colt got her message. In time, he knew they'd get there. She rubbed her hands across his back and he loved the feel over his palms on his bare skin. Instead of slipping the shirt off, like he normally would, he shifted to lay beside her.

"I'm happy with you."

"And I with you." He kissed the tip of her nose. She wrapped her hands around him and pulled him to her. He poured himself into their kiss. He wanted her to feel everything he didn't know how to say. She deserved that. His phone rang but he didn't want to end their kiss. Aly sighed and Colt knew she felt the same way. So, he let it go to voicemail. After a few moments, his phone rang again. Odd. He pulled back and looked at Aly.

"You should get that," she said.

Colt reluctantly rolled away from her and headed over to the kitchen counter. Aly sat up on the sofa and ran her fingers through her hair, fixing the tangles he'd made. Colt picked up his phone and saw that it was Frank. He never called this late. "Frank? Is everything alright?"

"No, Colt. It's your dad. He was moving some square bales and collapsed in the barn." Frank's voice was laced with concern.

Colt loved his father and the sound of Frank's voice made him fear the worst. "Where did they take him?" Colt asked as he grabbed his boots and slipped them on. Aly jumped up and was at his side. Frank gave him the location and hung up.

"What happened?" Aly asked

"It's my dad. He collapsed and they took him to the hospital." He slid on the second boot and grabbed his keys from the counter.

"Let me come with you." Aly slid her shoes on.

Colt pulled her into a hug. "No. It's okay. Mom and my brothers will be there." He felt her shoulders sag but didn't have time to think about it. "I'll call you." He kissed the top of her head and hurried out to his truck.

The hospital. Colt hated hospitals. He avoided them at all costs. The last time he was in a hospital he'd lost... *NO!* He couldn't think about that. He had to focus on his dad.

There was no telling what his father had been doing out in the barn. Colt knew he should've moved those bales into the hay loft that afternoon because they couldn't get the trailer in with them out. But he had wanted to go see Aly. He felt terrible that his father was still working so much when he was ready to retire.

Guilt. Anger. Dread.

Colt slammed his hand against the steering wheel. He knew his unwillingness to make a decision was to blame for his dad continuing to do some of the manual labor. If he'd been there his father wouldn't have risked hurting himself. It didn't matter now, he had to get to the hospital before it was too late. *Please don't let me be too late.*

Chapter 26

Aly finished mopping up the floor in the diner and while Jade cleaned the kitchen after a busy Friday night. She hadn't heard much from Colt after his father was taken to the hospital a week ago. Colt had called once to give her an update from the hospital and then once after getting him home.

The doctors said Mr. Teel had a mild heart attack. It took a few days to get his blood pressure under control, but he was doing much better. She knew it was a scary time and their family had a lot to take care of. So, she'd given Colt space. She wanted to be the one there for him through all of it, not just for a phone call. She wanted to hold his hand and drive him when he was too upset, but he didn't want that. Every time she offered anything, he refused it. Her heart ached at the thought that he didn't need her at his most dire time of need.

The front door dinged, Aly was surprised but realized she must've forgot to lock up when they closed. When she turned around to see who had entered she froze, stock still. Linda Teel stood straight as a board just inside. Aly pushed the mop bucket out of the way and slowly approached. "Mrs. Teel. We've closed already but I can see if Jade has anything still available to take home. It wouldn't be any troub—"

"I need a word with you personally, Ms. Meyers." Her voice was even, not giving anything away.

"Okay. We can sit at one of the tables," Aly said motioning to the booth closest to Mrs. Teel.

"I won't be that long." She pulled out what looked like a file folder with papers inside from her purse. "I know you have an interest in my son, Colt. I know that you two have been spending an awful lot of time together."

Aly swallowed but refused to see that as a bad thing. "Yes, ma'am. Colt has become a close friend."

"Do you hide things from your close friends, Ms. Meyers?"

"I'm not sure what you mean, Mrs. Teel."

"There's no need to act innocent." She held up the folder. "I have proof here that you are not the wholesome good girl everyone believes you to be. In fact, it's quit the scandal." Mrs. Teel raised an eyebrow toward her. Aly felt her heart drop to her feet. *No.* Mrs. Teel began flipping through the papers as she continued. "An office affair, kept secret for at least a year. It was with your boss none the less, your *married* boss."

"Mrs. Teel, it's not—" Aly started.

"Greg Winters of Winters Insurance, LLC." Her eyes were ice cold. "It appears that not only have you been involved in an affair but you're also associated with a number of rather questionable claims well."

What? She never messed up anyone's claims. She took it as the highest priority to handle every claim correctly. "I have no idea what you're talking about."

Mrs. Teel closed the folder. "In fact, one of those claims had to do with a business deal my husband and I are making. The errors have the potential to cost our family thousands of dollars."

Aly racked her brain searching for anything that might enlighten her on these accusations. But there was nothing. "Honestly, I don't—"

Mrs. Teel narrowed her eyes. "And you have some gall to try and get deeper into our financials through my son? What did you think, he would marry you?"

Aly was numb. Everything was spiraling out of control. "I'm not sure what claims you're talking about. I never mishandled any paperwork. I would never use Colt like—"

"I know my son cares for you a great deal. I'm not ignorant to that, but he has been through more than you know. And for your age, I don't expect you to even begin to understand." Mrs. Teel's words were sharp and sliced at Aly's heart, but she had the sinking feeling that they were correct. "By the look on your face, I'm positive you don't even know what I'm talking about. He doesn't let just anyone into that part of his heart."

Another stab.

Mrs. Teel swallowed and clenched her jaw. To Aly's surprise, when Mrs. Teel looked back at her there was a sadness in her eyes. "He is lucky to have had a once in a lifetime love and then he lost it in a way that even I cannot relate. He's never loved anyone as much as he loved Emily, probably never will."

Emily? She couldn't remember ever hearing that name.

"I know he's living in a fantasy world with you but that's not his reality," Mrs. Teel continued. "It's time to take over his responsibilities. That means ridding himself of those self-absorbed and foolish attachments."

Aly had no words. It was as if everything inside her had was splintering to pieces.

"I'm the first to admit that Colt hasn't lived a respectable life in the past and I'm not ok with it. He's always been one to indulge in things that distract him from his feelings. But he has unlimited potential." Mrs. Teel's features hardened again. "I'll never let someone as manipulative as you take advantage of him. You've already hurt our family. The least I can do is rid my son of your schemes in the future." She looked down at the folder in her hands. "I can't say the same for your family once this gets out. You know how small towns are. This..." She stuffed the folder back into her bag. "...is not what Colt deserves." Her eyes were stone and Aly felt the first tear fall down her cheek.

"Mrs. Teel, what you're saying isn't true. Colt means the world to—"

"He misses you. Actually, he told me he loves you."

What? "Colt told—"

"No. Greg. In fact, against my better judgements, I've met him personally. What you and he have done is disgraceful." Mrs. Teel adjusted the purse strap on her shoulder. "I would suggest you get reacquainted because there's sure to be a legal battle for you."

"Please, you're not even letting me speak." Aly's voice a desperate plea but Mrs. Teel was already out the front door. Aly's knees started to shake. The truth was out and she hadn't told Colt herself. Her family and everyone would hear it as lies not truth.

"I thought I heard the door." Jade stopped when she looked at Aly from the kitchen door. She pulled out her headphones and asked, "What happened?"

Aly couldn't find any words as her chest seized. Jade caught her just as her knees collided with the cold tile. Everything she was working toward—her fresh start, her business, her relationship with Colt—would be tarnished by lies of infidelity and fraud. A sob wrenched her body as she finally let go of everything.

******

Colt went to the fridge in his parents' house while his dad pondered over the checker board in the breakfast nook. The doctors believe his dad had a mild heart attack. Luckily, they didn't have to operate but his blood pressure took longer to get back under control. George hadn't been as disciplined about taking his medicines, for which Linda and Colt had both scolded him for. With a new prescription and rest, the doctor believed he'd be back to normal in no time. He was released after five days in the hospital. It had really scared Colt. There was never any question that his dad could take care of everything but this accident solidified in Colt that it was time to quit. Colt couldn't postpone the decision anymore.

His mom come in through the front door, entered the kitchen, and stopped when she saw Colt. "How's your father?"

"He's doing good. We're in the middle of a checkers game."
S

She motioned him toward the front door. "Can we talk in here for a minute?"

"Sure." He followed her into the entry way.

"Colt, there's no doubt now. Your father can't work like that anymore." Her voice was firm. "It's time for you take over the ranch."

On a breath he said, "I know."

"I'm being serious."

Colt felt his irritation spark. "I am too. I've been debating when but—"

"Your father could've died." She cut him off, her voice like a knife. "You have a responsibility. You made a commitment to the ranch and your family, not to some frilly little city girl."

His jaw clenched. "Don't talk about her like that."

"She's not right for you or for our family. She doesn't know the first thing about being a rancher's wife. You cannot possibly expect her to understand what you need."

He couldn't believe that his mother couldn't respect him in this one moment. They'd just had a family emergency for crying out loud. No, instead she's once again telling him how to live his personal life. "She has been the best thing to happen to me and all you want is to ruin that. You don't know *anything* about her."

"Do you know the real reason she left Dallas."

No. He didn't know the whole story but that wasn't a problem for him. She didn't know everything about him yet. They still had time.

"I can tell by the look on your face that I'm right in that statement." She pulled out a folder from her purse, and her face softened. "Colt, I know I'm hard on you. You probably won't believe this but I do want the best for you. I want the best for our family. But... I've never had a good feeling about Aly."

"You've never given her a chance. You always see her as an outsider and you've been pushing Olivia on me. Not because I love her but because of a partnership with her family. How can you possibly think that's what's best for me? Aly makes me happy."

His mother was quiet for a moment, looking at the folder in her hands. "I want to give you this and let you see what I've found out about her."

"You had her looked into? You were looking to dig up dirt on her?!" He felt his anger throbbing in his temple. Everyone had a past, why would his mother want to throw Aly's in his face?

"With everything going on concerning your father's health and this new partnership, we can't afford the baggage she'll bring into our lives. I'm sorry but we can't." She laid the folder on the entry table and then headed down the hall towards his father.

Colt didn't want to take the folder. He wanted to say that it didn't matter but deep down it did. He grabbed it off the table and hurried out to his cabin. He slammed the door behind him and collapsed onto his loveseat, gripping the folder. Part of him wanted to burn everything his mother had put in there. He wanted to wait until Aly was ready to tell him. The papers shook in his hand as he debated opening it.

His mother was right about one thing. Time had run out. He couldn't sit on the fence about when to leave the circuit, but that didn't mean he had to end things with Aly too. Colt felt sick to his stomach as he lowered the papers to the coffee table. He didn't have time to wait for Aly. Closing his eyes, he prayed for understanding and an open mind. Then he flipped open the folder.

Chapter 27

Aly dialed Colt for the hundredth time in hopes that she might reach him before she made it to his cabin. No such luck. She knew Colt probably already knew about Greg. Now she wished she'd just told everyone when she returned to Shaw Creek. There's no way to know how everything would've fallen out, but it surly would've been better than this. She parked next to Colt's truck that was parked in front of his cabin. Good. He was there. She knocked several times before she realized that the lights were off. She tried his cell phone again but it went to voicemail. She spun around on the porch and saw Frank hooking up a trailer to the back of a white truck. She shot off the porch and called to him. "Frank!"

He looked up and smiled at her. "Hello, Ms. Aly."

"Frank. Can you tell me where Colt is? He's not in his cabin."

Frank's smile faltered slightly but he recovered. "I believe he had to get feed and he took Dory. He should be back in about a half hour, though. Do you want me to tell him you stopped by?"

Of course, she hadn't thought about Dory. "I'll wait for a little while if that's ok."

Frank nodded. "Yes. It's supposed to rain in just a bit. Heavy thunderstorms, they say. You can sit on the front porch if you'd like, in case it starts before he gets back."

Aly looked up to the sky and saw that it was significantly darker than it had been when she left the diner. The sun would set soon and it would make seeing to get home more difficult, but she had to wait for Colt. There was no telling if his mother had spoken to him about Greg and the papers she had already.

"Thanks. I'll do that." She turned to head back when her phone began to buzz. She anxiously answered it immediately without looking at the name. "Colt?"

After a few seconds, she heard a voice she wanted to forget. "Aly."

Aly froze twenty feet from the cabin. "Greg." His name was a strained whisper. Why hadn't she looked at the screen before answering?

"I'm hoping this is a good sign since you're finally answering me." His voice was dripping with desperation. "I need to see you."

Aly sent a silent prayer to the heavens for strength. Taking a deep breath, she steadied her voice. "I don't know why you keep calling me. I thought I made it perfectly clear in your office that day, I don't ever want to see you again."

"Somethings happened and we need to talk. It's important." Greg paused. "I'm outside your apartment right now. Where are you?"

She clenched her keys in her hand. "How do you know where I live?"

"I spoke with Linda Teel."

Everything inside her splintered. She glanced towards the main house. Mrs. Teel was trying to get rid of her and she'd plotted with Greg to ruin Aly if that's what it took.

Greg continued, "She actually sought me out. She's worried about you and wanted me to help. So, I'm here for you. We need to talk and clear some things up. Meet me at Gorgio's, that Italian place on Main Street."

"Why should I meet you? There is nothing to discuss. You're MARRIED, Greg!" Aly scoffed. "How could you possibly think that I'd want anything to do with you?"

Greg was quiet for a few beats. "Please. It has to do with the insurance company. There could be legal problems and it will involve you."

Seeing him was the very last thing she wanted to do. However, she remembered the comments Mrs. Teel had said about mishandling claims. If there were legal problems that could involve her she needed to know what they were. "Fine."

Aly climbed into her car and hurried down the Teel's driveway. Everything in her life had finally been coming together and she was happy. Happier than she'd ever been. *Please give me strength and confidence to deal with Greg.*

Aly felt her heart clench. She didn't get the chance to talk to Colt and had no idea if his mother had spoken with him or not. Though she didn't mean to do anything wrong with Greg, she knew she was going to have to take part of the fall. In fact, she should've quit once it all started. Now she was going to be ruined because of her choices. All she wanted was the chance to start over and she thought she was getting that. She had believed that she deserved happiness and a love like Blake and Melissa had found. In the depths of her heart she knew she wanted that with Colt. Now because of her past and Linda Teel's desire to get her out of Colt's life, she was afraid it would all be lost.

Fifteen minutes later, she parked in front of the restaurant. She spotted Greg's fancy BMW a row over. The sun was starting to fall from the sky and it streaked the blue with a deep blood orange. Aly could see it through the breaks in looming storm clouds.

Greg was seated in the back corner next to the window and he rose when she entered. He tried to pull her into a hug but Aly shoved him away. He looked upset for a moment before flashing her that devilishly sexy smile that had charmed her in the past. Now it simply made her stomach turn.

"What's this about?" she asked.

"I've missed you more than I can say." He reached for her hand and she pulled it away. "You look as beautiful as ever, even in that waitress outfit."

Aly felt anger sizzle just behind her eyes. "I'm not the same woman I was two months ago. In fact, I like who I am now more than I ever have before. I don't really have any time to give you, so tell me what you want."

Greg hesitated at the harshness in her tone. Then his features softened and he actually looked sympathetic. "I'm sorry about how you found out about my wife, well, soon-to-be ex-wife."

"To bad," Aly said flatly.

"After you left, Angie returned home. I didn't lie to you about what I said. I do love you and want to be with you. We're getting a divorce."

"I'm sorry to hear that." Aly knew her voice dripped with venom. "I don't need to hear your sordid love story. It doesn't matter to me what happens in your marriage. What's happening with the company?"

Greg's face became serious. "When we started considering opening a third location, I made a bad business decision. We were struggling in the Dallas area."

Aly didn't know what he was talking about. "That can't be right. I know we were doing fine, the numbers we great."

"No. I wasn't giving you all the paperwork. I got in over my head and now the auditors believe I was hiding money. There was a partnership who were looking to get more insurance for the expansion they were planning and investing in. I made the decision to oversee it myself because of the amount of the policy. In doing so, I made a way to keep us a float but it was at the expense of that partnership."

Her gut flipped. Mrs. Teel was right. How could he hide this from her in the claim paperwork? "What did you do?" she asked harshly.

Greg ran his hand through his hair anxiously. "When they increased coverage, I doubled the actual rate and they believed me. Instead of signing them up for the better plan, I left them in the lower coverage option. Then I would make up the difference to their policy and move them into coverage they originally wanted, later. I didn't think they'd ever know but then they needed to file a claim and their policy didn't cover it."

She couldn't believe what he was saying. A panic festered in her chest. What did this mean for him? For her? "What did you do with the extra money?"

"I moved it into the reserve every month and then added it to our payments. When they needed the coverage, obviously their policy wouldn't cover it. I hadn't had time to build it back up and pay the difference. The policy holders had to pay for their loss."

Though she knew the answer to the next question she asked anyway. "What were the names on the account?"

"Franklin and Teel."

Aly shook her head in disbelief. "This can't be happening." It was all clear now. No wonder Mrs. Teel was livid. She associated Aly with the company who had stolen money from them. Pressure built up behind her eyes and her temple was pounding. "How could you?!"

"I know. I know. It was dumb and now I've got investigators breathing down my neck."

"Dumb?! No, Greg, it was psychotic! Why are you telling me this? I can't help you." Aly felt sick at the idea that he was forging paperwork. This could get ugly and she didn't want to be drug into it.

"It doesn't involve just me."

"If you changed papers or numbers that's on you. I simply filed what you gave me. I didn't do the balancing. It was all done before it reached me. I understand they may want to interview me and that's fine. However, don't you dare ask me to cover anything up for you. I did what my boss gave me. I can't help it if you changed the numbers." She studied the bags under his eyes, the way his clothes didn't quite fit his now thin body. No wonder he was so desperate.

"I know, but you're associated with this."

"I don't see how."

"I foraged your signature one some of the paperwork."

"YOU WHAT?!" Aly's pulse shot out the top of her head and her vision blurred.

"I'm sorry, so sorry." Greg raked his fingers through his hair. "I just… I can't do this alone. I love you. I do. I need your help."

"I can't even see straight right now! I could get fined or worse go to jail because you decided to scribble my name on some papers!" Her hands were shaking. She straightened her back and stood from the booth. "You're a liar, a cheat, and now a thief. Don't you ever contact me again." She headed for the exit. When she made it to the sidewalk just outside the door, Greg grabbed her and spun her around.

"Aly, please. I love you," he cried. She pulled her arm away. "When I was contacted by what turned out to be a private investigator, you can imagine my paranoia. I thought it had to do with the insurance company but the rumor around the office was that it had to do with you personally. They had been asking questions about you not the company. I did my own digging and found out from Stephanie that you were in Shaw Creek."

Aly felt vile rise in her throat. Stephanie was the one person who had kept her in the loop right after she left. "I don't know what to believe. It's so ridiculous."

"I made a deal with Linda Teel."

"You what?" Aly snapped. "Why would she want to make a deal with someone who stole from her?!"

"When she found out you were connected to me, she wanted nothing more than to get rid of you. Something about you being friends with her son." He took a step toward her and she retreated. "She wanted you gone and I wanted you back. So, I gave them all of the letters and emails we shared as a way to help her."

"Why on earth would you want to help her?!"

"Because the Teels and Franklins are going to hang me in court. I felt like if I gave them something they wanted—"

"She'd what?" Aly interrupted. "Go easy on you? Are you INSANE?! You stole money from them and cost them who knows how much in damages not covered by their policy! Nothing you're saying makes sense! Are you even listening to what's coming out of your mouth?!" She pressed her fingers to her forehead in an attempt to ease the pressure. Some people stared at them as they entered the restaurant.

Greg pulled her away from the entrance. "I know it sounds crazy but we need each other to get through this."

The words falling from his lips made her nauseous. He was so desperate to be with Aly that he tried to bargain with the very person he had wronged in order to maybe get on their good side?

"We're nothing, Greg. Your mistakes are all your own." She started to walk away but he spun her around and into a kiss. A flash of headlights passing them blinding her eyes for a moment. Her hands pressed into his chest and she shoved him with all her might. "Don't ever touch me again or you'll be hearing from my lawyer."

Greg stumbled back and called to her again, but she was gone. She dove into her car and locked the door. Her hands were shaking as she gripped the steering wheel and raindrops began to hit the windshield. Aly knew she had to get to Colt. Knowing that Mrs. Teel had sought to use Greg's information to hurt Aly tore at her heart. She had dug into Aly's past in order to get her out of Colt's future. Aly checked her phone one last time but there was still nothing from Colt. No matter how late it was going to be, she had to see him and tell him the truth. She loved him. She just hoped it wasn't too late.

Chapter 28

Colt sat down on the front porch of his cabin and tossed the folder on the small table between the two rickety old chairs. The thunder clouds dropped low over the ranch, like every hope he thought he finally had. There were so many things wrestling for a place in his mind. The papers in the file had validated things Aly had said about her ex. He was definitely someone she shouldn't have been in a relationship with: her *married* boss. Based on some of the notes Aly had given Greg, it was clear she had cared about the guy. In the conversations they had it was also clear that she was hurt by the situation. Had she known he was married? Was that why she was so hesitant to tell him? Guilt fell on his shoulders because he hadn't been as open with her either. He pinched the bridge of his nose, willing the increasing headache to leave.

How did his mother get all those personal notes and emails between Greg and Aly? He couldn't believe the lengths she'd gone to out Aly's secrets all because she didn't approve of their relationship. His phone buzzed in his pocket but he didn't care to look at it. Aly had tried to call him five times before he silenced his phone earlier. He needed to clear his head.

If she hadn't known Greg was married, he wasn't bothered by their affair. It wasn't her fault. His mother had a written letter from Greg that said he still loved Aly and had always wanted to be with her. Things with his wife had been strained for a while. *Typical story.* Along with the letter were notes from Aly to Greg. She said things in them that made Colt believe Aly loved Greg back. Things he'd hoped she might say to him someday. When he came across the documents about the money his family and the Franklins had lost he was shocked to see Aly's name on some of the paperwork. He had no idea that Aly had worked for Winters Insurance. The lost money and claim rejection had cost the ranch thousands in damages. It appeared that the two of them were the only employees who handled the account. Had she known about the fraud? If she had, did she know who he was all along?

The uneasy feeling that settled in his stomach reminded him why he didn't do relationships. It left a bitter taste in his mouth towards both of them. He knew there were things that tied her to Greg: romantic history and the obvious legal issue. He dreaded having this conversation with her.

He kicked his heel against the porch post in front of his chair. He didn't know what to think or feel. What if the legal battle they were about to wage found her guilty in some form? What if Greg wanting her back is what she secretly wants? Either way it would break him to lose her, regardless of her motives. He sent up a prayer to the heavens, "What do I do now?"

Suddenly lights flashed down the drive, creating a wave through the rain. His heart lodged in his throat when he realized it was Aly. She jumped out of the car and ran up to the cabin but stopped just at the bottom step when she saw him sitting there.

"Colt," she said not moving out of the rain. Her hair and clothes soaked, while her eyes were puffy and red. She looked drained and spent. The stress he had just experienced seemed to wash away just seeing her. They stared at each other for a long time before Colt realized he couldn't just let her stand in the rain.

"Come up out of the rain."

She carefully walked up the steps and stood a fair distance from him. He stood to hand her the blanket on the back of the chair and she thanked him.

Colt lifted his baseball cap and ran his fingers through is hair and down his face. He didn't know what to tell her or what she'd tell him. So, he remained silent and leaned against one of the posts on the porch. After drying off she placed the blanket on the second chair and turned to face him. He could see the tears swirling around in her eyes. "I-I've tried to call you a hundred times. I even came by but Frank told me you were gone."

Colt couldn't trust the tone he would have, so he kept silent. He wanted to go back a week, when they were teasing and laughing on the sofa in her apartment. They were so happy and carefree. Now all he felt was a desperate longing and sadness. He was at a loss at how to put those things into words. He sighed and looked down at the folder on the table behind him. Aly's eyes followed his and when he turned around they were wide with fear. She swallowed and wrapped her arms around herself, as if to keep herself from falling apart.

"I guess your mom gave you that." Aly bit the inside of her cheek, and Colt nodded. "She came to see me too."

Colt wasn't surprised that his mother had sought Aly out. He imagined the exchange wasn't pleasant.

Aly's shoulders sagged. "She told me that she knew about my relationship with Greg."

"Affair." Colt corrected and then hated himself at the devastation that reflected in Aly's eyes at the word. When she finally looked up at him again he spoke. "I don't know what to think about all of this."

"I didn't know he was married," she said quickly and locked eyes with him. "I resisted his growing advances for over a year before I finally had dinner with him. He didn't have anything personal in his office and never wore a wedding band." A tear slipped down her cheek. "He had a whole family—a wife and kids—and..." Her voice hitched. "I never knew."

That answered one of his questions and it was the answer he hoped for.

"I thought he was going to eventually ask me to marry him and move to Austin, where the headquarters are located. That's why I stayed there for so long." More tears fell and Colt hated to see her cry but didn't dare move. "I didn't find out about his wife until she showed up at his office to surprise him. That's the day I asked Jade if I could move in."

Colt turned to look out at the rain and sighed. "Aly, I believe you. You're not that kind of person, and we've all done things we're not proud of. My past isn't perfect either."

"What is it then?" she asked.

"I know about the fraud that had to do with my parents and the Franklins losing money."

She straightened her shoulders. "Greg confessed to me, just tonight, that he forged my name in a desperate attempt to cover his tracks. He needed the money to help save the Dallas office and gave me false paperwork that showed everything balanced. I had no idea he was capable of something like that."

Colt watched her for a few seconds and her eyes never wavered. He believed her. That was the answer to the second question. He rubbed the back of his neck, in an attempt to relax a little.

"What's the real problem, Colt?" Aly asked.

He watched the rain pool in the yard for a moment. "I read the notes you wrote to him."

"What notes?" she asked.

"The notes and emails between you and him. Greg gave them over to my mom. He also wrote about how much he loved you, how he still does." Colt glanced over at her and she hung her head. So, it must be true. She still loved Greg. Tears drenched her cheeks and her body shivered in the cool wind. He took a step toward her but she took one back, gutting him like a fish.

"Why did you read those?" she asked but didn't look at him.

"I debated reading them but I knew you were struggling to tell me things. I needed to know." He wanted to touch her so bad. "I just wanted to get it out of the way, then we could move forward."

"Those were personal." She wiped her eyes and looked up at him. "They were also from months and months ago. They don't even matter now."

Colt slid his hands in his pockets. "They do matter."

"No, they don't." Irritation soaked her words. "Everything has changed. That was before I knew he was married. Married, Colt!"

"You said things in there that..." He paused, scared to spill his feelings. "They prove you did love him, and I'm afraid you still do."

"But that was before you, Colt. You can't be mad that I cared for someone before I met you." Her voice shook from emotion or the cold, he didn't know. "I don't love him and I can't even think about being with—"

"Aly, he's getting a divorce and wants to be with you. I can't help but think that, if given the chance, you'd want to be with him too." He knew what it was like to love someone and then loose it. Granted his was in death and not by betrayal but that didn't change the heartbreak.

"How can you say that?" Aly asked breathlessly. "You honestly think I want to be with a man like that?"

Colt knew what he read in her notes. She loved Greg and gave up everything to be with him. "I know he hurt you. I could see it in your eyes every time anything about Dallas came up. You even said you didn't know if your heart could fully recover. How could that not be love?"

"I didn't know what love was back then. I thought he was everything I could ever want. He made me believe I was that for him too, but it was all a lie, Colt! He lied to all of us!" Aly brushed some hair out of her face. "I told you I didn't think my heart *had* recovered, not that it never would."

Colt placed his hands on the porch rail and watched the rain splash over the grass. "I just wanted you to believe in me enough to know that I wouldn't hurt you. I wanted you to be honest and then give me the chance to help you overcome it."

"Honest?" she questioned.

"Yes. I want to be enough for you that I can take whatever broken pieces you have and help you put them back together." Gosh he sounded like a sap but it was true.

Aly looked out at the yard, now covered in puddles. "I wasn't going to tell anyone. My family doesn't even know about Greg. Jade only knows because he kept harassing me, and I needed to talk to someone about it. But I tried to let you in, even if it wasn't in full detail. I told you about getting hurt and what it did to me. I trusted you enough to let you see how insecure and damaged I was." She took a deep breath. "You haven't even told your mother that you're seeing me. She just thinks I'm this selfish little girl looking to score another rich guy."

Colt scoffed at his mother's words. "You're nothing like that."

Aly looked over at him. "I want you to be a part of my family but I've not once been included in yours. They don't see me as someone special to you. And you know what Colt?"

He stared into her tormented blue eyes. Eyes he'd grown to love more than anything but right now were thunderous like the storm surrounding them.

"It feels an awful lot like Greg."

That lit his temper. He wasn't anything like Greg. "I would never—"

"You tell me I'm special and that you want to give a relationship with me a chance. But truth is, you're hiding me from the people closest to you. You're no different from him. I guess I'm not the type of girl you love in public but just a dirty secret you keep in private."

"I do that to protect you! I don't want you to feel belittled by my mother's criticisms." He knew his mother and he didn't want Aly to be made to feel like she wasn't good enough, because she was more than enough for him.

"Right," she scoffed. "So, in order to protect me, you hide me?"

"That's not what I meant. My mother has never thought I know what I want or how to love. And if you look at the last thirteen years of my life, that's true. But you changed all that for me. I didn't want her to ruin what we had together... what we've shared."

"You haven't shared the stuff that really matters. I want to know all of you, the good and the bad. You're afraid that if I'm still in love with Greg what do I have to offer you. The only reason that makes any sense to you is because that's how you feel about yourself."

Her statement hit it's mark. His heart seized at the truth in her words. The defenses he always had in place boarded around his heart. "You don't know what you're talking about."

"Oh really? I think I'm closer to understanding your constant deflection regarding the only relationship you say you've had." She took a step closer to him. "Who doesn't believe in who?"

Colt turned away from her and clinched his fists at his side. That wasn't the case at all. He didn't want her to be hurt by his mother's judgements or harsh words. He would take them all on himself just to keep Aly out of the line of fire. She was right about one thing, though. He knew he was just as guilty of not being honest with her. His voice was lost and he didn't know how to say it all, to let her know how he was feeling.

"Who's Emily?"

One question. Two words.

A name that carried all his lost hopes and dreams. The only person he ever gave his whole heart to. In a split second, he was twenty years old. The rain pelted the truck hood. Emily laughing next to him. George Strait playing on the radio. The yellow lines blurred. The horse trailer jackknifed. Screeching metal. Emily's screams. Colt's fists opened and his knees felt weak. He pressed his eyes closed, dropped his head and pleaded with God to help him.

I don't want to remember.

Then he heard Aly moving behind him.

"Colt, I want you to help me be stronger, but you have to let me help you too." Then he felt her arms snake around his waist. "Please," she pleaded.

He wanted her arms to give him comfort and possibly even love, but instead they made him feel caught in a snare. She made him feel again. She made him want to love again and he was beginning to think it was possible. But in order to give Aly everything she deserved, he would have to open up the last door from his past. He'd sworn to never let anyone into that part of his heart again. It was broken, bitter, and guilty. He was a coward and he knew it, but he couldn't let Aly see that part of him.

He gently unwrapped her arms and turned around. Her arms dropped to her sides, her face streaked with tears and eyes void of light. They stared at each other in silence for who knows how long.

"You're not going to let me." The statement breathless on her lips. It wasn't a question but an acknowledgement that she saw him building his walls. She took a shaky breath. "After everything, you're just going to shut me out and push me away?"

It's what he always did when a woman tried to get close to him. That's why free and easy had worked for so long. No commitment meant no love. No love meant no chance of losing it. He'd only let himself love one person and he could never get that back. He didn't know how to move past it and give someone else what he'd already lost.

As he watched Aly take the steps back down toward her car, because of his pride, he just lost his second chance at love.

Chapter 29

Aly turned out of the Big T Ranch drive. Between the hideously heavy rain storm and her own tears, she couldn't make out the road. The wind whipped around her and she gripped the steering wheel so hard her knuckles were white. Five hours. That's all it had taken for her relationship with Colt to completely shatter. All the hope she had in finding something lasting and believing she deserved it was gone.

She'd known Colt was a risk. He didn't do long-term relationships but with each passing day, she saw him take steps to build just that. Sure, the doubt she had at the beginning had caused some trouble but she'd done her best to put that behind her. And now she finally opened up to him and did her best to give him a glimpse inside of her broken heart, but it wasn't enough.

CRASH!

Lightening lit the sky and Aly could see the pools of water starting to cover the road. She felt the pull of the tires every time she drove through deeper water. Slowing her car to a crawl, she grabbed her phone and dialed Jade.

"Hey, I've been wondering where you are." Jade's voice was laced with worry.

"I'm on my way home from Colt's. It's going to take me a while." Aly flinched with another strike of lightening.

"Are you good to drive? You sound upset."

Aly cleared her throat. "I'm okay. It's been a rough night. I'll tell you about it later."

"Are you sure you don't need me to come get you?" Jade asked anxiously.

Aly wrung her hand on the steering wheel. "No. I'm going slow."

"Well, get off the phone with me so you have both hands on the wheel. I'll have ice cream and hot tea ready for you. If you're not home in thirty minutes I'm coming after you."

"Thanks, Jade." Aly hung up and focused back on the road. There were no other cars out which meant she was the only crazy one driving, but she couldn't stay at Colt's. Another sob wrenched her body. The tires skidded, she quickly wiped her eyes and blinked several times trying to see the road. A gust of wind caught her off guard and she over corrected the swerve. Her back tires hydroplaned, throwing the front of her car sideways. All Aly could do was hold her breath and send up a prayer, as she waited for impact.

Noise ceased to exist and everything turned in slow motion. Her eyes couldn't focus as everything became a blur. A flash of light cut through the darkness, so bright she had no idea if her eyes were open or closed. Then the tearing of metal grated her ear dumbs as it hit something solid. Her head flung forward and she hit the steering wheel. She felt a flood of water fall over her with broken pieces of glass. Another screech and then everything went black.

She summoned everything inside but she couldn't open her eyes. *God help me!* She tried to take a full breath but her lungs rejected the air. She couldn't move. She could taste iron in her mouth and something ran down her forehead into her eyes. Finally, she was able to loosen her right arm and wipe her eyes. *OPEN!* Her brain screamed at her eyes. With everything in her, she felt them flutter open, only to be slammed shut by the pounding rain. She lifted her hand again to cover them and blinked rapidly to regain her focus again.

Blurry. Blink. Seeing double. Blink.

She wiped her eyes again and looked down to see red smeared across her fingers.

Blink.

Finally, she could make out the rain pelting the hood of her car as her head lights beamed across a barbed wire fence and trees.

She still couldn't move her left side and slowly turned her head to see why. As she did, it felt like knives sliced through her head and she flinched. Blinking again, willing her eyes to stay open, she continued to turn to the left. Suddenly, the panic returned as she reached across, with her right arm and ran her fingers over the splintered bark of a tree. She was trapped. Her skin was cold from the rain. Her head throbbed uncontrollably. Everything inside her screamed to get out. If she stayed right where she was she would die.

Death.

A single word, she'd known all her adult life, but in that moment, it wasn't just a word. For the first time, she looked her own mortality in the face.

There was no telling what shape she was really in. She shifted in her seat and felt the seat give a little. She wouldn't die like this. Her eyes frantically searched the car for an answer. There didn't seem to be any way out.

Jade.

Aly turned quickly trying to find her phone. Her head spun and more blood ran from her forehead. She took several deep breaths before lowering her eyes to look for her phone. In the darkness, she searched with her free hand and came up empty. She felt the black close in around her and she knew she was going to pass out.

God, please!

Her eyes rolled back momentarily in hopes that it would calm the fear. The only sounds around were the rain and dinging of her car. Jade would come for her. Another attempt at a deep breath and she took a small plunge into the darkness, but Aly forced her eyes open.

Maybe she could pull herself out through the windshield. She griped the side of her door and the center console and pushed with all her might. Her knee screamed and her arms gave out. She took several deep breaths to calm the pain. Her knee was on fire and her whole leg throbbed. Another way. She had to come up with something else.

Tilting her hips to the right she was relieved when they didn't hurt. This created a little space for her arm to separate from the crushed door. She lifted her opposite shoulder as high as she could, separating her body from the door, it allowed her to free her trapped arm. It was sore and her elbow was swollen but she could move her fingers. She turned toward the passenger side and had to stop momentarily to allow the spinning in her head to slow down. Angling her hips so all her weight was on her good leg, she used the seat shoulder and dash board for leverage. She pushed with all her might. Another white light flashed across her eyes and pain shot from her knee to her hip. Gritting her teeth, she kept pushing up until she felt her hip rest on the center consol.

Her pulse pumped through her temple and she felt nauseous again. She leaned her head against the headrest and took several deep breaths. Her body shook with a mixture of adrenaline and cold. The rain hadn't let up one bit. Exhaustion fell over her like a brick wall. She tried to sit up but fell back. The darkness closed in on her again and her vision began to fade. *NO!* She strained to focus on the trees outside her car.

The sound of sirens in the distance gave her hope that there was a chance at rescue. *They're coming!* The car shook and it sent her head spinning again.

"Hey!"

Aly jumped but didn't see anyone. She could've swore she just heard someone and blinked trying to gain her bearings.

"Hey! Hold on! Help is on its way." There was a man standing over the hood of the car.

She took a deep breath and said, "Help."

"They're on their way. Hold on just a little bit longer."

Aly felt something warm run down the side of her head. She couldn't die, not here. She had so much left to do and so much she still needed to say to her friends, to her family, and to Colt. The rain soaked her hair through the broken windshield. Her body slid back into the driver's seat and she arched over the center console. Her head tipped back and her chest heaved with ragged breaths. There was no strength left. She felt a wave of nausea and couldn't be certain of how much blood she'd lost.

"Hold on!" The voice seemed farther away.

Another flash of white and her eyes darkened.

She gasped for air.

No! God, please! Not yet! I didn't get to tell him!

She gasped again.

He may not but I need to tell him...

White. Sirens. Rain.

I need him to know...

She desperately tried to fill her lungs with air.

I have to tell him I love...

The words fell away as she slipped into the black.

Chapter 30

Early the next morning, Colt shoveled out the horse stalls. It was two hours earlier than he usually got started but he couldn't sleep. In fact, he couldn't remember the last time he slept so poorly. Watching Aly drive off into the rain was harder than he ever thought possible. The more he thought about it the more he hated himself. She had been through so much and his mother hadn't helped the situation. But that's not what bothered him the most. It had been the realization that she laid out the biggest fear he had: that his heart wasn't capable of loving again. He was afraid of what he'd find when he looked at his heart. He'd given his whole heart to Emily and deep down he didn't believe he had anything left to offer Aly. What woman deserved that? Nevertheless, it didn't help the gut wrenching longing he couldn't seem to escape now.

"Colt?" His father's voice sounded through the barn.

"Yeah, Dad. I'm in here." He leaned the rake and shovel on the outside of the stall. George's eyes looked tired and the worry lines in his forehead were more pronounced. "You don't need to be out here. Are you okay?"

"I'm fine. I wanted to check on you. I heard about what your mother found out regarding Ms. Meyers."

Colt removed his gloves and slid them in his back pocket. "I figured you knew all about it."

"Look, I don't always agree with your mother's methods, but she does it because she loves you."

"I suppose so," Colt said sharply. His dad raised an eyebrow. "Sorry."

"Being the oldest has put a lot of pressure on you, both personally and with the ranch." His dad rubbed the back of his neck. "I know we could've handled everything differently."

Colt couldn't argue with his dad but at the same time, the choices he made were his own responsibility. He grabbed a bucket and started filling it with feed. "I'm responsible for myself, Dad."

"True." His dad opened the next stall so Colt could enter. They were quiet while they filled the rest of the feed troughs. When they reached the last one, George leaned up against it. There was no name plate on the door and no feed to be placed inside. There was no Jake. "Colt."

He sat the bucket down and stood in front of his dad. "Yeah?"

George looked tentatively in the empty stall. "I want to ask you a question that I haven't asked you in a long time."

Colt shuffled his feet. "Okay."

His father turned and studied him for a moment. "Are you happy?"

That wasn't what he expected.

He wanted to be happy and probably believed himself to be over all, but in that very moment he thought no.

George pressed his lips together. "That's what I was afraid of." He pushed off the stall and took a step toward Colt. "We go to church every weekend and pray at every meal together, but I never thought to really look at you and see if this is what you really wanted. What does that say about me as your father?"

"Dad, I *am* happy with our life. I can't imagine myself living anywhere else and it was time for me to quit the circuit."

"I'm worried you're just content with all this and you've just accepted your place. I haven't even asked what you want to do. " His dad tapped the empty stall door. "I want you to do something that brings you joy."

Colt looked at the dirt on his boots and bit the inside of his cheek. There was something that seemed like a far off dream of the past, train roping horses. He'd even told Aly that. *Aly.* The guilt and regret plundered him all over again. He looked up and was surprised by the tears forming in his dad's eyes.

"I can't tell you how hard it is on a parent to watch their child grieve the love of their life. You were just an empty shell, void of life. I worried you'd only fill it with meaningless exploits and relationships. Perhaps, that's why we seem to be so hard on you. We wanted something more for you than that." George took a few steps toward Colt. "You've had a lot more life breathed into you the past few months. I haven't seen you like that since you were in high school. It brings me such joy."

Colt knew his dad was right.

George continued, "Your relationship with Ms. Meyers has gotten a tad complicated."

Colt scoffed. "You could say that."

"Well, nothing worth having comes easy."

Colt took his cap off and raked his fingers through his hair. "She says he forged her name but I don't know what's going to happen."

"Do you believe her?" his dad asked.

Colt nodded. "I don't believe she's that type of person. She was really upset when she found out about the paperwork."

"I'll admit that when your mother told me everything she'd found out, I wasn't happy about you being associated with her. I'd like to believe she didn't know about it, especially since you care about her so much. I guess we'll have to wait for a judge to determine that."

"Well, it doesn't really matter now. We had a big fight last night."

"Fights happen."

Colt shook his head. "I don't think it's that simple."

"Does she know?" his dad asked.

"No."

His dad laid a hand on Colt's shoulder. "Emily was a good girl, but I've watched you build walls around yourself for years after losing her. You would rather risk your body riding bulls instead of roping because it's something you share with her." He squeezed Colt's shoulder. "In order to love again, you must be willing to share that part of yourself, whether that's with Aly or another woman."

Colt dropped his head and closed his eyes. "What if she doesn't like what she hears?"

"You both have a hard road ahead of you, and I'm praying she's cleared of all wrong doing. However, will you be able to forgive each other in the end?"

That was the real question. When the dust settled, would they be able to move past the secrets they each carried? His father pulled him into a hug and Colt gratefully accepted it.

"Colt! Colt!"

He turned to see Frank running toward them. "What is it, Frank?"

"Last night there was a wreck about five miles from here." Frank's face looked stricken. "It was Aly."

His heart sunk deeper than the top soil. "What?!"

"Her car hit a tree."

Colt looked at his father as he felt everything inside him splinter apart. Without a word, Colt ran out to his truck and peeled out of the drive. The sun was shining and the roads were beginning to dry. Limbs and leaves scattered around due to the strong winds. Everything and nothing ran through Colt's mind all at once. The truck moved on autopilot until Colt noticed what had to have been the crash site coming up on his right. He let up off the gas. There were deep tread marks in the ditch and it appeared to have spun her car until it met the large oak tree.

God, please no. Not Aly.

Colt hit the gas again and everything in and around him became a blur. His heart pounded in his ears and the pressure mounted behind his eyes. *Not again.* This couldn't be happening. He'd already been down this road once and if Aly... He couldn't finish the thought.

He had no idea how he made it to the hospital, but he quickly found a parking spot next to the emergency room. Gram was sitting with Blake and Melissa on the far corner of the waiting room, and Jade was reading a book to Wyatt. When Gram saw Colt, she stood and headed his way. Without a word, she reached out and embraced him. There was nothing like a grandmother's hug, and Colt needed it. Gram leaned back and looked in his face.

"How is she?" he asked in a whisper.

"She has a concussion. That's what the doctors are most concerned about and will keep her over night to monitor. She also has a dislocated knee." Gram squeezed Colt's arms. "It is truly a miracle."

It definitely was. He saw the evidence on the side of the road. Colt wiped down his face. "Thank goodness. I just found out before I drove this way. She left my house last night, and I didn't know—"

"Come with me." Gram took his hand. "She was moved to a room a few hours ago. They have her heavily sedated and she hasn't woken up yet."

God, please no.

Colt followed Gram down the cold stale hallway. Everything seemed so distant and he felt like he was walking in a fog. She stopped just outside the door and asked him to wait while she went inside. He leaned against the wall and took a deep breath. His nerves were heightened and anxiety gripped his heart. He closed his eyes to calm his heart. Then he saw her:

The room was dark and cold. The most beautiful girl in the world lay motionless in a white bed. The only signs of life were the machines connected to some kind of mask, tubes, and who knows what else all over her body. Her chocolate brown hair was tucked under her shoulders, face swollen and red from the wreck. Colt hurt to see her like this but couldn't look away. He walked slowly to the edge of the bed and sank in the empty chair. Why is this happening? She's full of life and beauty, she wasn't meant to be like this, broken. One minute she was happy and the next...

It was all his fault. He was ok and she wasn't. He turned his head away, unable to catch his breath. The echoes of the doctor's replayed in his mind.

"She's not getting any better."

"There's nothing we can do but wait."

"Her body is shutting down."

No. Not Emily. His Emily. They were supposed to have forever. With all his strength he turned back to look at the girl he loved, but instead he saw blonde hair not brown. ALY!

He jerked with a gasp from his memory. His brow was moist with sweat and his breathing shallow. Not again, this can't be happening again. He wasn't strong enough to lose the woman he loved again.

Loved. His heart skidded at the realization.

Gram exited the room followed by three people. "Colt, this is my son, Mark, Aly's mother, Sarah, and brother, Luke." He shook their hands with a nod. It was clear they were all exhausted by their rumpled clothes and heavy eyes.

"We're going to get some coffee and give you a chance to see her." Gram gave a comforting smile and they all headed back down the hall.

Colt looked back at the closed door, Room 2011. Behind the door, was the woman his heart longed for. The woman who brought him back to life. The woman he selfishly pushed away. Would she even want him here? He swallowed the lump in his throat and pushed open the door.

Chapter 31

*B*lack. *Why is everything black? I'm awake but my eyes won't open. There's something warm on my arm. I can feel it!*

Aly strained to get her eyes to open but they wouldn't.

What's going on?

Something moved over the back of her hand.

Someone's here. The texture is rough, like a callus.

EYES OPEN!

She tried to turn her hand over to touch whoever was there. Her body wouldn't move. Frustration started to rise in her chest.

I know I'm awake. I've got to let them know I'm here.

Then something warm and moist pressed against her hand.

A kiss! Someone's kissing my hand.

The pressure behind her eyes made her temples pound. There's no way she could move her head. She began to regain feeling down her body. Her arms. Her chest. Her stomach. He hips. Her— *KNEE!!!! Oh, it hurts!*

She summoned everything in her and forced her eye lids to open. The only light she could make out was from the window. She blinked several times, as her eyes made out the ceiling. She could hear the beeps from the machines above her head. There was still a weight over her right hand. Shifting her eyes to the right, her heart stopped. "Colt?"

He lifted his head at the sound of his name. "Aly!" His face lit up in the most amazing smile she'd ever seen. "Aly, you're in the hospital. You were in a car wreck last night."

She remembered the rain, the spinning, the tree, and... their fight. She looked him over and saw that his hair was disheveled, eyes red rimmed, and stress lines in his forehead. "You're here?"

He nodded. "I am. How are you feeling?"

"Tired. My head and knee hurt." She tried to move but winced at the sharp pain.

"Don't move. I'll go get the doctor and let him know you've woken up."

She gripped his hand as he stood and said, "Colt, wait." The look in his eye was a mixture of surprise and relief. "Thank you for coming. I didn't think you'd want to after—"

"I couldn't not come, Aly. We'll talk about it later, ok?"

She felt tears spring up in her eyes. "I need to fix this. Fix us."

"We're going to be ok. Now's not the time to worry about it. You're ok and that's all that matters." He placed a soft breath of a kiss on her cheek. "I'm going to go get them."

A few minutes later the doctor, her parents, and brother entered her room.

"How are you feeling, Aly?" the doctor asked.

"My head hurts the most."

He scribbled something down in his chart. "I'm going to check you out. You've been asleep for several hours." Once he checked her eyes, bandages, and vitals he said, "I'll order you some more pain meds and be back to check on you in an hour."

"Thank you." The doctor excused himself.

"Aly, praise the Lord you're alright." Her mom took the seat next to her where Colt had been. "We were so worried."

"How bad is the car?" Aly asked.

"Don't you worry about that." Her mother rubbed her arm. "We just need to focus on getting you better.

Her father asked, "Do you need anything, honey?"

"My throat is really dry."

"I'll see if you can get some water." Her father left the room.

Luke stepped up and rested his hands next to her on the bed. "Al, I'm so glad you're okay. You scared us."

She placed her hand over one of his and squeezed. "Thank you for being here."

"We wouldn't dream of being anywhere else."

Her mom pulled the blanket tighter around her. She was so glad to see her parents and brother. They were never in the same room together, it was just a shame it took an accident like this to make it happen. There was one other person she needed to see.

"Where's Colt?" Aly asked.

"He's out in the waiting room." Luke answered.

"Ok." Aly was still shocked that he had come especially after their fight the night before. So many things were said on both parts, not to exclude his mother's interference, but he had still come. Her heart ached at the thought of him pushing her away. She wasn't sure where they'd go from here but felt a glimmer of hope at his assurance that they'd be ok. Maybe, just maybe, they'd come out stronger on the other side.

******

The sound of the nurse coming into the room woke Aly. The lights were still dimmed and the clock read eight o'clock at night. Had she slept that long? She moved her arm and felt someone's cheek. Colt. He must've come in after she fell asleep the second time. Her family was gone and it was just him. Her heart swelled. They hadn't said the words but she knew she loved him. His actions made her hope that he loved her just the same.

"I'm just going to check your vitals and give you another round of meds." The nurse placed the medicine and a cup of water on her hospital bed table. "How are you feeling?"

Aly turned her head to watch the nurse record her blood pressure and was relieved that the room didn't spin. "Better."

"Good." The nurse motioned to Colt who was sleeping soundly. "Your grandmother vouched for him. Are you okay with him here?"

"Yes, he's fine." She took the medicine with her free hand, so not to move Colt. "Thank you." The nurse excused herself.

Aly looked down at Colt and ran her hand through his hair. He looked so peaceful. She knew he was probably going to have a horrible crick in his neck from the way he was positioned, but she couldn't bring herself to wake him. Instead she reclined her head and let the medicine relax her back to sleep.

The next time she woke up, Colt wasn't sitting next to her. He was looking out at the blue sky through the window blinds. He still had the same clothes on from the day before: his grey t-shirt and faded blue jeans. His jeans hung dangerously low and fell over a worn pair of brown cowboy boots. She could look at him all day. His shoulders flexed as he rubbed his neck. She could see the tension in his back as he took a deep breath. "Colt?"

He turned and smiled, the tension evaporated off his features. In two steps, he was back at her side and sitting down in the chair. "How are you feeling?"

"I'm much better. I guess I really needed the rest." She adjusted her pillow to sit up a little better. They watched each other for several beats, both seeming to debate on what to say. Aly decided to speak first. "I can't believe you're still here."

Colt brushed some loose strands of hair from her face. His eyes were glossy with unshed tears. "I'm so sorry, Aly." He shook his head in disbelief. "When I found out you'd been in a wreck after leaving me, my whole world stopped. I couldn't live with myself if something had happened to you and the last time we talked we were fighting. I want to fix this."

"I want to fix this too." She squeezed his hand.

"I know the way I handle things with my parents, specifically my mother, were wrong." His Adam's apple bobbed as he continued.

"I should've told her I liked you at the church luncheon, because I looked forward to see you all morning. I should've told my mother no and refused to dance with Olivia at the party, because you're the only girl I wanted to be with." Colt inhaled deeply. "I should've invited you to meet her one-on-one, because I respect you both so much. I should've refused that yellow envelope, because I trust you."

Aly felt a tear run down her cheek. "I never want you to feel like you have to choose between me and your family. That's selfish and I never want to become a problem between you and them. I'm sorry if I ever made you feel that way."

"You didn't. Forgive me for not handling them better?"

"Of course." She glanced to their hands linked at her side. "I'm sorry about everything that happened with Greg. You have to know that I don't love him. It was infatuation and lust. I don't think I've ever really loved anyone before. And I don't know what's going to happen with the missing money, but I had no idea about it. Honest. I'll fight him in court—"

Colt silenced her with a kiss. The kiss was tender and made everything inside her soften. He pulled back slightly and looked into her eyes.

"I need to tell you something." His voice a gruff whisper. "I don't take this lightly. I understand what it means and I still want to say it." The emotion in his eyes pulled at her heart. "I didn't think I'd ever be able to feel this way again. We may have a long legal battle ahead. We may be different in a lot of ways, but I don't care. We belong together. So, when I say this know that I mean it with everything in me."

"Colt." She barely got his name out. Her heart swelled and she felt as if it would explode from her chest.

"I love you, Aly." After he said the words his face lit up brighter than she'd ever seen it. "I don't want to look at the possibility of life without you in it ever again. Tell me you feel the same way."

His words were everything she had longed to hear. "I never thought I would find love so soon." She raised her hand up to cup his cheek. "But I did. I love you too."

He leaned forward and kissed her again. "We'll figure this out, you and me. I promise."

Aly felt a tear fall. Her whole life, she'd dreamed of falling in love. Never in a million years did she think it would be with this risk taking smooth talking bull riding womanizer. But as she looked into Colt's amber eyes, she was thankful for every part of their journey to each other. They had been tested and came out on the other side. Colt loved her. She loved him. The road wasn't going to be easy but it would be worth every bump.

Chapter 32

Colt made some popcorn, while Jade and Aly talked about changing the bakery's grand opening date in the living room. It had been three days since Aly was released. Her head was healing nicely and she wore a brace on her left knee for support. Colt had driven by the wrecker service yesterday and saw what Aly's car looked like. Mangled metal, bent in a 'V' from the tree. It was hard to deny what a miracle it was that Aly hadn't been injured worse. A flash of a memory from years ago appeared in his mind. Before it could formulate clearly, Colt shook it away. The microwave beeped and he poured the popcorn into a bowl.

"I think we could schedule the grand opening for one week from Monday. Do you think you'll be good to go by then?" Jade asked looking at the laptop.

Colt took a seat next to Aly on the sofa and loved how she leaned into him naturally. She had her braced leg propped up on the coffee table. "I think it'll be fine. I don't want to postpone it more than that."

"Great! I'll just update the dates on all the flyers, a new ad for the newspaper, and the Facebook page." Jade began typing and clicking away.

Aly took a handful of popcorn from the bowl on Colt's lap. "Thank you." She gave him a quick peck on the lips. Colt enjoyed the strawberry flavor she left there. He turned the football game on with the volume low, as the girls continued discussing the bakery. He loved how happy it made both of them.

The doorbell rang and Colt offered to answer it. When he pulled the door open, Luke Meyers was standing with a suitcase. Colt stepped back and welcomed him inside.

Luke shook his hand. "Is my baby sister behaving herself?"

"For the most part," Colt answered.

"Luke!" Aly looked over her shoulder from the couch. "What are you doing here?"

Luke dropped a duffle bag and sat down in Colt's spot next to Aly. "Hey, Jade."

Colt took a seat at the bar diagonal from the sofa. He could still see their faces but it gave them a little more space.

"Hi. Are you moving in?" Jade asked noticing the duffle bag.

"Well, I wanted to talk to you guys first."

"You're kidding?" Jade closed her laptop and sat in on the coffee table. "This should be good."

"No kidding," Aly added. "Are you living out of your car again?"

"Hey, that was just for a week after I got kicked out of my apartment for renovations. I hadn't found a new place yet."

Aly laughed. "Renovations for the damage your roommate inflicted on the place."

"And that's why we aren't roommates anymore."

Colt enjoyed the easy banter between Aly and Luke.

"So, why are you here?" Jade asked.

Luke stretched his arms along the back of the sofa. "Cami is due to have her baby any day now and I'd like to be here when it happens."

Colt loved the sass in Aly as she arched an eyebrow at Luke. "Okay... but I don't know why you need to stay here. You can just come to visit. Fort Worth isn't that far away. Besides, now that you finished your residency aren't you supposed to be setting up your own practice?"

Luke nodded. "I'm wanting to open a practice here in Shaw Creek."

"Really?!" Aly exclaimed and tried to give him a hug, but it was difficult with her leg still propped up. "You'll be moving here permanently?"

"Well, I've got a couple of options but it looks like I'm moving back to Shaw Creek for now."

Colt stood and shook his hand. "Congrats, man."

"Thanks."

"I think you just made her very happy." Colt tipped his head to Aly, who was talking to Jade about their rooming arrangements.

Luke slapped Colt's back. "Not as much as you do."

Colt appreciated Luke's support in their relationship. "I hope so."

"No doubt." Luke gave him a knowing grin and sat back down next to Aly.

"So, did you just assume we'd let you live with us?" Jade asked.

"No. I was going to check with Gram next." He smirked.

Jade rolled her eyes and Colt could tell they were going to have a lot of fun butting heads as temporary roommates.

"I guess that settles it. But, just until you find a place of your own," Aly said.

"Of course," Luke agreed.

"We can make room for you in the third bedroom, it's currently the catch-all room." Jade suggested.

"I'll try to find a place soon," Luke said.

Jade stood. "I'm not worried about it." She brushed her hand over his shoulder and winked as she passed. "For now."

Colt shared a sideways glance with Aly, who raised an eyebrow at him. *Interesting.* They must have a love-hate relationship.

"Thanks. I don't need a lot of space," Luke said.

Jade returned with a water bottle. "I'll help you move stuff around."

"Thanks." Luke hopped up and they both disappeared into the bedroom.

Colt couldn't help but feel excited for Aly. She'd been alone for so long in Dallas and now she would have more family around her. Aly looked over at him and pat the seat next to her. "Come here, cowboy."

Once he sat down, she reached for his face and pulled him down for a kiss. "I love you."

"I love you too." He kissed the tip of her nose. "That's good news about Luke."

"I know! I haven't spent time with him since we were in high school." Aly took another bite of popcorn. "How are things at the ranch?"

Colt shifted so he could look at her but keep his arm around her shoulders. "They're good. Everyone's been working hard, so I can be here to help you."

Her eyes dimmed slightly. "I'm sorry. You don't have to spend your afternoons and evenings with me. I'm sure you have more than enough to do out there."

"This is where I want to be. I get what I need to done every morning. Everyone understands."

"Everyone?" Aly questioned.

Colt sighed. His mother hadn't spoken to him since Aly's accident. She would get over it soon enough. Colt had pulled his name off the next two events and his dad was able to take a break. He figured she'd be ecstatic, but nope. There would always be something for her to gripe about. "She'll come around."

Aly nodded and turned her head back to the football game. "I'm sorry for the problems with your mom. It was never my intention to upset her and I know she probably thinks the worst of me because of Greg's scam."

Colt cupped her face and turned her back to him. "We've already talked about this. I don't care what she thinks. You didn't have anything to do with it and everything will come out in court. I'll handle her."

"But you shouldn't have to handle her. You guys are such a close family and you're their legacy." Aly looked down and fiddled with her bracelet. "I don't want to come between any of that."

"It's my choice. I'm happy for the first time in my adult life, because of you. If she can't accept you, that's her problem. She's the one missing out." Colt leaned in and kissed her gently.

Aly pulled back. "You make me so happy. Thank you for hearing me out despite everything. I promise to never keep anything from you again."

Colt's gut clenched at her words.

******

Aly couldn't quite figure out what just happened. Colt's eyes shifted and smile dimmed. Before she could analyze it more, he pulled her to him and kissed the side of her head. Despite her hesitation, she settled into his side.

Colt had been so amazing the past three days. He helped her do stretches to loosen and strengthen her knee. He waited on her hand and foot, so she didn't have to walk around a lot. He had really surprised her. Having a near death experience was bringing them closer than ever before. It was like a weight had been lifted off her. She felt relieved to have answered every question he had about her past so they could move forward. Facing Greg and the upcoming legal battle would be bearable because she had him to help her through it.

Luke and Jade came back into the living room laughing about something. Luke put a hand on Jade's lower back to allow her to pass. It was only for a second, but Aly didn't miss it.

"Anyone need a drink while I'm up?" Luke asked.

Colt raised his hand. "I'll take a water."

Luke settled in the chair next to Colt and they struck up a conversation about some football team. It made her so happy to see the two of them getting along. Colt was three years older than Luke, so she didn't think they had known each other very well in high school. The best part was that Luke seemed to approve of their relationship.

Jade propped up her laptop again and said, "Alright, girlie. I've got some advertisement ideas from the diner that could work wonders for the bakery."

Aly flipped through several examples Jade had for the diner. If there was one Aly liked, Jade would pull it up in Photoshop and start tweaking to Aly's taste. A short time later, her phone chimed. Colt looked over at her but didn't say anything. She knew what he was thinking and she was hesitant to look. Since seeing Greg at the restaurant, he had done what she asked and not contacted her. She figured he'd returned to Dallas or Austin to prepare with his lawyer.

She grabbed her phone and swiped, pleased when it was Melissa's name. She typed and quick response, letting her cousin know how she was feeling and returned it to the coffee table. When she looked up, Colt was still watching her. "It was Melissa checking in."

He nodded and turned back to the TV. While Aly was still looking at some flyers, Luke and Jade got into a lively discussion about a bad call the referee made. Colt leaned toward her and whispered, "You haven't heard anything from him, have you?"

"No." That was an answered prayer.

"You'd tell me if you did, right?" Colt's voice was quiet but firm.

Aly smiled, loving how protective he was of her. "Of course. I'm not going to keep anything from you anymore."

Colt's lips twisted and he looked uncomfortable. His Adam's apple bobbed again and he nodded. He turned back to the TV.

"You believe me, right?" she asked.

When he looked back at her, his features had softened. "I do."

Any trace of doubt she thought she'd seen before was gone. She wasn't going to over think it. They were still discovering things about each other and she was determined to not let her insecurities play any part of ruining things.

Chapter 33

Aly sat on the back patio of the Teel home alone with Mrs. Teel, watching all five of Colt's nieces run and play in the yard. The birthday dinner for George Teel had been wonderful and thankfully uneventful. Everyone was warm and welcoming to her, including her in conversation but not putting her on the spot.

Mrs. Teel rose from her chair without a word and went inside where both her daughters-in-law had gone. The tension in the air left with her and Aly let out a slow breath. There had been no words between them, other than the hello upon arrival. Aly was just fine with that. She was going to enjoy a quiet moment alone.

All the men had congregated together on the opposite side of the patio talking. She glanced over at the men and Colt shot her a wicked smile that made the butterflies take off. He never shied from telling her that he loved her and making time to see her every day. She wanted to show him that she loved him, so what better way than trying to build a relationship with his family. The light in his eyes when she mentioned coming that afternoon, verified her belief. No matter what Mrs. Teel thought of her, Aly was going to make it work because she wanted to be with Colt and he was worth it. He was like a dream and she couldn't believe how lucky she was. He winked at her and looked back at Scott.

Maria exited the house and sat down at the table followed by Matt's wife, Danielle. "We brought you some more sweet tea with lemon."

"Thank you." Aly took a drink. Maria and Danielle each had their hair fixed perfectly and wore designer clothes. If Aly compared their closets to hers, it would probably match. She could see herself enjoying shopping trips with them. Something they could bond over and that gave her some peace about being a part of the Teel family.

"Thank you so much for being so welcoming to me."

Maria beamed. "Of course! Danielle and I are so excited to see Colt find someone special."

Danielle nodded. "We love Colt and it's great to see him so happy."

"I'm glad too. He's the best thing to happen in my life." Aly paused, looking over at the men. "Matt and Scott are great too. You both are very lucky."

"Thank you. We are." Maria watched her husband run out to help dust off one of their daughters, who had fallen. The smile on her face said it all. Aly knew Colt would make a great father, after seeing how much he loved his nieces.

"Scott's still my dream come true!" Dannielle glanced over to the men. "It's exciting to see Colt with someone for more than one day. You're good for him."

Aly was happy they thought so. Maria and Danielle looked back out at the girls running to the play house. Aly looked over at Colt and sighed. They were good for each other.

"How are you feeling after the wreck?" Maria asked.

Aly crossed her left leg over her right and was thankful there was not more pain. "I'm doing good. Colt helped me with my stretches and I was able to get my strength back quickly. Luckily, the scar from my head injury is hidden above my hairline. Now I just have to get ready to open the bakery in a week."

"That's wonderful. I've told everyone about your baked goods," Maria said.

"I appreciate that," Aly said. The girls squealed, drawing their mothers' attention. They we spinning and then dropping to the ground. "Your girls are beautiful."

"Thank you." They both answered in unison.

"Do you want kids?" Danielle asked.

"Danni!" Maria scolded.

"What?" Danielle shrugged. "I've got to know more about the girl who's brought Colt to life. You know, I didn't think I'd ever see Colt this way, not since—"

"Danni!" Maria's voice was hard. "How about you go check on Linda? She'd been gone for a while."

Aly felt a rock drop in her stomach. *Since what?* The women shared a knowing look before Danielle excused herself and went into the house. Maria looked nervous. "I'm so sorry, Aly. I don't want you to feel hounded with personal questions like that."

"It's alright. I don't mind." Aly smiled at the idea. "I have such strong and wonderful mothers in my family. I pray that I can be like them someday."

"I'm sure you'll be a great mother." Maria nodded to Colt and the other men. "Colt's going to be an amazing dad. He's the best with the girls."

The conversation relaxed some and the tension from earlier was almost forgotten. They discussed Dallas, shoes and food, all things Aly loved. Maria was so sweet and Aly could see them becoming good friends. It had been at least a half hour since Mrs. Teel went inside when she emerged with Danielle. Aly smiled at Mrs. Teel and was pleasantly surprised to receive one in return.

Maria called the girls inside to clean up. The women stood and began making their way to the back door. Just as Aly was about to take the last step into the house, her favorite pair of strong arms circled her waist and guided her away from the door, just out of sight of everyone. Before she had time to think, Colt spun her and backed her against the side of the house. He silenced her surprised gasp with a searing kiss. One hand slid up her back and tangled in her hair. She got lost in the feel and taste of him before she remembered where they were.

She pulled her head back quickly. "Colt! Your family is just inside. You can't kiss me like that here."

234 · CHARITY CHRISTY

There was humor in his eyes. "I don't care. Let them see and then there will be no doubt that I love you."

"I love that you want that, but tone it back just a bit, cowboy." She skirted around him, barely missing his grip. She looked up at the darkening sky. "It's getting late and I have to be up early."

Colt groaned and said, "I would much rather just kiss you."

"I'd like that too."

He laced his fingers with hers and his face grew serious. "You know, maybe one day I won't have to worry about you going home."

Her heart skipped. Was he talking about a real future together? A permanent future? "Really?" she asked breathlessly. He nodded and that sexy smile spread across his gorgeous face. She felt her heart kick into over drive. "I like the sound of that too."

He pulled her into a quick hug and kissed the top of her head. This was just where she wanted to be and the idea of having forever with him made her world seem right. Then, he lead her into the house where they said their goodbyes to his family and he walked her to her car. "You have no idea how much it means to me that you came to have dinner with my family."

"Of course, I wanted to come. It's important to you which makes it important to me."

He embraced her and said, "Thank you." Then leaned back to look at her. "I meant what I said earlier. I want a real future with you."

"I want that too, Colt." She took a deep breath. "I've never felt this way about anyone."

"I'm glad."

She cupped his face in both hands. "So much has happened in the two months we've known each other, but the last eight days have made me the happiest I've ever been. I love you."

The look in his eyes melted her. "Remember what we promised in the hospital." He tucked a fly-away hair behind her ear. "Let me know if you ever have any doubt or are having second thoughts about anything. Don't push me away without talking. No matter if it has to do with my family or something dumb I know I'm going to do."

With all the love in her heart she said, "I promise."

"I love you." He lifted her chin so that she was angled perfectly to meet his lips.

This was where she belonged, with Colt. She had faith that all the trials they'd gone through were worth it. "I'll see you tomorrow?"

"Yep. I'll swing by. Drive carefully."

"I will. Good night."

The drive back to Jade's apartment was smooth and Aly didn't feel anxious at all. When she walked into the apartment, Luke and Jade were sitting next to each other on the sofa watching a movie. Luke looked over at her. "Hey, sis! Did you have a good time?"

Aly placed her purse on the bar and dropped down in the recliner. "It was a really good day."

"Mrs. Teel give you any problems?" Jade asked.

"Not at all. She didn't say much to me but it wasn't bad." Aly pulled a pillow on her lap and smiled at the memory of what Colt had said about wanting a future together.

"Is that some gooey look in your eyes?" Luke asked.

Aly looked over confused. "What?"

"You're in love."

Jade gasped and smiled real big. "Are you?!"

There was no point in hiding it but she was surprised at Luke's foresight. "How would you know anything about love? You've never had a serious relationship."

Luke rolled his eyes. "Not that I'm required to explain myself, but I know more than you think. You didn't answer my question."

Jade slapped Luke's arm and said, "If you don't stop, she'll never admit it."

Aly laughed at the two of them. "You guys need—"

"Answer," Luke said firmly. "Do you love him?"

A giddy feeling came over her and she smiled a cheesy girl crush smile. "I do. I really, really do."

"ALY!!!" Jade jumped up and landed on Aly's lap giving her a huge hug. "I think this is amazing!"

Aly hugged her back and laughed at her friend's excitement. She looked over at Luke who didn't seem near as excited for her. He must've noticed her looking at him because he walked over to her and pulled her up into a hug. "Good for you, Al. You deserve to be happy."

"Thanks."

"You promise you're ok with everything in his past?"

Aly was confident in what she and Colt had. They'd been honest and open to each other. "Without a doubt."

"Good. I know that we haven't been close since we both went to college, but I'm here for you. Just know that I will always support you."

Aly felt tears spring in her eyes. Luke was never one to be mushy and she almost couldn't find the words. "That means more than you know."

He ruffled her hair and took a step back. "I never would've thought you'd end up with Colt Teel."

Aly chuckled. "I know. It is pretty crazy, huh?"

"I'm glad you worked out all your differences."

"Me too. We've talked in length about everything and I'm ok with it. I wasn't fully honest about things but now he knows everything. It's just so amazing and I'm so glad that I've found someone to love and who loves me back."

"She's going to get mushy again." Luke smiled and sat back down on the sofa.

Jade found a romantic comedy on Netflix for them to all watch. Aly sent up a silent prayer of gratitude for the blessings in her life. She had her best friend, family, Colt, and the bakery opening. Her dreams were all coming true and she couldn't wait to see what happened next.

Chapter 34

Aly hummed away to the music playing on her cell phone. Jade convinced her to take Friday and Saturday off, so she could get everything ready for the bakery's grand opening on Monday. The kitchen had passed inspection and all the equipment was cleaned and ready for use. Aly thumbed through her to-do list when she heard the front door bell ring.

"Hey there, beautiful," Colt entered with a handful of wildflowers. She accepted them and gave him a kiss. "I missed you."

Aly placed the flowers in a glass. "You just saw me last night."

"True. But you've turned me into a sap." He pulled her into his arms.

"Oh. Is that right?"

"I don't let just anyone see me like this." He spun her out and then back into him. "Do you like it?"

"I love it. Thank you for the flowers. They've become my favorite." She stepped back to resume flipping through her list.

"You ready to open?" Colt leaned against the kitchen counter.

"I am. Still nervous about getting the timing right. I just don't want to run out of things too early. But it's really exciting and I can't wait for the first week."

Colt nodded. "I'm so proud of you."

"Thank you."

Colt's phone chimed and he checked it. "I guess I need to get out to the ranch. I just wanted to swing by and see you."

"I probably won't come out tonight. Jade and Melissa are helping me around here." She tucked a few bowls under the counter.

"Oh! We have the induction of the new deacon tomorrow. Are you going to be there?"

"Yep. Will you save me a seat?"

"You bet." She leaned across the counter and kissed him goodbye. "I love you."

"I love you too. Bye."

Looking around her kitchen, Aly had an indescribable peace about everything in her life. After talking with her lawyer, she felt very confident in clearing her name of any wrong doing in the lawsuit. With the support of Colt and her family, she knew everything would be alright. The past two and a half months hadn't been what she expected but they lead her exactly where she was meant to be.

******

The service had been amazing the next morning. The church inducted a new deacon and the whole congregation was invited to share in a luncheon in the east wing of the church. The recent rain made the lawn too wet for it to be held outside. Aly paused to wait for Colt but he was talking with several men, including his father. Melissa, Jade, and Luke were waiting for her at the sanctuary door, so she made her way to them.

"Are you ready for something to eat?" Jade linked arms with Aly.

"You know I can always eat."

"Well, Blake and Wyatt weren't willing to wait. They've already headed down there," Melissa said.

They all made their way down the hall and into a part of the church Aly had never been in before. They had built new classrooms and a gym about five years ago. There were lots of pictures lining the hall of all the pastors who served, along with the changes made to the building over the last fifty years. It was amazing to see.

The crowd headed into the east wing had come to a stop as people were joining the buffet line. Jade and Melissa were talking about a program Melissa's students were going to be putting on that week, but Aly wasn't really listening. Her eyes fell on a banner that said "Memorandum". She looked over each picture and plaque underneath, displaying the member's death date and family members' names. In the middle of the wall hung a picture of a girl with long brown hair and brown eyes. She was beautiful but couldn't have been much older than eighteen. Aly read the plaque under her picture. *Emily Ann Ross-Teel 1984 – 2003*

Ross-Teel? Wait. She'd heard the name Emily before. Aly checked the names listed as family. The first line read 'Spouse: Colt R. Teel.' Everything inside Aly literally froze and then shattered into a million pieces.

Colt. Married.

Jade tapped on her shoulder and said, "It's time to move."

Aly slowly turned to face her, tears clouding her eyes. Jade and Melissa looked past her and their faces grew pale. *They knew?!*

"Aly." Melissa went to reach for her but Aly recoiled bumping into Luke.

When he turned his eyes flashed with concern. "Aly, what is it?"

She felt her hands begin to shake as she glanced back at the plaque. *Colt had been married?!* Why would Colt keep something like this from her? If everyone else knew too, why didn't they think she should know? She could sense three pairs of eyes watching her. When she looked back at Luke it was clear he had known too. She shook her head and fled the line.

"Aly!" Luke called after her.

All she could think about was escape. The walls were closing in and her pulse hammered in her throat. When she reached the sanctuary door, she didn't even bother checking to see if Colt was still there. She burst through the front doors and down the steps, and struggled to take a deep breath of the clean air. Even the cool breeze didn't seem to help. She had to get to her car as quickly as possible but two arms circled her. She slapped at them trying to push whoever it was away. If she stopped she'd lose it.

"Aly, stop!" Luke said, desperation lacing his words. "Please, just stop."

Her legs crumbled and the gravel cut into her knees. Luke knelt next to her wrapping an arm around her. She took a labored breath before looking up into her big brother's grey eyes. "You knew?" she choked out. Luke nodded twice. "And you never told me. No one thought this was something I should know?!"

"I thought you knew. You said he had shared his past with you." Luke held her hands tight.

She shook her head. "No one said a word. *Married?*" Pushing Luke back, she stood on weak knees. "Everyone betrayed me."

"No, Aly."

"Yes! You said you supported me." She felt the tears get caught in her throat.

Luke looked torn. "I do support you. I didn't know he hadn't..." His voice faded with the wind.

She spun on her heal and was almost to her car when she heard Colt. The hair on the back of her neck rose. She glanced over her shoulder and saw him running toward her, Jade and Melissa were standing at the front door. "I can't do this," she said to no one.

Colt reached for her as she pulled open her car door. His touch had once made her feel alive, but now it seared her skin. She jerked her arm away from him and said, "Don't touch me."

His face fell. "Please let me explain."

Her heart cracked deeper. He's not denying it. She was crazy to think that he would since it was etched on the wall inside, but she still wanted him to say it wasn't true. How could she be fooled again? First Greg and now Colt. She gave him her whole heart and he still didn't open up to her. "How could you?"

"Aly—" Colt started.

"You still couldn't tell me about all your broken pieces." She didn't want to look at Colt's sad eyes but couldn't bring herself to move. "I bared myself in front of you that night and you kept a wife from me? A *deceased* wife?"

Colt took another step but she retreated again. "I'm so sorry. I couldn't bring myself to tell you."

"But apparently, everyone else in this entire town knows about it." She felt her anger billowing in her temple. "I don't understand how you could think we could have a real life together with *this* kind of secret between us?"

"It was a mistake, I know that. I didn't want to hurt you." Colt's voice shook slightly.

"So, instead you thought withholding this from me wouldn't do that? After you thumbed through my whole past, you were still hiding this from me. You had the chance to tell me everything. That was the plan, right? To get everything out there so we could move forward together." The pressure was rising behind her eyes. "You had the chance to build a future with me, but instead you just shattered my heart beyond recognition."

Without giving him the chance to say anything else, she ducked into her car and slammed the door. Without looking back, she pulled out onto Main Street. She didn't know where she was going or what she hoped to accomplish by leaving, but she couldn't stay there.

There had been so much joy in her life and in one second it all burst into a million pieces, scattering in the wind like a dandelion. *How could this happen, God?* They had overcome so much with his mother and Greg but now this? A secret, a big one just broke them all over again. Him hiding this was something she couldn't look past. What did that say about her that when she finally gave her heart to another man, he ended up deceiving her just like the others?

Chapter 35

At five o'clock the next morning, Aly finished filling all the displays for the grand opening in an hour. The joy she'd felt about this moment was nowhere to be found. Jade was working alongside her, being great as always to give Aly the space she wanted and help she needed. Aly finished placing all the cards in the display case and closed it up when she felt satisfied with the set up. The room looked just like she'd wanted. The menu signs and daily specials chalk board were hanging. The cash drawer was full and to-go bags unpacked for easy access. She was ready.

Jade emerged with another tray of scones. "This is the last of everything for now."

Aly thanked her and began laying the scones in their place. "Thank you so much, Jade. You've been here for hours helping me bake and I can never repay you. Once I get through this first day things will go smoother."

"It's no problem at all. You'll get your timing down on when to start making more. Stacy will be here in thirty minutes." Jade took the empty tray back to the kitchen.

Aly was so glad that Jade had suggested moving Stacy from the diner to help part-time in the bakery. There was no way she'd be able to do everything alone. It would work, since the bakery was only going to be open until two o'clock every day. Then Aly could work the evening shift in the diner for Jade. She heard someone approaching and looked up to see Gram.

"Good morning, dear."

"You're up early." Aly accepted her embrace.

"I couldn't miss your first day." Gram looked around the room. "This is beautiful. I'm so proud of you."

"Thank you, Gram. I think we're ready."

Gram rubbed Aly's arm. "I hope you got some sleep last night."

She hadn't slept much at all. "It wasn't the best."

Gram nodded. "I wanted to talk to you before things got crazy in here."

"Ok." Aly lead Gram over to one of the tables by the window.

"You know, when you were a little girl you sure were a spit fire. You drove Luke crazy and always kept your parents on their toes. So much energy and passion all wrapped up in a bubbling blonde girl. I just knew you were going to do something great. This…" Gram motioned to the bakery. "This is it."

Aly felt the joy in Gram's words filter through her body and charge her heart. Regardless of how she felt when she woke up that morning, this was her chance. The chance at something better and she wasn't going to let her discouragement about Colt hinder that. "Thank you, Gram."

Gram reached over and placed her hand over Aly's. "I missed you at the luncheon yesterday."

"I'm sorry. I just had to get out of there."

Gram nodded. "That's totally understandable."

Aly fiddled with her bracelet. "I was really upset. Still am."

"I don't blame you. You should take your time and pray about it."

"I'm not so sure I can understand why God would allow something like this to happen. After everything we dealt with, now I'm faced with a lie bigger than anything else. How can we ever have a lasting relationship when so far it's been nothing but mistrust and deception?"

Gram squeezed Aly's hand. "Sometimes I think God allows our hearts to break some. How else will light ever enter if there aren't any cracks?"

Aly looked out the window and thought about Gram's words. Did she want her heart to be filled with light and restored from everything in her past? Yes. In fact, she thought she'd already done that after her accident. She even attempted to do the right thing when it came to Mrs. Teel. She felt confident in herself and in what she and Colt shared. Now all of that was thrown off base. Her heart was broken, for the third time in just over two months. How was that possible? What could God possibly want her to gain from this?

Gram stood from her chair, pulling Aly out of her thoughts. "You pray about it and I promise God is going to use those cracks to shine the brightest light ever seen."

"Thank you, Gram. I love you." Aly hugged her.

"I love you too. Cami should be having her baby at any moment. You're going to have a new little cousin! I'll call you when it happens."

"I can't wait."

As Gram exited, Aly took in a deep breath. It was the first time she'd relaxed in almost twenty-four hours, and it felt amazing. Jade greeted someone at the back door, who Aly assumed was Stacy. It was time to help get her ready for opening day. Aly sent up a silent prayer for peace in every area of her life.

******

"Thanks for coming. Have a great day." Aly waved as the last customer left with a bag full of croissants for dinner that night. It had been an amazing day. She had sold out of a few pies and some of her bread. Pulling out her notebook, she quickly jotted down what was the most popular and made a note to talk it over with Jade that night. She checked her cell phone and realized it was about time to lock up. The front door bell rang and she hurried back to the front. One more customer wouldn't hurt.

"Hello, sorry I was—" Her throat seized at the sight of Colt standing just inside the door. His hair was rumpled and shirt wrinkled. There were circles under red eyes and the brightness that she'd grown to love was absent. He looked just like she felt.

There were no words and for a few deafeningly silent moments they simply stared at each other.

Colt pulled a small bouquet of wild flowers from behind his back and laid it on the counter between them. "I wanted to come by and congratulate you on your first day. I hear it's been a success."

She didn't want to make small talk with him. "What do you want, Colt?"

"I need to explain." His voice was desperate.

He had so many opportunities to be honest with her. She had wanted nothing more than to see inside the deepest part of his heart. "Explain?" she asked exasperated.

"Yes. I know you're angry but you need to know, I wanted to tell you—"

"You want to explain how you kept something as important as a *marriage* from me? A marriage that clearly everyone else knew about but me. The person you supposedly love." She could feel the vile rising in her throat. "After you got mad at me for not telling you everything about Greg, you want the chance to explain?"

"Yes. I know I should've told you but it's not something that comes easy for me." Motioning between the two of them, he said, "This is why I don't do commitment."

He's blaming me?! "So, it's my fault?" She balled her fits.

"No." He tilted his head back to the ceiling and closed his eyes. She could see the frustration and desperation shake his body. "It's mine."

"Do you not remember what we promised each other?" she asked. "I was lying in a hospital bed and we promised to never hide anything from each other, to be completely honest. Well..." She threw her hands up. "That promise was a lie for you, wasn't it? You looked me in the eye and promised me, knowing that I didn't know about your *wife*." Her voice broke on the last word.

Colt took a step closer to the counter. "I know. I never meant for this to happen. I wasn't supposed to fall in love again. I don't deserve it."

She turned away from him and walked back into the kitchen. She heard his boots on the tile and stopped when his hand cupped around her arm, like a vice.

"Aly, just give me the chance to explain it all to you."

Why did he have to touch her? She had longed for his touch but now she felt strangled by it. She looked over her shoulder at him. "I don't know if I can take it all. First Greg and then you, twice. My heart is broken. It's mangled and I'm not sure it can even beat anymore."

She pulled her arm away and went into the small office at the back of the kitchen. Her knees were starting to shake and she took a seat, hoping to regain her foundation. She loved him. Why did it have to hurt so much to love him?

"I've never felt so lost as I have in the twenty-six hours since you left the church. I can't eat. I can't sleep. I can't breathe. My life needs you in it, it depends on it. Can't you see that?"

"I don't know if I can do this."

He stepped forward and fell on his knees in front of her. "Please, listen to me. I want to tell you everything."

"Colt..." She couldn't find the words to say anything else.

He took a deep breath as if to summon all the strength he had. "I met and fell in love with Emily when I was seventeen years old."

Aly closed her eyes fighting the tears and turned away from him.

He gripped her hands to keep her near him. She wanted to pull them away but couldn't.

"We sat next to each other in our junior English class. She had just moved to Shaw Creek and I'd never seen her before. She was outgoing and beautiful. Every guy wanted her and I was no different, but I was too nervous to talk to her. When she showed up at the rodeo grounds with a horse, I took the chance."

Aly knew it was ridiculous that she felt jealous, since it had been seventeen years since he first met Emily, but she didn't want to think about it. She tried to pull her hands away but Colt's hold only tightened.

"She was a barrel racer and I was a roper. Somehow, it turned out she liked me as much as I did her. We went to the same rodeos and spent all our time together. She was all I ever wanted."

Aly felt sick at his words. She wished it didn't hurt so much.

"After we graduated high school, we got married with just our parents and a judge. Everything was perfect. Until..." Colt's features darkened.

Here is comes. Aly knew this was what she wanted to know more than anything and yet the look on his face terrified her at what he was about to relive.

"We were on our way home from a weekend rodeo and I was driving, pulling both our horses." His eyes dazed off as if he was in a dream. "George Strait was playing on the radio. I can see her face as she sang along. Her brown hair swayed as she danced in the seat next to me." Colt's smile dimmed. "The rain pelted the windshield and the trailer skidded every time we hit the water pooling on the road. I tried to focus but the double yellow line was a blur."

Aly felt herself shiver and shoulders tense. She'd just lived that.

"There was a flash of a deer across the headlights. The tires squealed and the horse trailer jackknifed." His voice faded on the last word and he shook his head ever so slightly. "I can still hear her scream. It was deafening even above the sound of scraping metal. The trailer rolled when it hit the ditch pulling the truck over with it."

Aly felt the floor fall out from beneath them. She didn't want to hear the rest but she knew it was coming.

"I didn't find out until I woke up in the hospital that she was in a coma. Both horses had to be put down because their injuries were too severe." Colt dropped his head. "She died a week later, having never come out of the coma."

Aly couldn't imagine how he felt. "I'm so sorry, Colt."

"It's all my fault. I'm the reason she's gone." he said it so soft.

She couldn't stand to hear the guilt in his words. "No, Colt. You can't blame yourself for that. It was an accident."

"I was the one driving. I'm the only one who walked away that night. I don't know how to really live with that." Colt fell back on his heels.

He'd been holding on to this guilt and pain for so many years, longer than Aly could imagine. "You didn't do it on purpose. Accidents happen, look at mine. You have to let it go."

Colt huffed in exhaustion. "That's what everyone tells me."

"It's true." She prayed he would really hear her. "You can be happy. I don't believe God wants you to live your life alone just because Emily lost hers. You're still here."

His eyes were cloudy as he focused back on her. "I never wanted to feel that way toward someone again. I loved Emily with everything in me but she was taken away. I didn't want to open myself up to that again. It was safer not to. That's been my life for the past thirteen years. Then I saw you fumbling for a set of keys in your pretty green dress. You weren't interested in my smooth charm." He bobbed both eyebrows. She rolled her eyes at that. Then his expression softened and he looked more vulnerable than she'd ever seen him. "But you're different, Aly. Special. You deserve more than I am, but I want nothing more than to try to be enough for you." His hand cupped her now wet cheek. "If I could go back, I'd tell you everything that happened. Please, forgive me. I love you and can't imagine my life without you."

Aly's heart warmed at his words. "Colt, I can't imagine what losing Emily must've been like for you." But he still didn't let her into that part of his heart.

He pulled her down toward him and pressed his forehead to hers. "Please, Aly. Give me, us another chance."

A feeling of peace settled over her, unexplained but comforting. Had Colt messed up? Yes. Had she? Yes. It was a guarantee they would in the future as well. What they both needed was grace. She wrapped her arms around his neck and she felt his body relax as she brought him to her. "I love you too. I told you that I've never felt this way before and I know you have."

Colt cringed at her words and whispered, "But I love you, Aly."

She pulled back and looked into her favorite amber eyes. "I know you do. I'm not mad that you loved Emily, I promise." She took a deep breath. "I want you to be my forever and I want to be yours too."

"You are."

She leaned in and kissed him softly. He didn't push her and let her lead, which she loved. It was slow yet passionate. "I love you," she breathed it against his lips. Kiss. "Only you." She kissed him once more. "Forever."

His face lit up brighter than the Fourth of July and his lips crashed onto hers. They each poured all their longing and love into the other. His fingers curled into her hair at the nape of her neck and she melted in his arms. All the loss and pain was worth it if it brought them together.

Colt pulled back and wiped her face before placing one last kiss on her forehead. He stood and helped her out of the chair. She looked up at him and Colt released a breath. "Aly Meyers, I promise to never lose faith in you and in what we have."

Aly tightened her arms around his waist. "Colt Teel, I promise to believe in you too."

Epilogue

One Month Later

Aly gripped the leather reins in her hand as Duke galloped up to her favorite spot on Big T Ranch. The trees broke and the ranch spread out in front of her. The grass was browning and trees were streaked in yellow and orange as the season shifted into fall. It was so beautiful. Colt slowed and dismounted his new Appaloosa, Gene. Aly did the same and took Colt's hand as they walked over to the edge of the hill.

"How's he doing?" Aly asked nodding toward Gene.

"He's great. I have a good feeling about him."

Aly took a seat next to Colt. He'd finally taken her to the horse sale and found a new one. He'd been spending all his free time working with Gene to build the unbreakable bond she knew he missed from Jake. It was beautiful to watch.

A hawk cried as it soared overhead and Aly watched it glide past them.

"Are you happy?" Colt asked.

She looked at him. "Never more so."

He gave her a quick kiss. "It's hard to believe I've converted you."

"Converted me? From what?"

"City to country." Colt winked.

Aly rolled her eyes. "That may be somewhat true, but you can't say I'm a complete convert." She clicked the heels of her black and brown Timberland knee-high boots.

"Yeah, those aren't the best for the ranch."

"Hey, they have hardly any heel. I got these when I received my bachelor's degree."

"They're *very* nice." He winked. "Hey, I've got something for you."

"Ok." She watched him walk back to Gene to try and see what it was, but he just grabbed a duffle bag that was tied to the saddle.

Colt returned and knelt down behind her. He leaned forward over her shoulder and whispered, "Close your eyes."

Aly felt the goosebumps race across her skin as she lowered her eye lids. "They're closed."

The sound of the zipper on the bag only heightened her anticipation. Then Aly felt something press against the top of her thighs. It wasn't just one thing but two. Aly gasped and opened her eyes. In her lap was her very own pair of Ariat cowboy boots. They were a dark chocolate brown with a sky-blue paisley pattern up the leg.

"Colt, they're beautiful!" He laughed at her excitement and helped her change shoes. She stood up and held a leg out to the side to inspect the boots. "I love them!"

"I'm glad. I figured since you're going to be my girl, I better get you a proper pair of boots. Now they aren't work boots, but I know how much you love to dress up. I guess you could call them your dress boots. They're a little bit of city to add to your new life here in the country."

Aly threw her arms around Colt's neck and kissed him deeply. "Thank you. I love this place, as long as you're with me."

"Me too." He hugged her close to him and she knew she was home. "You want to go for another ride?"

"You know I do."

She had been given a real new beginning, her happily ever after. She'd learned to forgive herself, give grace to those who'd hurt her, and found happiness in the most unlikely place. The craziest part, this city girl felt most like herself nestled into a saddle riding with her cowboy. And she was never going to give him up.

About the Author

Charity Christy writes contemporary clean romance designed to inspire, encourage, and tug at your heart strings. She believes the art of writing is one of the most powerful ways to share the power of forgiveness, the expanse of love, and the importance of your own story. Charity lives in Oklahoma with her husband, Brent, and their two boys. She received her Bachelor of Arts from Northeastern State University in Oklahoma. She loves blogging, traveling, photography, and genealogy. She finds the most enjoyment being outside, drinking hot tea, with a pen and paper, overlooking their family farm.

To get to know Charity more visit www.charitychristy.com. You can also find her on Facebook, Twitter, Instagram, and Pinterest.

Acknowledgements

First, I want to thank my Lord and Savior, Jesus Christ. I know that at the age of 14 He stirred in my the desire to write. He gave me the ability to express myself to Him and others through my pen. I thank Him for lighting the fire inside my heart and making my dream of writing books possible. My prayer is that through my writing, I'll be able to play a small part in inspiring and encouraging others.

Brent – If it wasn't for you I'd not have a real love story in my own life. Thank you for telling me I can do this no matter how many times I tell you I feel like I'm struggling. Thank you for listening to me rattle off random conversations in my head, sitting quietly while I type next to you, proofreading chapters, and watching the boys when you get home all so that I can pursue something God has placed on my heart. You are better than I deserve and I'm so thankful you're who I get to do life with!

Mom & Dad – I've been beyond blessed with parents who have always encouraged me to do whatever I wanted. Thank you so much for always allowing me to share everything that was bouncing around in my head as a kid and even now. No matter how long my dreams, rants, or brainstorming is you listen and offer me feedback. I can never repay you for the continued love and spiritual encouragement you give me.

Rachel & Hannah – Being the oldest of three girls is such a blessing. You two are a huge blessing in my life. I want to thank you both for listening to my never ending stream of ideas. Thank you for the late night debates about my plot or an idea I want to emphasize in my story. You're support through this process has meant the world to me!

COMPEL Small Group – You ladies have been amazing as I've taken the journey through two books! When I had no idea how to go about finding an editor, how to publish, or how to write my book summary you offered a never ending supply of help and prayer. Thank you!

My LifeGroup – For over three years you have been the most influential people in my life. Your spiritual encouragement and accountability has sustained me through every part of my life, including my writing. Thank you for your honest living, prayers, and true friendships. I don't know where I'd be without you. I love you all.

Nikki – Here's to book number two! You've been such an amazing support through both of these books. Thank you for reading through my manuscript. I appreciate you!

Tasha – Thank you so much for taking time out of your busy amazing life and reading my manuscript! I miss all our fun college days doing nothing but reading and writing. You are such a dear friend.

Lauren – I absolutely love the photos you took for my book cover and advertising! It means the world to me that you've joined me on this journey!

Victorine – Like always, you've done an amazing job designing my cover! I love it!

Suzie – There's so much I could say to you but it would probably take up an entire page. ☺ Thank you so much for editing this manuscript. I feel like I grew and developed as a writer more than any other time in my life. You're encouragement and honesty have taught me how to push outside of my box and look at the delivery of my message in a new light. I owe you more than you know!

www.ingramcontent.com/pod-product-compliance
Lightning Source LLC
Chambersburg PA
CBHW061602170626
46811CB00001B/287